BATON ROUGE
BINGO

Reviewers Love Greg Herren's Mysteries

"Herren, a loyal New Orleans resident, paints a brilliant portrait of the recovering city, including insights into its tight-knit gay community. This latest installment in a powerful series is sure to delight old fans and attract new ones."—*Publishers Weekly*

"Fast-moving and entertaining, evoking the Quarter and its gay scene in a sweet, funny, action-packed way."—*New Orleans Times-Picayune*

"Herren does a fine job of moving the story along, deftly juggling the murder investigation and the intricate relationships while maintaining several running subjects."—*Echo* Magazine

"An entertaining read."—*OutSmart* Magazine

"A pleasant addition to your beach bag."—*Bay Windows*

"Greg Herren gives readers a tantalizing glimpse of New Orleans." —*Midwest Book Review*

"Herren's characters, dialogue and setting make the book seem absolutely real."—*The Houston Voice*

"So much fun it should be thrown from Mardi Gras floats!"—*New Orleans Times-Picayune*

"Greg Herren just keeps getting better."—*Lambda Book Report*

By The Author

The Scotty Bradley Adventures

Bourbon Street Blues

Jackson Square Jazz

Mardi Gras Mambo

Vieux Carré Voodoo

Who Dat Whodunnit

Baton Rouge Bingo

The Chanse MacLeod Mysteries

Murder in the Rue Dauphine

Murder in the Rue St. Ann

Murder in the Rue Chartres

Murder in the Rue Ursulines

Murder in the Garden District

Murder in the Irish Channel

Sleeping Angel

Women of the Mean Streets: Lesbian Noir
Men of the Mean Streets: Gay Noir
Night Shadows: Queer Horror
(edited with J. M. Redmann)

Love, Bourbon Street: Reflections on New Orleans
(edited with Paul J. Willis)

Visit us at www.boldstrokesbooks.com

BATON ROUGE BINGO

by

Greg Herren

A Division of Bold Strokes Books

2013

ISBN 13: 978-1-60282-954-1

This Trade Paperback Original Is Published By
Bold Strokes Books, Inc.
P.O. Box 249
Valley Falls, NY 12185

First Edition: October 2013

"What Was the Deduct Box?" reprinted with permission of the Long Legacy Project. "Huey Long's Life & Times |Governor/What is the deduct box." http://www.hueylong.com/life-times/index.php.

CREDITS
Editor: Stacia Seaman
Production Design: Stacia Seaman
Cover Design by Sheri (graphicartist2020@hotmail.com)

Acknowledgments

In all honesty, I never planned to write another Scotty Bradley book after *Who Dat Whodunnit*. Someone asked me after that book came out if I was going to write another Scotty, and my response was, "If I can figure out a way to write a book and work Mike the Tiger and Huey Long into it, I'll think about it." And sure enough, a few weeks later at the gym it came to me just exactly how I could do that—and here we are.

A special thanks must be given to Audra Snider of the Long Legacy Project, the nonprofit organization that operates hueylong.com. It is astonishing how his name has been blackened in the eighty years or so since his murder, especially considering his remarkable accomplishments while serving the people of Louisiana. I strongly encourage anyone interested in the legacy of Huey Long to visit the website and to read T. Harry Williams's brilliant biography, *Huey Long*. Huey Long was a remarkable, remarkable man, and Louisiana would be a far different place had there never been a Huey Long. Forget what you've been told, and educate yourself. The more I learn about Governor Long, the more I admire him.

Everyone at Bold Strokes Books has been an absolute delight to deal with ever since I signed my first contract with them five years ago. Thank you, Radclyffe, for bringing me into the family, and thank you to Cindy Cresap, Stacia Seaman, Sandy Lowe, and everyone else who makes writing and publishing with BSB a most delightful experience. The BSB authors and editors are also an amazing group of people—especially Anne Laughlin, Carsen Taite, Lynda Sandoval, Nell Stark, Trinity Tam, Rachel Spangler, Lisa Girolami, Karis Walsh, and my darling Ruth Sternglantz.

My coworkers at the NO/AIDS Task Force not only do amazing work, but they deserve accolades for putting up with the unpleasant creature I turn into as deadlines approach—and pass by. Josh Fegley, the Evil Mark Drake, Brandon Benson, Drew Davenport, Alex Leigh, Nick Parr, and Jean Redmann are some great people. I also got to attend Jean's wedding to her longtime partner, Gillian Rodger, while I was working on this book, which was an amazing experience. Thanks for letting me be a part of it.

Julie Smith, Lee Pryor, Nevada Barr, Michael Ledet, Pat Brady, Butch and Bev Marshall, Susan Larson, the gang at Garden District Books, and the rest of my New Orleans krewe are the best friends and cheerleaders and support system any writer can have. I am truly blessed to know some of the most amazingly talented people, and even more blessed that I can call them friends.

Paul Willis has made my life worth living for the last eighteen years. Anyone who has managed to put up with me for that long deserves a Nobel Prize.

And of course, the always enabling instigators, who keep my eyes firmly on those sneaky squirrels and somehow manage to make me feel special. Were it not for you, I would have never tasted red velvet cupcake vodka—and that's just one of the many ways you've all made my life richer.

This is for JESSE AND LAURA LEDET.

"Well, sooner or later, at some point in your life, the thing that you live for is lost or abandoned, and then...you die, or find something else."

—Tennessee Williams, *Sweet Bird of Youth*

PROLOGUE

L eo Tolstoy opened his novel *Anna Karenina* with this wonderful quote: "Happy families are all alike; every unhappy family is unhappy in its own way."

Tolstoy clearly had never met *my* family.

Then again, I doubt he could have even conceived of a family like mine.

Don't get me wrong—I have a *great* family. My parents are amazing, but they're a little odd. Okay, they're a lot odd; I've never met anyone with parents even remotely like mine. They're what would have been called hippies in the sixties, and no one's ever come up with a word that fits people like them more accurately. Even *hippies* isn't really accurate—but calling them left-wing radicals isn't really accurate, either. They are both very passionate about their beliefs—vegetarianism, nuclear power and nuclear weapons should be banned, gays deserve full equality, sexism and racism are societal evils that need to be eradicated, etc. They also are huge fans of marijuana—they always buy it in bulk, always have the best stuff you can imagine on hand, but they don't sell it. Anyone who wants some can have some; I don't think I've ever paid for pot that I can recall. I think my parents' sense of social justice comes from growing up remarkably privileged. My mother's family, the Diderots, trace their history in Louisiana back to 1720—the Diderots might not have been original settlers, but they arrived in New Orleans within five years of the original settlement on the riverbank. There was a plantation before the Civil War, and the Diderots made a lot of money in shipping. My grandparents have a beautiful old mansion in the Garden District, and I have an enormous trust fund Papa Diderot set up for me when I was born. I've never touched the principal, and frankly, the quarterly interest payment is more money than I need. I give the leftover money to charity.

My dad's family, the Bradleys, are newer money than the Diderots; they made their money in oil in the 1930s. The Bradleys feel inferior to the Diderots; my mother's family has a long societal lineage, and Papa Diderot loves making Papa Bradley feel inferior. The Bradleys are more conservative than the Diderots, which of course means I am much closer to my mother's family than my father's. They have a big house on State Street—which to the Diderots might as well be outer space.

New Orleans is a horribly snobbish city, all things considered.

My name is Scotty Bradley, and I am the youngest of three. I have an older brother, Storm, and an older sister named Rain. Yes, that's right, my parents named their eldest children Storm and Rain. (Rain has renamed herself Rhonda, but no one in the family calls her that.) The story is that they were going to name me River, but both sets of grandparents gathered around my mother's hospital bed and demanded she name me something more normal. So Mom decided to name me after both grandmother's maiden names. So far so good, right?

Except that Maman Diderot's maiden name was Milton, and Maman Bradley's was Scott. So on my birth certificate my name is Milton Scott Bradley. Yup, Milton Bradley. I'm sure she thought it was highly amusing, but grammar school was an absolute nightmare until Storm started calling me Scotty.

I've been Scotty ever since.

My own home life isn't exactly normal, either. I have two boyfriends who live with me. Yes, I am in a three-way relationship, which often confuses people when they try to wrap their minds around it. I met both my guys over the same weekend, and I was crazy about them both. I couldn't decide between them, and they made it easy for me. There have been some bumps and bruises over the years, but for the most part it's worked beautifully and we're very happy together.

My guys are Frank Sobieski, who's a retired FBI agent (he retired after twenty years so he could move to New Orleans) and is now a professional wrestler. Frank is tall and lean, with big, well-defined muscles. He has an angry scar on one of his cheeks, which makes him look mean and threatening, but when he smiles his blue eyes light up and he looks so handsome my knees get a little weak—even after all this time. We have a private detective business together—Bradley and Sobieski—but we don't get a lot of business. Fortunately, between Frank's pension and my trust fund, we don't really need anything else.

The third side of our triangle is Colin Cioni. Colin is shorter than me—maybe about five-seven—and has curly bluish-black hair, dimples, olive skin, and an amazing body. He is solid muscle and is built like a little tank. Colin used to be a Mossad agent but now works for Blackledge, an independent CIA-like agency for hire. He's gone a lot on assignments he can't tell us about. I worry, of course, but always hope for the absolute best. He's always come home so far.

As for me, I'm a college dropout. Yes, sad but true. I have sandy blond hair (that recently started thinning a bit in the front) and was a wrestler in high school. After I dropped out of college, I became a Southern Knight—a male stripping troupe that got booked all over the country for shows. I did that for a few years before giving it up and getting certified to be a personal trainer and to teach aerobics. I still stripped every once in a while, but as an independent contractor. In fact, the weekend I met Frank and Colin I was dancing at the Pub/Parade on Bourbon Street during Southern Decadence. Someone slipped a computer disc into one of my boots, and a friend wound up dead at my front door—and we were off to the races. I showed an aptitude for police work, so I became a private eye licensed by the state of Louisiana.

That's pretty much it, I guess.

On with the show!

CHAPTER ONE
SIX OF SWORDS
Journey by water

The GPS in our brand-new Explorer announced that it was about ninety miles to Baton Rouge from New Orleans when Frank punched in the coordinates into it before pulling away from the curb at the airport.

I stifled a laugh. It might only be ninety miles, but to a New Orleanian it's like being sucked into a wormhole and winding up in another dimension.

Of course, New Orleanians are horrible snobs about the city's *suburbs*, always making snarky jokes about needing shots and a passport to head over to the West Bank or out to Metairie, so it should be no surprise that we also look down our noses at the rest of Louisiana. We act like there's no intelligent life outside of Orleans Parish; nowhere decent to eat, no art or culture to speak of, and certainly no one we'd want to associate with could possibly live out there. It's not true, of course—but we like to pretend it is.

As my Louisiana History teacher at Jesuit High School once sniffed contemptuously, "President Jefferson offered Napoleon ten million dollars for New Orleans, and for an extra five million he threw in the rest of the continent west of the Mississippi."

Needless to say, this snobbish disdain for the rest of Louisiana was hardly endearing—which quite frequently means New Orleans gets screwed over by the state legislature.

So when Frank first mentioned this trip to Baton Rouge, I reacted the way any true New Orleanian would. I scrunched up my face like I'd smelled something really awful and said, "Ew. Do we have to?"

He rolled his eyes. "Yes, we do, and we need to buy a new car."

This was even more horrifying to me than going to Baton Rouge, to be honest. I hate to drive—I *always* have. I don't even like *riding* in cars. Given the way people drive in New Orleans, it's understandable. Most drivers in New Orleans don't use their signals, ignore street signs and traffic laws if inconvenient, and no one here knows how to make a left turn properly at an intersection. It always amazes me that there aren't more traffic fatalities.

Fortunately, I grew up in the French Quarter and rarely had to leave my *neighborhood*, let alone the city limits. The only time in my life I'd ever owned a car was when I went to college at Vanderbilt University—a car I sold after I flunked out and moved home. When I was on the stripper circuit with the Southern Knights, I simply caught a ride with one of the other dancers, flew, or borrowed my dad's car. Once I was off that circuit, I never needed to own a car. The Quarter was kind of a self-contained neighborhood—there was the A&P on Royal Street (now a Rouse's) and any number of mom-and-pop corner groceries. There was Mary's True Value Hardware on Bourbon (now on Rampart), plenty of places to eat, and if I needed to buy new clothes, there were plenty of places around. Mom and Dad both had cars I could borrow any time I needed one, and in a pinch I could always take a cab. And my best friend David was always willing to cart me around whenever I needed to go somewhere.

Well, until the time we were chased down I-10 by a gang of artifact thieves who wound up running us off the road, totaling his car, and breaking his nose. After that, he probably wasn't quite as willing anymore, but I also never asked him for a ride again.

Besides, by then I was already involved with both Frank and Colin, and both relocated to New Orleans and moved in with me. Colin owned a black Jaguar that seemed like something out of a James Bond movie. It was only a two-seater, but the three of us rarely needed to go anywhere in a car.

But resistant as I was to the notion of buying a car, I had to admit Frank had a point. His professional wrestling career was taking him all over the Gulf Coast, and the Jaguar ate gas like it only cost a quarter a gallon. Our friends Lindy and Rhoda—the Ninja Lesbians—were also coming in for a vacation, and they wanted to do plantation tours, so we needed something bigger. Why he settled on a Ford Explorer was beyond me, but as long as I never had to drive—and Frank promised he would *never* make me drive—I was fine with it.

And much as I hated to admit it, it was kind of a comfortable ride.

So I settled into my seat as Frank pulled away from the curb at the airport. We'd just dropped off Colin and the Ninja Lesbians. Rhoda and Lindy were heading back to Tel Aviv, and Colin was off on yet another spy job, the Goddess only knows where.

Rhoda and Lindy were Israeli nationals, employed by the Mossad. Colin had gone through training with Rhoda and was Lindy's trainer when she'd joined the Mossad. Colin had left the Mossad to work for the Blackledge Agency, one of the top undercover guns-for-hire organizations in the world. He'd been trying to get Rhoda and Lindy to join him there, but without much luck. Frank and I had met them when we were all looking for Kali's Eye, a jewel stolen from a temple in a very small country during the Vietnam War. They'd become a part of our extended family since then, and had become masters at finding reasons to visit New Orleans.

I loved them.

I tried not to think about what their jobs entailed. It was the only way I could handle it. I just told myself whenever I did think about it that they were all three highly trained professionals.

I knew Colin was very good at his job, and whenever I worried about him, I just reminded myself over and over again he'd come home safely.

He had every time so far, after all.

"It's a shame they couldn't stay another few days," I said as Frank signaled and swung around a slow-moving pickup truck. "The Ninjas have never seen you in the ring."

That was another reason Frank wanted us to get a car—his professional wrestling career was *really* taking off. He was currently champion of the Gulf States Wrestling Association and had to travel a lot for appearances and title defenses. The reason we were heading to Baton Rouge was because Frank was defending his title against his archenemy, Kid Karisma, there. The GSWA was doing a live broadcast from the Pete Maravich Assembly Center on the LSU campus. The center had sold out less than a week after tickets went on sale. This was a big deal for the league—their biggest show thus far, *and* it was going to air on pay-per-view. Stephen Wamsley, the promoter, had said the subscriptions were so high he was already planning another one in a few months at the New Orleans Arena.

When Frank first started with them, the shows had been at Knights of Columbus halls and high school gyms, with the occasional show at a casino. They taped some of the shows for broadcast on a little-watched regional cable network. But Stephen, who'd taken over for his father shortly after signing Frank, was a hustler. He'd moved the broadcasts to a national cable network, and they were starting to catch on. Every time the ratings went up, more money flowed into the GSWA coffers. This meant better production values for the broadcasts and more money for the guys.

I was so incredibly proud of Frank. It was hard enough for someone to start a career as a professional wrestler in his late forties. Not only had Frank done so, but he'd become the biggest star in his promotion. He was always swarmed after his matches with adoring fans wanting autographs and pictures. Stephen was even talking about adding a merchandise page to their website, which was getting a ridiculous amount of hits.

Frank had over five thousand fans on his wrestler's Facebook page.

It was no surprise to me that Frank was becoming such a big star.

Of course, Frank looked phenomenal in his shiny black pleather trunks with the lightning bolt across his perfectly shaped hard ass, the knee pads, and the shiny black leather boots.

I loved sitting in the crowd listening to them cheer for my guy, you know? And always smiled to myself when I heard the women talking about how sexy he was.

If you only knew, I would think, *how sexy he looks out of the tights.*

"Yeah," Frank replied, accelerating as he pulled back onto I-10 West. "It was good seeing them again."

"Are you nervous?" I asked, putting my knees up on the dashboard and scrunching down in my seat. The match wasn't until tomorrow, but Frank *always* experiences a little stage fright before a match—and this one was bigger than any other show he'd ever done.

Hell, *I* was nervous for him.

"Not really," he replied as we left dry land and headed out over Lake Pontchartrain. He glanced over at me and smiled. "I'm actually feeling remarkably calm. It's going to be a great show, I think. Jeff and I have worked out some pretty great stuff for the match." Jeff was Kid Karisma's real name. Despite the big feud that was the main part of their current story for the promotion, both Frank and I were really fond of Jeff Protheroe. He was in his late twenties, was former military, and lived with his wife and baby daughter near Pensacola in the Florida panhandle.

He was also really good-looking, with an amazing body.

"Nothing too crazy, I hope—nothing where either of you might get injured," I said, glancing over at him.

"Nah." He looked in the rearview mirror and fell silent again.

"You've been acting kind of weird all day, Frank. Want to tell me what's going on with you?" It was true. Frank always got weird on days when Colin was leaving for a job—he generally just kind of shut down. It was how he dealt with *his* fears about Colin not coming home. But today had been a different kind of weird, a kind of forced cheerfulness that was somehow worse than his silence.

Frank glanced over at me and gave me a rather faint smile before turning his attention back to I-10, where it belonged. "You know me too well." He turned down the volume of the car stereo, cutting off Amy Winehouse in mid-lyric. "I've been trying to figure out how to tell you something all day, and really, there's no better way than just coming out with it." He exhaled. "I got an e-mail from my sister this morning."

That got my attention. I sat up and leaned against the door, giving him my full attention.

I didn't really know much about Frank's sister. I knew her name was Teresa; she was married, had three kids, and lived somewhere in north Alabama. She sent Frank a birthday card and a Christmas card every year. The Christmas card often included a photograph of her family in front of a Christmas tree wearing Christmas sweaters; Frank always threw it into the garbage after opening it. (I am not proud to admit that I dug it out to look at the picture and read the note written inside every year—it was always innocuous and impersonal.) Whenever I asked Frank about his sister, he always brushed the question away. This, of course, drove me insane with curiosity. I'd been tempted, more than once, to research her and her family—I *am* a licensed private eye with an insatiable—some might say obsessive—curiosity. But I knew Frank would be pissed if he ever found out I'd snooped, and reluctantly I always decided to wait for him to discuss her with me when he was ready. I did know that his parents had both died in a car accident when he was in his early twenties. Teresa and her family were the only living relatives he had left.

I also knew they hadn't spoken in over ten years.

"Oh?" It took all of my self-control to make that one syllable sound innocent and calm.

Frank glanced at me out of the corner of his eyes and had the decency to start laughing. "You're not fooling me a bit, Scotty." He reached over and patted my left knee with his right hand as we loomed up behind a slow-moving U-Haul truck over the Bonnet Carré Spillway. "You're dying of curiosity, aren't you?"

"Not in the least," I sniffed, resting my head against the car window as he swung the Explorer into the next lane and passed the U-Haul.

"*Riiiiiiiiiiiiiiiiiiiiiiiiiight.*" He laughed. "Because you don't have a curious bone in your body, right?" When I didn't answer, he went on. "Seriously, Scotty, I appreciate you never pressing me about my sister." His hand was still resting on my bare leg, and I put my own hand on top of it. Frank has gorgeous hands. They were big, with strong thick fingers. He always kept his nails clean and trimmed. I traced a vein from his wrist up to his elbow. "I've never really wanted to talk much about her. It hurts still, after all this time. We used to be so close when we were kids. But she said some pretty awful things to me, unforgivable things, really." He swallowed, his Adam's apple bobbing in his tanned neck. "She's very religious, very fundamentalist Christian." The knuckles on the hand gripping the steering wheel whitened. "She loves me as her brother, but just can't condone my *lifestyle choice*." His voice tightened on the last two words. "And she just can't be a part of my life until I recognize my sin, ask God for forgiveness, and follow a righteous path."

"Oh, how awful. She actually said that to you?" I grimaced. *That* explained it.

He nodded. "Yeah, and I wasn't exactly nice to her. I may have told her to shove her Leviticus up her self-righteous ass." The corners of his mouth twitched.

"Why didn't you invite her down to meet me and Colin?" I asked. "Surely, once she met us…"

"I didn't want to put either of you through that. And besides—she doesn't approve of my being gay. You think having two partners would win her over?"

"But, Frank, you've braved the Bradleys. You *know* how awful Dad's family is. She couldn't be any worse than Papa Bradley."

He laughed. "You always think Papa Bradley is a lot worse than he really is. He's not that bad, Scotty. He's always been very nice to me."

It took a lot of effort not to roll my eyes. I'd finally come to a kind of détente with the Bradley side of the family, but it was an uneasy truce. "If you say so."

"Anyway, that's beside the point now." He sped up to go around a pickup truck with furniture in the bed tied down with what looked like bungee cords. "It seems silly now, to have gone so long without speaking to her." He glanced over at me as he maneuvered back into the right lane. "She's my only family, really. Since Mom and Dad were killed…" He shook his head. "Maybe that's why I got so angry with her, I don't know. We'd always been close. She's only two years older than me." He laughed. "We drifted apart when we got older. Anyway. She *is* my sister, even if her religion tells me I'm going to hell."

"So, why did she e-mail you out of the blue? To make peace, finally?"

He drummed his fingers on the steering wheel for a moment as Amy continued to claim she didn't have an addiction problem in the background. Finally, he said, "She wants me to take in my oldest nephew. He's thinking about transferring to either Tulane or UNO."

"But, Frank, that's great!" I burst out before realizing that he was clenching his jaw so tightly that a muscle was jumping in his cheek. "Isn't it?"

He sighed. "Yeah, it is, I guess. It's just—aw, hell." We passed the turnoff to take I-55 north to Jackson. He signaled to take the Laplace exit. There was a big hotel there, and a mega gas station. He pulled in next to one of the pump islands and switched off the engine. He turned and looked at me. "I haven't seen my nephew since he was about six years old, Scotty. I don't know him at all, but much as I want to, I can't say no to her, I'm sorry." He took a deep breath and shook his head. "My nephew's gay, Scotty."

Poetic justice for a homophobe flashed through my mind immediately, and just as instantly I regretted thinking it.

It always bothered me when anyone wished a homophobe would have a gay or lesbian child as *punishment* for being a homophobe. Yes, that might be an apt punishment for *them*, but it never takes into consideration how hellish that would be for the child. It assumes that having a gay child would magically transform a homophobe into a banner-carrying member of PFLAG.

Sadly, it doesn't always work that way—and the one who truly suffers is the child.

"How old is he now?" I asked.

"He's eighteen, just finishing his first year at the University of Alabama." Frank sighed. "He came out to his parents...and my brother-in-law has disowned him."

I bit my lower lip and counted to ten silently in my head.

Nothing makes me angrier than a parent whose love for their child can be switched off like that.

"So my sister wants him to come down and visit me for the summer, you know, check the schools out, see if he likes New Orleans," Frank went on. "Since he can't go home, and he doesn't have anywhere else to go. She's actually hoping my asshole brother-in-law, once he's over the shock, will accept Taylor and they can put all of this behind them." Frank sighed. "He'll be heading down here this weekend, if it's okay with us. Please tell me you don't mind. I just can't turn my back on Taylor."

"Of course we can't! He's welcome as long as he wants." I folded my arms. "But why is he out of school so early?"

"He did a semester in Paris—he's taking a minor in French and is actually fluent, apparently." Frank grinned. "He's majoring in political science—he wants to work for the State Department."

I whistled. One of the only regrets in my life is I don't speak a second language. "Impressive."

"Anyway, the semester in Paris finished, so he's been back home for the last week or so. Apparently, he met a boy over there…that's kind of what triggered the whole coming-out thing. I don't know the whole story—but my brother-in-law went away on a business trip and told Taylor he had to be gone by the time he gets back. He'll be back this coming Monday. My sister seems to think her husband will change his mind eventually—which I doubt. He's really a sanctimonious holier-than-thou asshole, but she thinks it best if Taylor isn't there when he gets home."

I'd noticed that Frank carefully avoided referring to his sister and her husband by name. "Well, he can stay in the upstairs apartment," I said as Frank took off his seat belt. "But is it really a good idea to bring an eighteen-year-old newly out gay boy to the French Quarter?"

Frank grinned as he opened his car door to get out. "You grew up in the Quarter and look how you turned out." He shut the car door and started filling the Explorer with gas.

"Exactly my point." I mumbled, slumping down in my seat.

To be honest, now that my outrage at how Taylor's parents were treating them was wearing down a bit, I was starting to get a little concerned.

I know I'm luckier than the vast majority of gay American men. I grew up in the French Quarter, for one thing, with its embrace of difference and diversity and uniqueness. I also grew up with far-left parents who most definitely would have been hippies had they been old enough in the sixties—parents who not only accepted me for being gay but were genuinely *delighted* their youngest child was a big old 'mo. I was getting into the French Quarter gay bars when I was seventeen. I was dancing on the bars in a thong when I was twenty. I haven't exactly had the most conventional life.

Was I a good role model for a teenager freshly out of the closet?

I rather doubted Frank's sister would think so—but then, in banishing her son from her home, even if it turned out to be just for the summer, hardly gave her a moral high ground from which she could cast judgment on *my* past.

And I was hardly going to encourage Taylor to become a go-go boy.

Keeping him out of the gay bars—and the bathhouse—was going to be a full-time job.

Listen to you, getting all parental and responsible, a voice jeered in my head. *It didn't harm you, so who are you to make decisions for what's right for this kid? As long as he knows about safer sex and to always use a condom, who am I to stop him from getting some world experience? And it's not like kids nowadays have to go to bars anyway. He's probably got Grindr on his phone and a Manhunt profile. If he was seeing some guy in Paris, he's probably not a virgin, either. Besides, you don't want to be one of those judgy adults he won't talk to. Isn't it better to be his friend? Let Frank be the authority figure.*

I was so completely lost in thought I didn't notice Frank had gotten back into the car and started the engine until he looked over at me and said, "Earth to Scotty? You okay?"

"Yeah," I replied, forcing a smile as he drove back up the on-ramp to I-10. "It's pretty cool of Teresa not to send him to some kind of 'don't be gay' camp. I mean, that's what I would have thought she'd do."

His knuckles tightened on the steering wheel, but he didn't say anything for a while. He sped up and merged onto the highway. "She might be religious, but she isn't stupid," he finally said as we drove off the swamp bridge and back onto dry land again. "She has a college education, you know. Not that she's ever used it, of course. All she ever wanted to do was be a wife and mother." He shook his head. "And as hard as our parents tried to keep us out of Alabama, that's where she wound up."

"You're from Alabama?" I glanced over at him in surprise. "I thought you were from Chicago?" I racked my brain and couldn't remember him ever mentioning Alabama before, except in regard to his sister.

"I grew up in Chicago." He sighed. "I was born in Alabama, Scotty, that's where we're—my family—is from. I really don't like to talk about it much." He put his big hand back on my knee. "I'm sorry—I should have told all of this to you before. But I don't have any really pleasant memories of Alabama."

Quelle surprise, I thought, but aloud said, "I figured you'd tell me about your past and your family when you were ready to. I didn't want to pressure you."

"Yeah, well, I hated Alabama when I was a kid. We used to go there every summer to visit." He made a face. "I have a ridiculous number of relatives there—I don't know many of them, really, but that's where we're from, and I have a lot of aunts and uncles and first cousins. I was really skinny as a kid, and not very athletic. Sports were important to my dad, and of course, my cousins were all jocks." The muscle in his jaw was twitching again. "They used to make fun of me. And my dad was always *why can't you be more like your cousins?* He made it very clear I was an enormous disappointment."

"Frank—I'm sorry." I put my hand down on top of his and interlocked my fingers with his.

"Yeah, well. My parents moved to Chicago when my sister and I were young—I was only two, so I don't remember ever living there—and that's where I grew up. We lived in the city until my parents bought a house in the 'burbs. My sister and I both went to the University of Illinois. Tommy Wheeler was my cousin Bobby's best friend, so he was always around when we were kids. She started dating Tommy Wheeler when we were in high school and went down there for the summers and it got serious. After she graduated from college she married him and moved back down there, started having kids." He shook his head. "I've never had any desire to ever live there. Never. I went to work for the FBI right out of college, as you well know. Then Mom and Dad died...and I met you, and retired and wound up living in the South." He smiled at me and patted my leg again. "I never had any doubt about wanting to live with you, you know— but I worried that New Orleans was too close to Alabama." He laughed. "Every time I have to go to Mobile to wrestle, my stomach knots up when I cross the state line into Alabama—even after all this time!" He shook his head. "I'm sorry, I probably should have told you all of this years ago."

"No worries." I smiled back at him. It *was* weird, now that I thought about it. We were going on eight years together—*eight years*—and how did I not know any of this?

Then again, we still weren't 100 percent sure we knew the third side of our triangle's real name, either.

Yeah, we were going to be *great* role models for Taylor Wheeler.

We rode along in silence, listening to the stereo, until we hit major traffic just after we got into Baton Rouge—just before the place where I-12 merges back into I-10. Interstate 12 is a New Orleans bypass—it cuts from Baton Rouge to Slidell across the north shore of Lake Pontchartrain and cuts at least an hour out of the east-west trip by not swinging south into New Orleans.

Baton Rouge is notorious for its traffic. About the only time you can ever pass through the capital of Louisiana without coming to a dead stop is around three in the morning—if then. I've never really understood why that is—probably something to do with the way highways merge right before the bridge across the river, and that the college campus is also right there on the banks of the Mississippi. God forbid you try to get through the city after an LSU football game lets out—I made *that* mistake once when

I was driving back from a go-go boy gig in Houston. It took me about an hour to get from the river to where I-12 splits off.

"Jesus, this is worse than game day," Frank commented as we inched forward.

I switched the car stereo to the radio and searched for a station.

"At this time, all students, including those living on campus, are asked to leave the campus as quickly as they possibly can. The bomb squad from the Baton Rouge police department are currently working their way across the campus. As soon as there is an all-clear and it is safe to return to the campus, we will make an announcement…"

"That explains the traffic," I said, switching the stereo back so it was playing the music on my iPod again. "But why would terrorists target the LSU campus?"

"I seriously doubt this is terrorists," Frank commented as we inched forward another couple of feet. "No offense, but I doubt very seriously a college in Louisiana would be a high-priority target."

"Yeah, it's probably some douchey frat boys trying to get out of a test," I replied, looking out the window at the car beside us. It was a green Chevrolet. At the wheel a woman was talking into her cell phone with a cigarette dangling from her lip. "It's going to take forever to get to the 110." The 110 turnoff was the way to downtown Baton Rouge and the capitol building; we were staying in Storm's condo along the riverfront near the capitol.

At that moment my cell phone started ringing, and a picture of a pig's face showed up on the screen. "Hello, Storm," I said as I accepted the call.

"Where you boys at?" Storm sounded a little out of breath.

"We're on the 10, stuck in evacuation traffic." I looked over at the woman, who smiled at me as she tossed her cigarette out of her window. "I've no idea how long it's going to take us to get there. If you want to get dinner, don't wait for us."

"I'm not at the condo," Storm replied. "I'm at the police

station. I wanted to let you know in case you got there and were wondering why I'm not there. The doorman can let you in—I let him know you were coming when I left."

"Why are you at the police station, or should I ask?"

"I'm trying to bail Mom out."

"What has she done now?" I looked over at Frank, who was giving me an odd look.

"She's been arrested for assault." He sounded like he couldn't decide whether he should be irritated or amused. "She punched the attorney general."

CHAPTER TWO
NINE OF SWORDS
Defending oneself stoutly

"Dufresne is lucky all I did was slap him," Mom said, defiantly tossing her waist-length salt-and-pepper braid over her shoulder. "He's an utter and complete asshole. No, wait a minute—an *asshole* actually serves a purpose, and that's more than anyone can say for Troy Dufresne."

Storm strode across the living room to the wet bar and poured himself a healthy slug of Jack Daniel's. He tossed it back and refilled the glass, adding a couple of ice cubes. He gave me a broad, fake smile. "See what I'm dealing with? She was even more fun in front of the judge. News flash, Mom: it helps to show a little contrition in front of the man setting your bail. After your little outburst in the courtroom, it's a wonder he didn't lock you up as a menace to society." He took another slug from the glass. "I'm not completely convinced you aren't one."

"At least you got her out in the end," I pointed out as Mom sat down next to Frank on the couch. They'd just arrived at Storm's condo—Frank and I could hear them arguing the moment they got off the elevator.

It had taken us over an hour to get there in the bumper-to-bumper crawl of traffic. I'd started wondering if we were going to die there on the highway, trapped in traffic, when we finally reached the turnoff for the 110 and downtown Baton Rouge. The traffic hadn't let up much, but eventually we found our exit and headed for the parking garage of Riverview Tower. We'd managed to get our bags up the elevator to the twelfth floor and tossed them into one of the two spare bedrooms before deciding to order pizza. The drawer in the coffee table was filled with delivery menus, as I knew it would be. Storm didn't cook, and I also knew, without having to look, that the only thing I'd find in his kitchen cabinets would be potato chips or pretzels—maybe both. I'd just hung up on Capital Pizza when I heard the argument coming down the hall.

I'd barely had time to take in the condo before they burst in. It was nice, as I knew it would be. The living room took up most of the floor plan of the place—the spare bedrooms were tiny, and the kitchen was little more than a galley. But despite the small bedrooms and a kitchen that was barely usable due to its size, the selling point of the condo was the stunning view from the living room. The entire wall facing the river was glass, and when I pulled the white curtains back, I literally gasped. The Mississippi River spread out before us, and off to the left I could see the big bridge across to the west side. A massive barge was heading past on its way downriver to New Orleans. There were two doors that opened out to a balcony that ran the entire length of the living room. There was some cheap white plastic furniture out there, along with a couple of dying palm trees in enormous planters.

The afternoon sun was undoubtedly murder on the balcony, but it was probably lovely out there in the mornings.

"So, why did you slug the attorney general?" Frank asked, his blue eyes twinkling. He was trying really hard not to smile. I glanced over at Frank, who had an amused look on his face.

I couldn't help but wonder what his own mother had been like.

Frank and Mom had hit it off after a slightly rocky start. I'd met Frank over Southern Decadence weekend, when he was still working for the FBI. He'd actually been in New Orleans on a job, investigating a gubernatorial candidate's rumored ties with a homophobic neo-Nazi group. I'd stumbled into the middle of his investigation—and he'd not exactly been thrilled when a gay go-go dancer was so deeply mixed up in the whole mess that it proved to be easier to involve me rather than extricate me. Mom already had a rather dim view of the FBI and was definitely not too thrilled when they used me as bait to draw out the bad guys and I wound up being kidnapped. But everything worked out in the end—the bad guys went to jail and I ended up with Frank. Mom, ever the pragmatist, welcomed Frank into the family like he was a long-lost son. Mom is pretty hard to resist, and it didn't take long before Frank worshipped the ground she walked on. He was wrapped around her little finger, and she could get him to do things for her that her own kids wouldn't do.

I also knew Mom would embrace his nephew and make him feel like a part of the family.

Taylor Wheeler had no idea what he was in for when he got to New Orleans.

Honestly, I still wasn't completely comfortable with taking on the responsibility of a teenager. But I couldn't just let Taylor wind up homeless and broke, not as long as I had breath in my body and money in the bank. I wasn't raised that way. And if Mom and Dad had the slightest hint that I *considered* not helping Taylor—well, I may be in my thirties, but Mom did like to remind me every once in a while that I wasn't too big to be spanked. Besides, I'd read too many articles online about parents throwing their gay kids away like so much garbage, and every time I did, it broke my heart a little. I was so lucky to have my parents. The least I could do as a karmic payback to the universe would be to help Frank's nephew and welcome him into the family. And it wasn't like he was some wide-eyed innocent from a small town in Alabama coming to New Orleans for the first time. He had a year of college behind him, including a few months living in Paris. New Orleans might even seem provincial to him after the City of Light. With Colin off on a job for who knows how long, we did have that empty apartment upstairs for him to use.

Yeah, there was no way I could live with myself if we turned our backs on Taylor.

Besides, Mom would kill us both if we didn't take him in.

"Yes, tell us what triggered your latest crime spree, Mom," I added, with a broad wink at Frank. "I mean, really. The state attorney general?"

Actually, I already had a pretty good idea why she had smacked him one. She'd been railing about him ever since he was elected. Troy Dufresne had run as a moderate Democrat, promising to work together with the opposition to solve Louisiana's problems. He had some interesting plans about increasing law enforcement and regulating businesses— especially oil companies operating out in the gulf. The Deepwater Horizon disaster was still pretty fresh in voters' minds, and Mom herself had railed against BP and how the legislature was owned by corporations and special interests for years. Dufresne painted himself as a tireless crusader for the people, prepared to come to Baton Rouge and root out corruption and clean up the state from one end to the other.

That lasted about five minutes after the votes were counted and he was elected by a huge margin.

Almost immediately he started talking about switching party affiliations. No sooner was he sworn in than he went ahead and did it. Almost every person he appointed to work for his office was a tool of special interests and corporations—including an attorney who'd worked for BP. Everyone who'd voted for him was livid. Editorials all over the state, regardless of political affiliation, trashed Dufresne. The nicer ones claimed he'd defrauded the voters, others claiming he'd sold his soul to the very people he'd run against. For a man in his mid-thirties who obviously had higher aspirations in politics, he'd pretty much destroyed himself in Louisiana. Louisiana voters were willing to overlook a lot from their politicians. You could be reelected after being exposed as a regular patron of a bordello. We'd elected a governor who was serving a jail sentence at the time for taking bribes *when he'd been serving as governor before.*

But Louisiana voters don't trust politicians who switch parties.

Go figure.

To add insult to injury, once Dufresne had been sworn in, he started throwing his weight around in an attempt to out-conservative the governor, who could best be described as an arch-conservative. (An über-conservative?) In his move to the far right, he passed many religious right leaders and left them brushing off his dust. He stated, in a speech at Loyola's New Orleans campus, that he supported amending the state constitution to permanently prevent any "equal pay for equal work" legislation. He also went on record as saying he would defend the state's horrible "right to work" laws with his dying breath. Despite the Supreme Court ruling in *Lawrence v. Texas* overturning sodomy laws and decriminalizing gay sexuality once and for all, Attorney General Dufresne seemed intent on enforcing Louisiana's sodomy law, which had never been officially repealed. A gay couple in the small town of Rouen, on the north shore and Troy Dufresne's hometown, had recently been arrested for sodomy—and Troy Dufresne had given a press conference, claiming it was time for Louisiana to take a stand against godlessness. I hadn't taken it too seriously—a federal appeal would certainly overturn any conviction, and the couple was going to have one hell of a lawsuit on their hands against the sheriff in Rouen and the state of Louisiana, and rightly so.

However, as far as Mom was concerned, it was like Dufresne had waved a red flag in her face.

"What kind of asswipe would want to enforce that archaic sodomy law? The goddamned Supreme Court of the United States overturned every goddamned state sodomy law in the country! What kind of lawyer disregards a Supreme Court ruling?" Mom's eyes narrowed as she plopped down in an easy chair. "He'll be coming after abortion clinics and Planned Parenthood next, you just mark my words—and we need to be ready for the son of a bitch." She sighed, almost visibly deflating as the anger drained out of her. "I didn't go there to slap him, you know. I just wanted to see if I could talk some sense into him, make him realize he was killing his own career. No one is going to vote for a man who made Louisiana the laughingstock of the country, and that's what this is going to do. But he's such a smug bastard I just lost my temper and let him have it." She shrugged and pointed an index finger at me. "Wipe that grin off your face, Scotty, this is serious. You and Frank could just as easily be arrested next, you know. If he really intends to keep enforcing this law—"

"The New Orleans Police Department would never even try, Mom, and you know it," I reminded her, trying not to smile. "The gay tourist dollar is too valuable."

"He doesn't care, Scotty." She shook her head, the braid moving back and forth. "He's trying to make a name for himself as a conservative politician—he thinks this is his ticket to higher office. I'm serious. He's already gone after the gays—it'll be abortion next. We have to stop him *now.*"

I opened my mouth, but Storm cut me off. "What makes this even worse is she used *my* name to get in to see him." He gave me a dour look. "I can't wait to see the headline in the *Baton Rouge Advocate* tomorrow morning: 'Freshman Senator's Mother Slugs Attorney General.'" He rolled his eyes and refilled his glass. "I'll have to see if I can get him to drop the charges when he calms down."

"At least it'll play well with your constituents," I pointed out.

"I hope he doesn't drop the charges." Mom set her jaw.

Frank stood behind her chair, reached down, and hugged her from behind. "Please don't ever change, Mom," he said, his face lighting up with a smile. He met my eyes and winked.

Seeing the two of them together, and how much they obviously loved each other, made my heart happy.

I couldn't help but wonder what his mother had been like.

Although I could be reasonably certain she was *nothing* like mine.

She closed her eyes and rested her head against one of his arms as Storm picked up the remote control and turned the television on. He sat down on the couch. "Might as well see what they have to say on the news." He put his feet up on the coffee table. "What a day—a bomb threat on the LSU campus, my mother slugs the attorney general...I wonder if the bomb squad found anything?"

"Who would want to blow up LSU?" Frank asked, still standing behind Mom. "It just doesn't make any sense."

"I'm betting it was a frat prank," I replied.

"Hush," Storm said, turning up the volume as the commercial break ended and the news came back on.

"And now, with the latest on the bomb scare on campus today, is Annetra Tyler. Annetra?"

Annetra Tyler was a beautiful young African American woman with shoulder-length hair. She wore a blazer with the station's call numbers on it and held a microphone with the logo on it as well. She was standing in front of the tiger habitat on the campus, where the school mascot Mike lived. The habitat was across the street from Tiger Stadium and was one of the biggest and most expensive tiger habitats in the world. LSU had had a live tiger mascot ever since the 1930s, and Mike was a point of pride for almost everyone in the state. Every Saturday in the fall it seemed like the entire state came to a complete halt during the LSU football games. The current Mike was the sixth one, and one of the most exciting traditions for the games was when Mike and his cage were driven into the stadium and around the field with the cheerleaders on top. Everyone in the stadium jumps to their feet and cheers.

I've only been to a few games in Tiger Stadium, and there's *nothing* like it.

"Thanks, Aaron," Annetra was saying on the television.

"University administration has announced that it is now safe for everyone to return to the campus, but classes are officially canceled for the rest of the day. The bomb squad and dogs found nothing suspicious, but the campus administration, the campus, city, and state police are all working together to get to the bottom of this scare. But I've just been notified and have confirmed that Mike the Tiger has been kidnapped."

"What the hell?" Mom gasped. "Who kidnaps a tiger?"

"*How* do you kidnap a tiger is a better question," Frank said with a frown.

"For more on this breaking story, here's Brandon Hardy. Brandon?"

The picture on the television switched from the newscaster to a young white man holding a microphone. In the background was a large Chevrolet pickup truck. There was steam coming from under its hood, and the back tires were still on the country road, the front end down in a ditch running alongside the road. Given the thick forest on either side of the road, Brandon Hardy was clearly broadcasting from out in the country somewhere. He was rather good-looking, with curly dark hair and broad shoulders underneath his station jacket. His eyes were opened wide, and he spoke in that hushed, barely-able-to-contain-my-shocked-excitement tone newscasters must learn in college.

"Thanks, Annetra. As always, the veterinary students and university police evacuated Mike the Tiger before the full evacuation of students, faculty, and university employees began. The plan was for Mike to be moved to a secure facility just outside of town, which the university built for just these kinds of emergencies. But things didn't go according to the careful plans made for just such an occurrence."

Brandon Hardy started walking along the road, the camera following him. "When the truck towing Mike in his trailer reached this point in the road, they were cut off by a white panel van. Once the truck stopped, masked armed men jumped out of the van, tied up the veterinary students and campus security, and knocked them unconscious. They apparently unhooked the coupling and took Mike and his trailer. When the students and security regained consciousness, the trailer and the van were gone. One of them was able to call for help on his cell phone. The state police have put out an APB on the van and are asking anyone who may have seen the van—or Mike's trailer—to call." Brandon Hardy stopped walking and looked back at the camera. "Apparently, there have been some threats made about Mike in the past few weeks."

The camera cut to a young woman's face. There was a bandage on her forehead, and she looked distraught. A caption appeared under her face, reading HOPE PORTERIE, LSU VETERINARY SCIENCE MAJOR. Mom gasped as Hope started speaking.

"We've been getting some threatening letters and calls," Hope Porterie was saying to Brandon Hardy. "But we get that sort of thing from time to time, you know, cranks and pranks— drunk frat boys from Ole Miss or Arkansas or Alabama, saying they're going to kidnap Mike, but you know, who's going to kidnap a Bengal tiger?" She shook her head, and her eyes filled with tears.

"We've also been getting some threats from an animal rights group, saying it was inhumane to keep a tiger on a college campus and drag him out for football games, but you know, we get that kind of stuff all the time and it never means anything, you know, it's just people trying to make a point." Her voice broke. "Mike is very well cared for, and we keep him healthy and fed and happy. Who would do such a thing? Why? I hope the people who did this are aware of how dangerous he is. He's used to people, but he is still a wild animal and can do a lot of damage." She wiped at her eyes. "Please, whoever did this, if you're watching, *please* let us bring Mike back home."

The camera zoomed in on Brandon Hardy's face as he solemnly said, "Who would kidnap a tiger? That's the question on everyone's lips tonight, Annetra. Back to you in the studio, Aaron."

"Do the police think that maybe the bomb threat was a decoy, to get Mike moved off campus so he could be taken?" the news anchor asked, a concerned look on his face.

"The state police are looking at every possibility, Aaron."

"Thanks, Brandon." The camera went back to Aaron in the studio, and he smiled at the camera. "After the break, a ruckus at the state capitol today brought legislative business to a standstill."

We all just stared at the television as a Subway sandwich commercial started. Storm picked up the remote and muted the sound. He whistled. "I can't believe someone kidnapped a two-thousand-pound tiger in broad daylight and *got away with the tiger!*"

"This is just terrible, absolutely terrible." Mom moaned, rubbing her eyes. She looked at me and then Storm. "Poor Hope. Storm, you have to do something."

"You know her, Mom?" I asked, starting to get that wretched feeling in my stomach. *Of course Mom knows her.*

Mom nodded. "She's Veronica Porterie's daughter."

"Oh, good God." Storm buried his face in his hands, and the knot in my stomach tightened.

"Veronica Porterie?" Frank looked confused. "The woman who runs that crazy animal rights group?"

"AFAR," I replied, taking a deep breath. "She was Mom's best friend in high school."

AFAR stood for "Army For Animal Rights." It had started as a group trying to keep cats and dogs in California shelters from being euthanized. But as Veronica Porterie raised more and more money, AFAR's vision expanded and its members became more and more aggressive and belligerent. They became known for breaking into laboratories and setting test animals free. They protested against zoos and hunting. They called wearing fur murder, and as more and more time passed, Veronica Porterie seemed less connected with reality.

I hadn't seen her in years, and I'd never known she had a

child; she always seemed to be too busy saving animals from humans to be bothered with marriage, family, or kids. She was tried for murder in California a while back—they'd broken into a testing facility to release animals and a security guard had wound up dead. There had been a hung jury—afterward, the jurors who'd voted against acquitting her felt the prosecutor hadn't proved she was the actual killer or had even been there, which she denied. After the trial, AFAR kept a low profile for a few years, but they'd been getting more active again lately.

"Wait a minute," I said slowly. "One of the vet students who takes care of Mike just happens to be the daughter of a militant animal rights activist? That can't be a coincidence."

"She's going to be their top suspect once they figure it out." Mom buried her face in her hands. "It won't matter to them one bit that Hope hasn't seen her mother since she was a little girl."

"Why not?" Frank asked.

"After Veronica was tried for killing that security guard, her parents sued for custody of Hope and won," Storm explained. "They also managed to get a restraining order against Veronica so she couldn't even see the child."

"That seems a bit extreme." Frank frowned.

"That poor child—Storm, she's going to need a damned good lawyer, and I know you'll do the right thing and represent her." She stood up and walked over to the window. "This is really bad. Hope wouldn't be involved, I just know she wouldn't."

I was about to ask why when the phone buzzed. "That's our pizza," I said, heading for the door. "No one says a word until I get back."

When I got back upstairs with the hot pizza, the news was back on and there was a picture of Mom on the screen. "Mrs. Bradley has been arrested before, mainly for disturbing the peace or resisting arrest, but this is her first arrest for assault," the news anchor was saying as I kicked the door shut with my foot. "Attorney General Dufresne's office has not returned any of our calls asking for a statement."

"Terrible picture," Mom said as Storm turned off the television. "I've never taken a good mug shot."

"There's something to aspire to," Storm replied sourly. "I'm sure if you get arrested enough times, you're bound to take a good one sooner or later."

Mom gave him a dirty look. "You're not too old for me to spank, you know."

Frank interrupted before Storm could say anything. "Mom, you said you went to high school with Veronica Porterie?"

"McGehee." Mom nodded, making a face as she said the word. Mom hated that she went to McGehee, which to her symbolized privilege, power and snobbery—everything she believed was wrong with our country and society. When it was time for college, she refused to go to Vanderbilt—the traditional school for the Diderot family—and went to the University of New Orleans instead. She'd started dating Dad in high school. Since the Bradleys were an LSU family, Dad went to LSU for a year before transferring down to UNO. He and Mom have been together ever since. "Veronica and I were in the same class, we started kindergarten together. I don't remember how we first met or how we became friends—all I know is we were inseparable until we graduated." She smiled, her eyes a million miles away, lost in memory. "She always liked animals. She always wanted to be a vet or something, you know, work with animals. She always liked animals better than people. She went to Berkeley, and she really changed there—I don't know what it was. I mean, she was in Greenpeace for a while"—she inhaled—"and I joined because of her, you know. But Greenpeace isn't the same as AFAR. But AFAR wasn't originally what it is now, either. Your father and I were two of the original members of AFAR, and we donated a lot of money over the years. But as much as I believe animals should be treated ethically, I don't believe you have the right to destroy personal property. Or harm people to prove your point. That pizza smells good."

I flipped open the box. "Help yourself. But it's not vegetarian."

"I'm so hungry I don't care," Mom said, grabbing a slice and taking a healthy bite, strings of mozzarella stretching from the slice to her mouth. "Storm, I wish you'd give Hope a call. She's really going to need some help. You know the police are just going to turn on her once they find out who her mother is."

"After I eat, Mom." Storm took a slice.

"How come I've never met Hope?" I asked. "Or ever heard of her before today?"

Mom sighed. "Veronica has never married, you know. She's never, as long as I've known her, had a long-term relationship with a man. It's like she always thought all they were good for was sex." She laughed. "And some aren't even good for that. I was really surprised when she told me she was pregnant. AFAR had already started liberating animals from testing labs by then, and your father and I were distancing ourselves from the organization. She wasn't married, and she didn't tell me who the father was." She took another bite of the pizza. "The baby was about three when that security guard got killed. Her parents sued for custody and won, like I said, and got that restraining order against Veronica so she couldn't see her own daughter. Her father died shortly after—your grandfather believes knowing his daughter was a murderer is what killed Albert Porterie—and his wife moved away from New Orleans. I think she wanted to get away from where everyone knew they were related to Veronica. I can't say as I blame them." She tossed the crust back into the box. "Funny that she wound up a veterinary student, don't you think? Just goes to show, you can't escape your genes."

"So, you do know her, Mom?" Frank took another slice of pizza and wiped grease from his chin.

Mom nodded. "I made a point of inviting her down to New Orleans when I found out she was coming back to school here." She glanced at me. "I stayed in touch with Veronica's mother, even after she…after that security guard was killed. She was my friend, I wanted to make sure, you know, that her daughter was okay. Veronica never tried to get in touch, in all of those years…" She glanced over at the television. "Taking the tiger—it is the kind of thing they'd do." She sighed. "But how do you kidnap a tiger in bright daylight? Surely someone had to *notice* them driving that tiger around; it's not like his cage isn't garish."

"All you'd need is an eighteen-wheeler." I shrugged as I took a drink of my soda. "With a hydraulic lift, I guess, you could haul the trailer into the back, and once you pull the door down, voilà. No one can see the tiger, and you're just another truck driving down the road. The question is, where can you keep a tiger that people wouldn't notice?"

"A barn somewhere," Frank pointed out. "If you're out in the country and you have a barn on the property, you can just leave the tiger in the cage and, you know, throw meat in to it. And if the barn is far enough away from the road…no one would hear it roaring."

"Yes, that makes some sense," Storm mused, muffling a burp with his hand. "But AFAR couldn't be responsible. Their thing is to return animals to their natural state. So they wouldn't keep a tiger captive in a cage somewhere. They'd want to return it to Africa or India or wherever the tiger is indigenous."

"But Mike wasn't a wild tiger," I replied. "He was raised as a cub in captivity. He wouldn't know how to survive in the wild."

Mom's lips compressed into a tight line. "AFAR doesn't care about that sort of thing." Her face looked severe, like she was trying to hold on to her temper. "Veronica always claimed that animals were instinctive, that a tiger or any animal raised in captivity will instinctually know how to survive if returned to the wild, like how a housecat will go feral if it escapes, or a dog will go wild." She shook her head. "I don't know if it's true or not, but…it just seemed wrong to me. So many things they believe… are wrong. That's why your father and I finally had to just walk away from AFAR. It really broke my heart, you know. Veronica was my best friend. But people change."

I closed the now-empty pizza box and folded it up for the recycling bin. "So, Storm, are you going to call her?"

"Well, I don't think it would hurt her to have some legal advice." He yawned, stretching his arms overhead.

"I'll call her." Mom got up, digging for her cell phone in her purse before going out onto the balcony.

Storm gave Frank and me a strange look. "Somehow, I have the feeling this isn't going to be the last we've heard of this. Things never seem to go easily for us."

He had a point.

CHAPTER THREE
STRENGTH, REVERSED
Discord in one's affairs

Although I'm the one who has some psychic ability, Mom's prediction about Hope needing a lawyer came true the very next morning.

Storm was on his way out the door when I staggered out of the room Frank and I were sharing in desperate need of coffee. "There's coffee made in the kitchen," he said as he went out the front door. "I'm running late for the session. See you tonight at the match if not before." The door closed behind him.

I walked into the kitchen with a sigh. I dumped the coffee and made a fresh pot—Storm made coffee so awful that there aren't proper words to describe it. I'd hoped Mom was already up—no one made coffee good enough to match hers. It wasn't quite eight yet. I yawned again while the coffee brewed. I hadn't slept very well, tossing and turning all night while trying not to wake Frank up. He needed his sleep—he needed to be totally on his game tonight, and I wasn't going to be responsible for him not being on his A game. When there was enough coffee in the pot for a cup, I went ahead and poured myself one. I walked over to the window and looked out at the muddy river.

We hadn't stayed up too late—even Mom, who usually doesn't go to bed until the sun is rising, was yawning and wandered off to her bed around eleven. I was feeling pretty worn out myself. It had been a rather long day, and Frank didn't need to be convinced when I said it was time for us to go to bed as well.

Frank, like always, was sound asleep almost the moment his head hit the pillow.

But not me—the best I managed all night was that awful half-sleep where your mind is still very much aware it's awake but your body thinks it's sleeping. I couldn't seem to get comfortable in the bed—it was a little too soft for my liking—and every time I seemed to be about to fall into a deep restful sleep, Frank would turn over onto his back and start snoring.

Of course, when he does that at home I just put my hand underneath him and lift a bit—he always rolls right over onto his side and it stops.

But I was afraid I'd wake him—and then what if he couldn't get back to sleep? Then he'd show up for his big match all tired and worn out and unable to focus. And when a professional wrestler is tired and unfocused, that's when injuries and disasters in the ring are more likely to occur, and I wasn't about to be responsible for that.

An overactive imagination can truly be a bit of a curse sometimes.

I finished my cup of coffee and had just poured another when Frank came wandering into the kitchen in just his black Calvin Klein briefs. He smiled at me sleepily before getting a cup down from the cupboard and pouring himself some coffee. "I don't suppose there's anything to eat around here?" He leaned back against the counter and took a sip of the coffee.

"Not likely. Storm doesn't cook. That's why he has all those delivery menus."

Frank walked over to the window, giving me a lovely backside view of the muscle development in his back, his narrow waist, and his perfectly shaped ass. "You don't suppose there's a diner somewhere nearby?" He absentmindedly scratched his leg. "I really am starving."

"I guess we can find out."

Mom was still asleep when we finished washing up and getting dressed, so we went foraging for breakfast on our own.

We found a nice little greasy-spoon diner a few blocks away from the condo. Frank had an egg-white mushroom omelet, while I indulged with blueberry waffles. "You nervous about tonight?" I asked when he finished and pushed his plate away.

He shook his head and beamed at me. "No, it's going to be great. You're going to be amazed." He winked at me and sighed. "No, I'm worried about my nephew." He rubbed his hands over his head. "I was thinking I should e-mail my sister and have him come down right away, don't you think?"

"It's fine with me," I replied. It wasn't completely a lie—I hated the thought of him being stuck up there in Homophobia County, and said so. "The sooner he gets out of there, the better. I still have some reservations, but they aren't about *him*, they're about *me*, if that makes sense?"

Frank grinned at me. "We've been together how long? Of course it makes sense." He put his hands down on top of mine. "Thanks, Scotty, I appreciate this."

I got some toast and jelly to go for Mom, and we walked back to the Riverview Tower. We kissed in the elevator on the way up, and I was thinking it might not be such a bad idea for him to have sex the day of a match when the elevator opened on Storm's floor.

But as we walked down the hall to Storm's door I imagined all kinds of awful things happening to Frank in the ring because I'd worn him out.

Stupid overactive imagination.

Mom was sitting on the couch with a cup of coffee watching the television when we walked in. "Hey, guys," she said, not looking away from the television screen.

"We got you some toast," I said, handing her the bag and sitting down next to her as she started spreading jelly on her toast.

"I need to jump in the shower and head down to the arena," Frank said, kissing the top of her head.

I considered joining him, but decided not to. It would be

weird with Mom in the living room, for one thing, and there was that whole "day of the match" thing.

Tonight, though, was going to be a different story.

"What are you watching?" I asked after the bedroom door closed.

"I keep hoping there's going to be some more news about Mike," she replied between bites. "They're calling it a tiger-napping." She rolled her eyes at me and gestured to the coffee table where the morning paper sat. "I suppose that's what everyone is going to call it now," Mom said with a sigh. "Tiger-napping. Seriously. Why must they always invent words?"

"I don't know. I guess *kidnapping* didn't seem dramatic enough." I picked up the paper. The headline on the front page of the *Baton Rouge Advocate* screamed MIKE KIDNAPPED!!! Right below that was a photo of him in his habitat, yawning and looking totally bored. "Besides, it's not every day a tiger is kidnapped. Did it make the national news?"

"Shh." She turned up the volume just as the video of a frightened-looking young girl being walked up the steps of the police station by two uniformed cops played on the screen. Across the bottom of the picture was the caption VETERINARY STUDENT IN CHARGE OF MIKE HAS TIES TO ANIMAL RIGHTS ACTIVISTS.

"Hope Porterie is the daughter of the notorious Veronica Porterie, who founded the AFAR group back in the 1980s." The newscaster's voice was breathless, her tone screaming *Can you believe this?* A really horrible photo of Veronica Porterie—her mug shot from her arrest for the security guard's murder—popped up on the screen. "When AFAR broke into the animal-testing facility for Flax Cosmetics, they released all the animals, but a security guard was killed. Veronica Porterie was tried for his murder, but the result was a hung jury. The district attorney chose not to try her again." Now her voice was disapproving: *Can you believe he didn't throw the book at this lunatic?* "And we here at WBRZ News have recently learned that AFAR has been threatening to 'free Mike' for more than a year. And the group founder's daughter somehow managed to insinuate herself into caring for Mike—and was with him when AFAR kidnapped him. Things are not looking good this morning for Hope Porterie. Back to you, Jim."

"That's really bad," I said as Mom muted the television. "But I suppose it was just a matter of time before the connection turned up."

"Guilty until proven innocent," she said, picking up her cell phone. "I'm going to text Storm."

"You don't think there's a connection?" I replied, a little dubiously. "I mean, come on, Mom. Her mother runs AFAR."

"Nobody knows for a fact that AFAR took Mike, Scotty. What kind of private eye are you, anyway? Automatically assuming guilt based on circumstantial evidence?" Mom replied. "Besides, don't you think the FBI has had Hope's phone tapped for years now?" She fumbled with her phone for a moment before giving up and dialing.

I was glad Frank was in the shower. Frank adores her, but as a retired FBI special agent, Mom's paranoia about the Bureau sometimes got a bit under his skin. He never said anything when Mom went on one of her tears, but his face would always flush a bit and that vein in his forehead would start throbbing. Both Dad and I had talked to Mom about it—to at least ease up on the feds or just bite her tongue in front of Frank—and she *had* gotten a lot better. But once she's wound up there is no turning back the tide.

"Storm, it's your mother. The cops have taken Hope in—we just saw it on the news. You need to get down there!" She paused, listening, and started talking again. I got up, tuning her out, and walked over to the bedroom. I didn't hear the shower running, so I went inside. Frank was shaving, naked, in the bathroom with the door open. He turned his head and smiled.

"I called my sister," he said, going back to shaving. "I told her to send Taylor down as soon as possible. She's going to put him on a flight from Birmingham to New Orleans." He smiled back at the mirror. "I called Rain, she's going to pick him up tonight for us and take him home with her. She'll bring him over once we get back home tomorrow."

I sat down on the bed. "Wow." That was quick.

He rinsed the lather off his face and walked over to me, kissing the top of my head. "It'll be fine, Scotty." He started getting dressed. "I haven't seen Taylor since he was a little boy." He pulled on a pair of sweatpants and laughed. "You should see your face—you look like you've seen a ghost." He finished getting dressed and walked back over to me.

"It'll be fine," he said, stroking my arm and kissing my head again. "We can't just abandon him. Where else will he go?"

I nodded. I knew he was right, and really—how awful could an eighteen-year-old gay boy be?

But I still had a knot in my stomach.

I followed him out into the living room.

"Taylor's coming down tonight on a Southwest flight," he announced.

Mom grinned and bounded over to him, her braid bouncing. "That's so wonderful!" She hugged him and looked at me with a strange look. She reached over and took my hand. "You really don't need to worry so much about Taylor," she said. "You and Frank—and Colin, when he's here—are great role models for him, you know."

"Yeah," I replied, not convinced.

"I have to get going," Frank said, kissing me on the cheek. "I'll see you guys at the arena, okay?"

I smiled until the door shut behind him. I let out a sigh. "Mom, I'm terrified."

"You're being ridiculous, you know." She shook her head. "You're going to be fine. Really. He's just a kid, and think about where he grew up. He has a lot to learn."

"He spent the last few months in Paris. He could probably teach me a few things." I walked over to the sliding glass door and put my forehead against the glass. I knew I was being ridiculous, but I couldn't help myself. "I—I have nothing to show for my life, Mom." I blew out my breath and looked back at the river. A barge was slowly passing, on its way to New Orleans. "Before I met Frank, what was I? A personal trainer and stripper who could barely pay his bills—and wasn't even capable of having any kind of relationship with another guy. I was sexually active, I slept with total strangers who picked me up in bars, I used to dance on bars in a thong for dollar bills. I mean, yeah, that's exactly the path Taylor should take, don't you think?"

Mom patted my hand. "Are you ashamed of your past, Scotty?"

I thought about it for a moment—the one-night stands, the nights spent dancing on Ecstasy until the sun came up, and grinned. "Well, no, not really."

"You were always a good person, Scotty, and isn't that really the most important thing?" She gave me an odd look. "What's this all about, anyway? Are you really that nervous about Taylor coming down here?" She smacked the side of my face lightly with her hand. "Think about this poor kid for a minute, Scotty. He's grown up in some horribly repressed small town in northwest Alabama, where everyone goes to church and acts holier-than-thou while sinning in the worst possible ways behind closed doors. He's probably hated himself for most of his life, having to hide who he really was because he was afraid of exactly what has happened—his family turning on him. I don't know much about the University of Alabama other than they have a good football team, but I can't imagine anywhere in Alabama being really gay-friendly, can you?"

I shook my head.

"So what Taylor really needs is acceptance and to see that gay people aren't evil, aren't going to hell, are decent human beings who live their lives without hurting anyone else. And I can't think of anyone better to show him that than you and Frank."

"Thanks, Mom." I put my head back. "What did Storm say about Hope?"

"He's on his way to the police station." She scowled and sat up. "What time is Frank's match?"

"The show starts at seven," I replied, raising an eyebrow. I didn't like the determined look on her face, or the tone of her voice. She was up to something. "Frank's the headline match, of course, so he probably won't be on until at least nine thirty. The whole broadcast is supposed to be over by ten. Why?"

"You mind taking a little drive with me?" Her face took on an air of affected innocence. "A little adventure with your old mom? Come on, it'll be fun."

"Where to?" I raised my eyebrows. "What are you up to, Mom?"

"We'll be back in plenty of time to have dinner and make it to Frank's match," she said in a wheedling tone, ignoring my question and glancing at her watch. "Come on, I just have a hunch I want to check out." She patted my arm and gave me an enormous smile. "If it doesn't play out, well, we'll get to spend some quality time together."

Now I was really suspicious. "Quality time" almost *always* meant doing something I didn't want to, and without fail it turned out to be something terribly unpleasant.

But truth be told, I didn't have anything to do until it was time to head over to the arena.

And I *hadn't* spent any time with Mom alone in a while. "Okay, I'm up for whatever. Let me get cleaned up—just a quick shower."

Less than fifteen minutes later, we were in her car flying down I-10 heading back in the direction of New Orleans.

"Where are we going?" I asked for probably the thousandth time since we'd gotten into her car. "I'm in the car, Mom, so it's not like I can change my mind."

"I have a hunch, okay?" She glanced over at me and back to the road as she swerved into a lane and around a slow-moving Cadillac. "The Porteries had a cabin on the north shore, just outside of Rouen, in the Manchac Swamp near Lake Maurepas.

Her father and his buddies used to use it for hunting and fishing. If Veronica was behind the tiger-napping, she had to have a place to take the tiger, right? And it had to be somewhere relatively close but out of the way. What's more out of the way than the Manchac Swamp?"

She had a point, I had to give her that. "But, Mom, the swamp is almost all the way back to New Orleans."

She rolled her eyes at me. "It's an hour drive, at most. We're just going to head out there, take a look around, and head back, okay?" She patted my leg. "It makes sense, though, doesn't it? The tiger was taken on a back road—a back road that might have been on the way to Rouen. No one has seen Mike since he was kidnapped. How is that possible? How do you hide a tiger? Wouldn't it make sense for Veronica and her goons to take him to the old hunting cabin?" She moved over into the left lane. "It's easier to get there from I-12, if I remember correctly. We take the Pumpkin Center exit, and take 22…" She wondered for a moment. "I think I can remember where the turn into the swamp is…I just know it's easier from I-12 than from 55." She laughed. "I always thought her father's devotion to hunting had something to do with why Veronica became such an animal rights activist." She grinned at me. "Kind of like how you're such a determined meat eater because your dad and I are vegetarians."

"That's not why—most people eat meat," I protested. "And once you've had bacon—well, there's no turning back." When we were kids, both sets of grandparents were horrified that Mom and Dad were raising their kids as vegetarians, so they fed us meat at every opportunity.

I swear to God if I never eat tofu again it will be too soon.

"I do miss bacon," Mom replied in a dreamy voice. "Sometimes I dream about it."

"You don't *have* to be a vegetarian, Mom."

"I know you find it hard to believe, but your father and I actually *like* tofu." She winked at me. "But every once in a while, I slip down to the Rouse's and buy some bacon, okay? And if you tell anyone I said that I'll call you a liar." She shuddered. "I don't even want to think about how awful your brother would be if he knew."

She veered off to the left—cutting off an enormous pickup truck on jacked-up tires that blared its horn at her—and got onto I-12. She reached down and turned up her satellite radio, which she had set on a classic rock station. I rolled my eyes as we hurtled along I-12, through the towering pine trees lining both sides of the highway. She flipped open the ashtray and pulled out a half-smoked joint.

"You are *not* going to get stoned and drive," I said, grabbing it out of her hand. "Seriously, Mom. Do you want to get arrested again?" I dropped it into my shirt pocket. "We can smoke it when we get back to Baton Rouge." I leaned back into my seat as she passed another eighteen-wheeler like it was standing still. "So, tell me about Veronica Porterie."

"I've pretty much told you everything already."

"Sure you have." I smirked at her. "Do you really expect me to believe you haven't spoken to her since that security guard was killed? I know Storm didn't believe it, either."

"You're too smart for your own good," she snapped. "Yes, I've spoken to her from time to time. I've even given her money sometimes, when she needed it." She sighed. "The security guard was an accident—they thought the lab would be empty. They didn't want anyone to die. It was an accident, Scotty. I believe her. Veronica might be a little unhinged when it comes to animals, but she's not a killer." She bit her lower lip. "I *have* to believe that."

I didn't know what to say to that. We sped along in silence for a while. We passed cars and exits at a pretty fast clip while the stereo blared Foreigner's "Cold As Ice," followed by "Carry On Wayward Son" by Kansas. Mom slowed down—not enough for my comfort level—to take the exit marked PUMPKIN CENTER with BAPTIST below it. She didn't slow down even as we flew down the off-ramp, even though there was a stop sign clearly visible at the bottom of the ramp. She slammed on the brakes, throwing me forward—if not for my seat belt I probably would have gone through the windshield.

I come by my bad driving habits naturally. It's clearly in my DNA.

"Drama queen," Mom said, turning right and flooring it to pick up speed as we passed a gas station and a building with a sign that—and I am not making this up—read FORMAL WEAR AND BAIT.

"Now, that's a reality show just waiting to happen," I commented.

"Don't give them any ideas." Mom rolled her eyes as the car picked up even more speed. "It's bad enough they're doing one of those *Grande Dames* shows in New Orleans."

I chose not to tell her Frank, Colin, and I watched the *Grande Dames* shows religiously and were looking forward to the New Orleans version like kids waiting for Christmas. The road we were on dead-ended at State Road 22, and Mom turned left, speeding up again as we passed through a more residential area. I glanced at my watch—it wasn't quite noon yet. There was still plenty of time for us to get back. The odds that Mike the Tiger was at this old hunting cabin were slim—hell, for that matter, the cabin itself might not even be there anymore. Mom hadn't been out there herself since she was a teenager—and that was a lot longer ago than she wanted to think about. Even in a worst-case scenario, I didn't have to be there for the first matches—I didn't have to be there until Frank got into the ring—but the truth was I'd been getting into the matches somewhat over the years as Frank's star rose.

To be honest, I had thought it was kind of silly that Frank had wanted to become a professional wrestler. I would never say that to him, of course—I'm not that big a dick. But I was a wrestler in high school and had always seen the professional style to be rather silly and cartoonish. But it took all of his courage to tell me he wanted to try it. It was in the days after the storm when the city lay in ruins and we didn't know if New

Orleans was going to rebound from the horror. I don't know how long it took him to drum up the courage to bring it up, and he was so absolutely adorable when he told me—I didn't have the heart to tease him or say it was ridiculous. He got accepted into a top training school in the Midwest and was gone for about two months.

And when he started e-mailing me photos of him in the outfits—well, he looked fucking smoking hot in the trunks, knee pads, and the boots.

Porn star hot.

And who knew Frank, so quiet and reserved, was charismatic enough to win the fans over and rock the interviews where he threatened maiming mayhem for his next opponent?

She slowed and made a right turn on a dirt road.

"How much farther is this place?" I asked. "Are you sure it's still accessible?" Dirt roads leading into swamps didn't exactly fill me with confidence. "We're not going to get stuck out here?"

"Relax already." Mom waved her hand dismissively. "We'll be back in plenty of time. I don't want to miss it, either. Dad's taping the pay-per-view, too." Mom and Dad were two of Frank's biggest fans, taping every broadcast. They'd even hung a signed poster of him in trunks and wearing his title belt in their tobacco shop, the Devil's Weed.

"If you say so," I grumbled. Mom was not the best when it came to time management, so I knew I was going to have to keep an eye on the clock and nudge her along.

About twenty minutes later we were definitely getting into the swampy area nearer the lake. The road narrowed until there was barely room for our car. Less than a foot from the side of the road on either side was murky water and marsh grasses. Spanish moss hung from the huge limbs of massive live oaks. She was driving slower now. I couldn't get over how silent it was out there. Finally, she turned into a dirt driveway with a rusted metal mailbox on the side of the road. The door hung open, and the little plastic red flag was hanging at a weird angle alongside. Mom didn't speed up, and dust rose behind us in our wake. I saw an alligator's head in the water alongside the road and shivered a bit. I've never been a fan of swamps, and that long-ago Southern Decadence weekend when I first met Frank, I'd been kidnapped by some very bad guys and taken out into a swamp to their camp. I'd had nightmares about that experience for quite a while afterward. Even though it had been eight years, I still got squeamish around swamps.

Eventually, though, the driveway turned back toward I-12, and the swamp was left behind a bit as we moved into a thick pine forest. Everything was so silent that the tires sounded really loud crunching on the dirt beneath us. "This is their hunting place?" I said, barely above a whisper.

Mom nodded. "We used to come out here a lot when we were in high school, you know, to drink and get laid and all the stuff teenagers do."

"You don't really think she brought Mike here, do you?" It seemed a little too pat to me. "I mean, wouldn't this be the first place the cops would look? She doesn't strike me as the type who'd make it this easy for the cops."

"I told you it was just a hunch, Scotty." She shook her head. "It certainly isn't hurting us any to check it out. And you have to admit, if you were going to kidnap a tiger—this would be the perfect place to hide him, isn't it?"

We went around another turn in the driveway, and a small cabin came into view. There was a beat-up, rusted Chevrolet Bel Air parked next to the little building. A big propane tank stook just a few yards away from the house. The cabin, raised about four feet from the ground, had a screened-in front porch.

Mom nodded. "Someone's here." She grinned at me. "I *told* you."

"Maybe we should just get out of here," I replied, still whispering. "I don't have a good feeling about this, Mom. Really, let's just turn around and get out of here."

Mom pulled up right behind the Chevrolet with its Idaho plates and turned the engine off. "We've come all this way—we might as well see who's here." She unbuckled her seat belt and gave me a look. "You can stay here in the car if you're afraid."

I hate it when she does that.

With a sigh I removed my seat belt and opened the car door. I stood up and stretched, my vertebrae popping as I arched my back. I walked over to the Chevrolet and looked through the dirty windows into the backseat. It was filled with empty food containers and empty water bottles. The front seat was just as bad, and the dashboard was covered in dust. The front windows were open a slight bit, and I caught a whiff of a musty smell from inside. The Chevrolet had been sitting there for a long time, I was willing to bet. The windshield was spiderwebbed with cracks, and the shocks on the left side were shot—it was listing a bit. "This car's been here a while," I said. "I don't think it's been driven in a really long time."

"Someone's been here, though," Mom insisted, pointing down into the dirt. "See those tire marks?"

I looked where she was pointing and had to admit she was right. There was also an oil spot in the dirt. "Maybe we should call the parish police…" My voice trailed off as Mom walked up to the cabin and climbed the sagging wooden steps to the porch. She opened the screen door and let out a bloodcurdling scream.

My heart pounding, I ran up to see what was wrong.

A woman's body was lying facedown on the porch, a dried puddle of blood spread out beneath her head. Flies were buzzing around, and I gagged a bit from the smell.

"It's Veronica!" Mom gasped the words out, and her right hand clutched my arm.

Crazily, I realized the chances of making it to Frank's match just got slimmer.

Chapter Four
The Moon
Unforeseen perils

It was after two in the morning when Mom and I finally got back to Baton Rouge.

Frank was waiting up for us in the living room, watching *Double Indemnity* on TMC, when I unlocked the door and we walked in. He immediately muted the television and jumped to his feet. He was wearing a tight white tank top over black sweatpants with the word *SAINTS* written up the side of one leg in gold lettering. The depth of his worry was written all over his face. "Are you both all right?" he asked.

I've never loved him more than I did in that moment.

The drive back had been worse than a nightmare. Mom was far too upset to be trusted to drive, so there was no choice—I had to do it, and I am a white-knuckle driver under the best of circumstances. Fortunately, at that hour there wasn't much traffic for me to deal with, other than speeding eighteen-wheelers trying to run me off the road. But I was so physically and mentally fatigued that it took what little energy I had left to stay focused on driving. I'd drunk so much awful sheriff's office coffee that falling asleep wasn't a concern. I'd called Storm to tell him what was going on when it became clear we weren't getting out of the Tangipahoa sheriff's office to get to Maravich Center on time for Frank's match. All I could do was hope Frank wouldn't notice we weren't out in the audience and wonder where we were until it was all over.

The last thing I wanted was to distract him before his big match, which was why I called Storm instead. Of course, Storm had wanted to jump in his car and rush over to Rouen to rescue us, but I'd told him not to bother. We hadn't done anything wrong, so I figured we didn't need a lawyer present.

I sagged in relief as Frank gave me a big hug and squeezed me until I could barely breathe. I'd been so terrified he'd be mad at me, and he had every right to be mad. I pressed my face against his strong chest and listened to his heartbeat for a moment. I could have stayed there forever—it felt so nice and comforting there in his arms—but he let go of me after kissing the top of my head and gave Mom a big hug. As he hugged her, he said, "Mom, you look like you could use a drink. What can I get you?"

"Bourbon. No water, just ice," she said, her voice still shaky. He helped her over to the couch and she sank down onto it with a heavy sigh.

I bit my lower lip. I was more than a little worried about her, to be honest. Usually, nothing brings out the fire in her soul more than dealing with the police. I'd never seen her like this before— so drained and lifeless, with no spirit or fire in her eyes. The deputies hadn't let us ride together to the station, putting us into separate cruisers, and another deputy drove Mom's car. When the Tangipahoa Parish sheriff's office finished with us and had let us go, Mom seemed completely out of it as we walked out to the car. The only thing she'd said was when she told me she didn't trust herself to drive. This worried me, given my reputation in the family as a lousy driver. No one ever let me drive if they could possibly help it.

She hadn't spoken in the car during the drive either. She just closed her eyes and rested her head on the passenger window. I kept glancing over at her to make sure she was okay. She seemed paler than usual.

It was the first time she'd seemed her age to me. Her youthful spark was gone.

But to be fair, it *had* been a rough day. Mom had never come across a dead body before, let alone the corpse of a childhood friend, and as the car hurtled through the dark Louisiana night, I'd wondered if she was going to be all right.

I'd been through an emotional wringer myself since we opened the door to the cabin's screened-in porch and saw the body lying there.

It seemed like we stood there forever, like time had somehow come to a stop. We stood there, unable to move, just staring at the body. Neither one of us said anything. There was no sound other than the humming of cicadas and an occasional splash from the bayou directly behind the cabin.

The woman had been shot in the back, and I could see at least two bullet holes in her red-and-black sleeveless flannel blouse. She had a flip-flop on her right foot, but her left foot was bare. The other flip-flop was a few feet from where she lay. The force of the bullet had probably carried her forward a few feet before she'd gone down face-first on the warped wood. Her gray shoulder-length hair was fanned out around her head. Bluish-green bottle flies were circling her body, landing on her or in the sticky puddle of blood spreading around her torso before taking flight again. The air was thick with humidity, so it would probably take the blood longer to dry. I calculated she'd been dead somewhere between eighteen and twenty-four hours. She was wearing jeans shorts and hadn't shaved her legs in a while.

"Is it Veronica, Mom?" I asked, finally breaking the silence.

Mom moved beside me. I heard the screen door slam shut behind her and then I heard her throwing up in the yard.

I didn't know what to do—other than the standard *don't touch anything, it's a crime scene.*

I took a deep breath of the thick, fetid air. *Stay in control, Scotty, don't get sick yourself,* I thought, fighting against the gorge rising in my stomach. I took another deep breath and focused. *Be professional, Scotty, it's just another case. What do you see?*

I opened my eyes and switched into investigator mode, making mental notes.

I could tell she'd been trying to escape her killer—that was apparent from the position of the body. She'd almost managed to reach the corner where the screen porch turned at a ninety-degree angle to continue around the side of the cabin when she'd been shot. The screen door hadn't been latched, and I turned my head to look out at the dirt driveway through the screen. There were any number of tire tracks out there in the dirt—I'd have to leave all of that to the cops.

It stood to reason that someone had driven up, I realized. She'd probably been inside the cabin, waiting for someone. A car had pulled in, and she'd come outside to see who it was. The killer had come onto the porch—so it was most likely someone she knew. She hadn't been nervous at first—but then the killer had pulled a gun and she'd tried to get away. I narrowed my eyes, turning around and taking it all in. *Why didn't she try to get into the house? Wouldn't that have made the most sense? Why did she try to run around to the side porch?*

I stepped toward the front door of the cabin. It was slightly ajar, and I could feel cold air coming through the crack. I was probably right—she'd probably come outside when she heard the car pull up. She hadn't shut the door all the way—it looked like the wood of the door and its frame had been swollen by humidity so many times they both were a little warped, so the door had to be slammed in order to shut. I couldn't see anything through the small opening—it was dark inside. I resisted the temptation to go in and poke around—the cops wouldn't appreciate that—so I turned my attention back to the crime scene itself.

The porch itself needed painting, as did the cabin, and the screens had rusted. The wooden planks, once painted a pale blue, were rotted through in places and warped in others. There were some solid metal chairs, the kind that sit on metal pipes and can rock a little, placed at regular intervals. They too had rusted in the heavy swamp air over the years, and looked like they hadn't been moved since they were put there—sometime during the Eisenhower administration, if not earlier.

I got out my phone. Trying to move as little as possible, I took pictures of everything I could see on the porch from every conceivable angle before pushing the screen door open with my foot and walking down the steps.

Mom was still bent over, her hands on her knees. The remnants of her breakfast lay in the tall grass in front of her.

"You okay, Mom?" I said softly, putting my hand on her lower back.

She straightened up and nodded. She turned and wiped her mouth with her left forearm. She gave me a weak smile. She still looked pale and clammy, her eyes bloodshot and watery. "I can't swear to it without taking a better look, but I hope you don't mind if I don't take another look, okay?" She breathed in deeply. "I'm pretty sure that's Veronica, though." She shook her head and gave me a pleading look. "Damn. I don't suppose we can just get in the car and just head back to Storm's and pretend we were never here?"

"I wish we could do that, believe me." I put my arm around her shoulders and gave her a comforting squeeze. "But someone may have seen us come out here, and if we don't call the cops, they'll want to know why. It won't look good."

"We could say we never went up to the porch at all."

I looked at her. This wasn't like Mom. "Is there something you aren't telling me, Mom?" I asked. She didn't answer, and I kept looking at her. Then it dawned on me. "You knew she was here, didn't you?"

She bit her lower lip and nodded. "Yeah, I knew she was staying out here." She took another deep breath. "Damn, I've got a nasty taste in my mouth." She looked back toward the cabin. "You don't think the cops'll care if I rinse my mouth out with that hose, do you?"

"They'll probably consider the whole place a crime scene, Mom." I sighed. "But go ahead." *And then you're going to answer me some questions.*

I watched her walk over to the side of the cabin and turn the spigot on the side of the building. She picked up the hose and rinsed her mouth out.

I checked my phone. I didn't have much of a signal, but I figured I couldn't just call 911 out here. I pulled up my web browser and did a search for the Tangipahoa Parish sheriff's office.

I didn't know whose jurisdiction this would fall under—state or parish or the town of Ponchatoula, but figured calling the parish sheriff was the safest bet—better to let them sort out jurisdiction. It took a lot longer than I would have liked for the information to come up, but finally it did and I called. After I told the dispatcher my name, our location, and that we'd found a dead body, I hung up and slipped the phone back in my pocket.

"So, you want to tell me what this little trip was all about, Mom?" I asked.

She wiped sweat from her forehead and squinted at me in the bright afternoon light. "I saw Veronica on Saturday. She called me, wanting to talk to me." She held up her hand. "Stop right there—she didn't say anything about kidnapping Mike, okay? She wanted to talk to me about Hope." She exhaled. "She told me she was staying out here and she wanted to see Hope, wanted to know if I thought Hope would want to see her. I knew Hope was in the veterinary school, Scotty, but I swear I had no idea she worked with the tiger. I had no idea AFAR wanted to steal the damned thing." Her voice sounded bitter. "So of course, once I heard about the tiger theft, it all made sense. I thought I could come out here and reason with her, surely she wouldn't want to have Hope take the fall for her..." She let her voice trail off.

I didn't say anything. I appreciated Mom's loyalty to her friend, but Veronica Porterie's track record wasn't that great.

And there were any number of people who wouldn't be in the least bit sorry to hear she was dead.

We wound up not having to wait more than about twenty minutes or so before a parish police car came rolling up the dirt driveway with its lights flashing. A ridiculously tall young deputy got out—he had to be at least six foot five in his bare feet. He couldn't have weighed much more than one hundred and fifty pounds on a good day. He was gangly—all elbows and knees and angles. I couldn't imagine where he could find pants to fit his tiny waist and lengthy legs. He had strawberry-blond hair, cut in the traditional Southern small-town way—short and standing straight up like a bristle brush. His hairline was a perfectly straight line running across his reddish forehead maybe an inch or two above his eyes. He had an enormous Adam's apple in a really long, storklike neck. His ears stuck out from either side of his heavily freckled, reddish face like the handles on a coffee mug. His wide-set eyes were his best feature, almond shaped and a bright green with golden flakes. "Hey, you the ones who called?" he drawled as he shut the car door behind him. "You say you found a dead body?"

I stepped forward and held out my hand. "Scotty Bradley. I'm the one who called. The body's on the porch." I gestured with my head in the direction of the cabin.

His hand was damp and enormous. It was mostly bone and skin, yet still he had a good strong grip. Up close he was even younger than he'd seemed when he got out of the car—I figured him for about twenty-two, twenty-five at most. He spoke in a deep, mellifluous voice, and the beautiful green eyes looked intelligent. His accent seemed almost put on, like he wanted us to underestimate him. He certainly did look every inch the stereotype of the wet-behind-the-ears hayseed deputy, though.

"Deputy Donnie Ray Tindall, Tangipahoa sheriff's office, nice to meet you, Mr. Bradley." He looked over at Mom. "Ma'am?"

"Cecile Bradley." She took a hesitant step forward, holding out her hand. He took it, gave it a quick shake and let go.

"My mom," I said. "She's a friend of the deceased."

"Sorry you had to see that, ma'am." Donnie Ray tipped his cap at her. His voice was gentle. "You want to go have a seat in my car, get out of this heat, cool down a bit?"

Mom shook her head. "Thank you, I'm fine."

I wasn't so sure about that—she still looked a little green to me.

Another sheriff's department car pulled up and parked next to Donnie Ray's. Two older men wearing the same uniform got out of the second car. One was short and had a huge gut that hung over his belt, and he hitched up his pants as he shut the car door. He was bowlegged and seemed to have more authority than the others. He crooked a finger at Donnie Ray, who gave me a little shrug and walked back over to where his peers were standing. The other deputy was taller than his companion, but strongly built with the body of a high school athlete who'd kept himself up in the years since. He wore mirrored sunglasses and stood slightly behind the short one, his arms folded. I couldn't tell who he was looking at—I hate mirrored sunglasses.

They talked in voices too low for me to hear, and then the two newcomers headed to the cabin while Donnie Ray walked back to where we were standing.

"So, what are you folks doing out there?" He said it in a friendly tone, but his eyes were cold and hard. He pulled out a little notepad from his shirt pocket, flipping it open expertly and getting a pen from his pants pocket.

"Like I said before, my mom went to school with Veronica Porterie," I said, trying to keep my voice neutral and non-threatening. "When we heard about the tiger being kidnapped on television, and that AFAR was taking credit for taking him, Mom remembered the Porteries had this place out here. We thought we'd come check it out. It made sense, you know? I mean, they had to have a place to hide the tiger, right?" His face took on a strange look, and I added quickly, "I'm a private eye." I pulled out my wallet, hoping I had one of my business cards in it. I breathed out a sigh of relief as I saw one, which I slipped out and handed to him. He examined it skeptically. Out of the corner of my eye I saw the taller deputy come tearing out of the cabin, run over to his car, and start talking on the radio.

Donnie Ray gave me a weird look as he slipped my business card into his shirt pocket. He jerked a thumb over at the ancient Chevrolet. "You don't know whose car that is, do you?"

"No," I replied. "I assumed it was Veronica's."

He nodded and jotted down the license plate. He gave me a curious look, his thin lips widening in a smile. "So, you and your mother just decided to come out here to the Porterie place to look for Mike the Tiger, huh? A good hunch, I suppose, but as you can see there's no place around here to keep or hide a tiger. No barn or pen or anything." One of his thick red eyebrows slid upward. "No one's been out here in years. It always surprised me a little that the Porteries kept paying the taxes on the place. I figured they'd eventually sell it."

"You're familiar with the place?" I was a little surprised. It seemed to be pretty well off the beaten path. The cop who'd been on the radio came walking over to us. Donnie Ray held up a finger again with a slight smile and went to meet him. Once again, they talked in voices too low for me to hear anything, and then both came walking over to us.

"This is Deputy Howie Landers," Donnie Ray said. "He's going to be asking you some questions, Mrs. Bradley, while I keep talking to Scotty here."

Howie Landers smiled at us both. Up close, his teeth were yellow and crooked, and he reeked of stale cigarette smoke. He was a little taller than me, and now that he was so close, I could see that he'd let his body go a little to seed. He had love handles and a bit of a soft tire around the middle. His arms were strong and beefy, though, and he took his sunglasses off to reveal bloodshot brown eyes that were set a little too close together.

His cheeks were riddled with acne scars. "Nice to meetcha," he drawled. "You want to come join me over by the car, ma'am? We can sit in the air-conditioning if you like—if you don't mind my saying so, you look a little green around the gills."

"That would be lovely, thank you," Mom replied in a very small voice, and followed him across the sparse lawn.

I stared after them.

"You okay?"

I turned back to Donnie Ray. "I'm worried about her. I think she may be in shock."

He glanced over at them. Mom was talking, gesturing with her hands and looking a lot more animated. She seemed to be more herself, so I muttered a quick prayer for Howie Landers and turned my attention back to Deputy Tindall.

"She looks like she's going to be fine," he said. "It helps to talk. Howie's a good guy, he'll get her mind off what she saw."

"Yeah, I guess so." I nodded. "You sounded like you know this place pretty well."

"Like I said, the Porteries don't come out here that much anymore. But kids come out here to party," he admitted, lowering his voice and glancing from side to side to make sure no one could hear what he was saying. "It's quiet and out of the way, and they can be as loud as they want to be and no one would ever know." He shook his head. "One of these days some drunk kid's going to drive his car off that driveway into the bayou and drown himself, and there's going to be hell to pay, you mark my words. The Porteries need to gate the damned driveway." He shook his head. "Absolutely no reason for anyone to be able to get back here that easy."

"Did you use to come out here when you were in high school?" I asked, unable to help myself from smiling.

He bit his lower lip. "Maybe. Maybe not. So, you and your mother drove out here from New Orleans?"

"I didn't say we were from New Orleans."

"Your business card said you were." He inclined his head.

"Besides, when you called in, Howie ran you, found your private eye license in the system. And your mother's arrest record." His eyes twinkled a little bit. "Got arrested yesterday in Baton Rouge, even." He made a little noise. "Punched the attorney general, did she?" He winked at me. "Troy's from Tangipahoa Parish, you know. I went to high school with his little sister."

"Yeah, well, Mom's kind of feisty." I shrugged and returned his smile. "You see why I was worried about her. She's usually a spitfire."

"There are worse things." He shrugged. "How well did you know the deceased?"

"If the deceased is Veronica Porterie, I didn't know her well. I haven't seen her since I was a little boy. She was my mother's best friend in high school."

"It's Veronica Porterie, all right," he admitted, writing in his little notepad. "Or someone who looks a lot like her."

"Sounds like you knew her."

He smiled. "There's a lot of Porteries in Tangipahoa Parish, Mr. Bradley. Being related to the crazy lady who runs AFAR's not exactly a point of pride for them." He scratched his chin with his pen. "My fiancée's a Porterie, so you can say I'm pretty familiar with what Veronica Porterie looks like."

"Call me Scotty." I filed the information about the Porteries away in my mind. "That must be kind of awkward, after AFAR took credit for kidnapping Mike."

His face tightened. "That tiger is not in Tangipahoa Parish, I can tell you that for a fact, Mr. Brad—Scotty." He relaxed. "So, you and your mother came out here to look for the tiger?" There was a bit of amusement in his voice—which, despite being a bit insulting, was probably understandable.

"I'm a private eye, like I said," I replied. "We didn't think it would hurt anything to come take a look around. We thought maybe even if Mike wasn't here, Veronica might be, and we might be able to talk her into returning him, you know?" I held up both hands in a "couldn't hurt to try" way. "So, anyway, we came out here—Mom remembered coming here when she was a kid—and when we went up on the porch to knock on the front door, we found her. We backed right down the steps without touching anything."

His eyebrows came together. "Didn't it occur to either of you it might be dangerous?"

"Dangerous?"

He flipped his notebook closed. "Veronica Porterie and her gang are murderers, you know. They've killed before—you mean to say it never occurred to you and your mother that you could be walking right into danger? What if they really *did* bring Mike here?"

"It never occurred to me," I admitted, feeling my face starting to turn red. "I suppose it wasn't very smart."

"To say the least." He flipped his notebook closed.

We eventually had to go back to the Rouen police department to swear out statements, and after what seemed like a million years, they finally let us go.

As Frank poured a good stiff bourbon for Mom, Storm came out his bedroom in his robe, rubbing his eyes. "Don't glare at me," I said, plopping down in a reclining chair and pulling the lever so it popped into a more prone position. "It wasn't my idea to go out there. I went along thinking I was going to keep her out of trouble." I rolled my eyes. "I should have known better."

Mom took the glass from Frank gratefully. She took a healthy drink before sitting down on the couch. "How many times do I have to say I'm sorry?" She shuddered and took another sip. "Frank, I'm sorry we missed your match. I assume you won?"

"I always win," he replied, giving her a worried look. "But I'm more concerned about you, Mom. Are you sure you're okay? Death isn't pretty to look in the face." He sat down next to her and put his arm around her shoulders, and she put her head down on his.

Storm handed me a glass of vodka with a few pieces of ice floating in it. I took a sip and grimaced. It was smooth with a bit of a cold bite, and I felt my throat starting to warm up. "Thanks." I smiled up at him as the vodka started relaxing me. "Did you talk to Hope?"

"Of course I talked to Hope." He sat down in the other reclining chair and the footrest popped out. "The cops weren't too happy about me showing up when I did, and getting her out of there, but they didn't have anything to hold her on in the first place...and I didn't like the idea of her giving them anything they could use against her at a later time." He shook his head. "I don't really think she gets just how bad this all looks for her. And it's worse than we thought." He sighed. "I've written a check out to you guys—I'm retaining you to work on the case, so everything we say here is protected."

"What about Mom?" I glanced over at where she and Frank were talking in low voices.

"As long as she doesn't hear us, we're good. I already briefed Frank while we were waiting for you two." He took a swig of his own drink and put it down on the end table. "Hope is in some seriously deep shit and has no clue. I'm calling in Loren McKeithen—I don't have the time to deal with this until the legislative session is over." He rubbed his face with his hands. "She's been in touch with her mother. Well, *was* in touch with her mother."

"But I thought—"

"Yes, Mom wasn't aware—and I'm pretty sure Hope's grandmother didn't know about it, either. But about a year ago Veronica made contact." He rubbed his eyes again. "Hope didn't want anything to do with her, of course—she was raised on how horrible her mother was, after all, and she was abandoned. But she was curious, so she agreed to meet her. At the hunting camp."

"Oh, that *is* bad." I rubbed my eyes and took another slug from the vodka. It really was good.

He nodded. "But she swears she had no idea AFAR was going to take Mike or had anything to do with the tiger-napping—it was just as big a surprise to her as it was to everyone else moving him. She's quite upset, honestly—she really loves that tiger." He yawned and stood up. "I'm beat—I'm going back to bed. We can talk about this more in the morning."

His bedroom door shut behind him. Mom finished her drink and put her glass down on the coffee table. "I think that's a good idea—I'm pretty worn out." She stood up and yawned, leaning down to kiss Frank on the forehead before going to her own room.

I followed Frank into our room. Once the door was closed behind us, he put his arms around me, kissing me with such force I backed up against the door. "So glad you're okay," he whispered in my ear, putting his hands into my armpits and lifting up.

I helped him by giving a little hop and put my legs around his waist. "I'm so sorry we missed your match, I wouldn't blame you for being pissed," I said, letting my hands drift down his back and coming to rest on his hard butt. I smiled at him. "Can't wait to watch the recording. Was it awesome?"

He started nuzzling my neck. Some chills went down my spine, and I shivered. "You have no idea." He turned around and walked over to the bed, still carrying me. He grinned at me, a devilish glint in his eye. "I'm still a little wound up. Up for some bed wrestling?" He pushed me down onto the bed and yanked his T-shirt up over his head.

Damn, but he is one sexy stud! I thanked the Universe again for my incredible good luck.

I winked. "I thought you'd never ask."

CHAPTER FIVE
PAGE OF WANDS
A young man with blond hair and blue eyes

The drive back to New Orleans that Wednesday morning seemed to fly by. Storm was already gone by the time we got out of bed, so we just showered and packed up what little we'd brought with us. We were on the road by ten. I checked in on Mom before we left, but she was sound asleep, so I didn't want to wake her up to say good-bye.

I hadn't slept well, even though the night had run late and Frank wore me out before we finally went to sleep. I kept waking up every half hour or so, still wrapped in Frank's strong arms. I would lie there for a few moments, my eyes adjusting to the dark, until I drifted off into a miserable, unrestful half-sleep. I gave up around seven, made some coffee and took a shower. We stopped for a quick breakfast at Dunkin' Donuts, and I slid down in my seat once we got back on I-10 East. I didn't have to talk much, which was good because I wasn't sure I could maintain a conversation. Frank filled in the gap by taking me through last night's matches, which was a relief. I was proud of him, and listening to his descriptions of how the crowd cheered his every move made me regret missing the match even more than I had already.

Before I knew it, we were passing over the marshy lake estuary, which meant we were getting very close to the city.

A knot formed in my stomach. I took a deep breath. What if

Frank's nephew didn't like me? What if I couldn't relate to him? What if staying with us made things worse for him?

Get over yourself, bitch, I reminded myself. *This isn't about you, it's about what's best for Taylor. You are who you are, and anything is going to be better for him than spending the summer in rural Alabama around a bunch of right-wing homophobic religious zealots. Mom and Dad did a pretty good job raising you—just follow their example and he'll be fine.*

Although the thought of an eighteen-year-old gay boy turned loose in the French Quarter after a lifetime of repression was more than just a little bit scary.

Rain had checked in with Frank last night after picking Taylor up at the airport, and that was all Frank had said about it. My sister is pretty cool, and since she's not as wacky as the rest of the family, she would serve as a nice intro to the family for him. She's married to a surgeon at Children's Hospital, and they have a big house on State Street in Uptown. She does all the proper things a surgeon's wife with society connections should do—charity work, food drives, fund-raisers, all of that. She is a member of the oldest ladies' Mardi Gras krewe, Iris, and rides in their parade every year. (She always buries us in beads every year.) She is very well-liked and respected because she is very efficient and never lets any detail slip through the cracks.

She's also a pretty awesome sister. She used to worry about me when I was single, and was always setting me up with guys she thought would treat me well and take care of me properly. It got annoying sometimes—Rain really had no idea of what I was looking for in a man—but I couldn't get mad at her because she was coming from a good place.

We took the 90 West/Claiborne exit from I-10. Traffic was light, and in just a matter of minutes Frank was making a left turn onto State Street, right by the Ursulines Academy and the Our Lady of Prompt Succor church. State Street is a hidden delight of New Orleans that few tourists ever see, big beautiful homes with highly manicured lawns. The Bradley side of the family have had a ridiculously enormous house on State Street for well over a hundred years. Rain lived a few blocks away from them, closer to St. Charles Avenue.

"Don't be nervous," Frank said as he pulled into the driveway, grinning over at me. "He's a teenager, not some kind of alien from outer space." He shut the car off and unbuckled his seat belt. "Okay, I'm a little nervous. I haven't seen Taylor since he was a little boy."

Rain's house is an enormous stone building sitting on a perfectly landscaped lot. There was a circular driveway, and her white Lexus SUV was parked by the front steps. The half-moon between the sidewalk and the driveway was filled with flowers and a small marble fountain with water shooting out of the mouths of the Three Graces. I never understood why they bought such a big house, frankly. It had five bedrooms and four bathrooms, and there were just the two of them and their dogs. Rain had never had any desire to have children, and her husband Jake pretty much went along with whatever Rain wanted. She had a maid come in twice a week to help keep the place clean.

I pulled out my keys and unlocked the front door. I also rang the doorbell to let Rain know we were here. Of course, ringing the doorbell set off a cacophony of dogs barking. Rain has two adorable (if incredibly spoiled) cavalier King Charles spaniels. She'd only meant to get one, but there were two puppies left when she visited the breeders—a lovely couple who lived near Monroe—and she couldn't bear having to choose between them.

"Rain!" I called as the dogs came tearing down the front hall and leaped on me and Frank, their tongues out and tails wagging.

There was no answer. I could smell baking bread, so I walked down the hallway to the enormous gourmet kitchen in the rear of the house. Rain spent most of her time in the kitchen, despite the ridiculous size of her home and the fact my brother-in-law had given her one of the guest bedrooms as an office. Rain's kitchen was the control center of the house. It was huge, almost as big as my entire apartment. There was an enormous island in the middle with a sink and butcher top. Copper pots and pans hung down from a lowered ceiling above the island that also served as a vent. She had two large refrigerators, as well as a stainless steel freezer in one corner of the room. The back wall was almost entirely made of windows, so there was plenty of natural light. A glass sliding door led out to a screened-in porch, which then opened out onto a deck with a enormous sunken hot tub. The backyard was an enormous tropical garden that Rain had designed herself and required a team of gardeners to prune, cut back, weed, water, and maintain. The kitchen's view of the backyard made it seem like the house was in the middle of a forest, rather than a city—even the back fence was hidden by towering bamboo stalks.

In one corner of the kitchen was a sliding panel behind which was Rain's computer desk, where she paid the bills and organized her charity work. She owned every conceivable kitchen gadget. She loved to cook and was always experimenting with new recipes. I never understood why she'd majored in business administration at Baylor—I always thought she should have gone to a cooking school. As I walked down the hallway I could hear voices talking in the kitchen, and the smell of the baking bread was overpowering. My mouth started watering and my stomach growled. I walked into the kitchen with Frank right behind me. A tall boy was standing with his back to us, shelling peas in a crimson T-shirt and long navy-blue board shorts. Rain was sitting on one of the stools at the island, sipping coffee from an enormous mug with *QUEEN* written across it in gold leaf.

She raised an eyebrow when she saw us. "Exciting trip to Baton Rouge, huh, guys?" She put the mug down and slid off the stool, offering her cheek to me.

I kissed her on the cheek as the tall boy turned around. I laughed. "You know us, Rain. Never a dull moment for the Bradleys, even when we're in Baton Rouge."

Out of the corner of my eye I saw Taylor turn around.

He was tall, six feet four at least—a few inches taller than Frank. Frank always said he'd been ridiculously skinny when he was a teenager—apparently it was in the Sobieski genes. Taylor was lean, probably prone to being thin with great difficulty gaining weight. His crimson T-shirt had the big script *A* that was the symbol of the University of Alabama on the front, and hung on his thin frame. He had blond hair bleached almost white by the sun, with bangs that curled slightly at the ends. His hair was cut in a short pageboy, and it was darker underneath. He had wide-set, round blue eyes so bright they almost glowed. A strong nose had dimpled cheeks on either side, with a strong chin and a wide mouth. He was tanned a dark golden brown, and the hair on his forearms was also bleached white. His shoulders were wide, and he had really long, gangly arms. His legs were slender and crisscrossed with veins and muscle striation, like his forearms.

He looked so much like Frank it took my breath away. I'd never really thought about what Frank must have looked like when he was young, but looking at his nephew I got a very clear picture.

He blushed and looked down at his feet. He mumbled "hey" in a quiet, adorably shy way.

Frank crossed to him swiftly in a few steps and hugged him. After a few seconds, Taylor hugged him back.

Rain nudged me with her elbow. "Let's go out to the porch and give them a few minutes to get acquainted, shall we?"

I poured myself a cup of coffee and followed her out onto the screen porch, closing the sliding glass door behind me. The ceiling fans were turning, and I plopped down on the couch.

"Mom just called," Rain said, crossing her short tanned legs. "Dufresne isn't pressing charges. He says he just wants to forget the whole thing. Storm's pretty relieved." She laughed. "Mom really needs to mellow out a bit. I don't like Dufresne either— he puts the *hole* in *asshole*—but she can't go around slugging people."

"She's never going to change," I replied, leaning back. We'd had some variation of this conversation any number of times over the years. "But I don't know if I'd want her to."

Rain is two years older than me and a year younger than Storm. Storm and I had been sent to Jesuit, an all boys' school, while she went to McGehee, a school for wealthy society girls located on Prytania Street in the Garden District. Mom and Dad were avowed Wiccans and hated the pretensions of society, but also recognized the value of the education the private schools could provide. Every night over dinner they would "deprogram" us from the "lessons of privilege" we got at school. It was in junior high school that Rain started calling herself Rhonda. This rebellion against her hippie-style name at first was a huge concern to our parents until they realized she was just rebelling against her parents in the time-honored tradition of teens, and it was an expression of individuality rather than conformity.

And how else could you rebel against pot-smoking parents who pretty much let us do as we pleased?

Privately, she told me it was because "Rain's just a fucking stupid name."

She further rebelled by not only refusing to follow family tradition by going to Newcomb for college, but unlike Mom, who'd really rebelled by going to UNO, she'd gone to Baylor, where she met and married a poor country boy from the back country—the Rio Grande Valley near Harlingen—and put him through Tulane's medical school. Now he was a surgeon based at Children's Hospital, and she kept busy with her charities and the dogs.

And I couldn't imagine a better older sister. She was *awesome*.

She also adored both Frank and Colin.

"How did Mom seem about," I hesitated, "about finding Veronica's body? I was really worried about her last night. I've never seen her like that before."

"She was upset still, but about Veronica being murdered

more than anything else, I would say." Rain sipped her coffee. "She was also pretty upset for missing Frank's match." She leaned over and patted my arm. "And making *you* miss it. Don't worry, I DVRed it and can record it onto a DVD for you." She winked at me. "He was amazing! I was so proud of him. And he looks so good in those trunks." She leaned back with a sigh. "I'm thinking about getting Tom some."

"Tom would never wear a Speedo, would he?" I tried to picture my brother-in-law in a Speedo, and couldn't. Tom was in really good shape—he worked with a trainer three times a week and did a lot of cardio—but he was really reserved.

"He wouldn't in public." Rain giggled. "But he's a bit of a freak in private."

I held up my hand. "Stop. TMI. There are some things about you I'd rather not know."

"Fair enough." She sighed. "I feel so bad for Hope," she went on, not missing a beat. "No matter how crazy our mother gets—and she gets pretty crazy—I can't imagine how awful it must have been to have that nutjob as your mother. And then to have her killed…" Her voice trailed off, and she shook her head sadly.

"You know Hope?" I stared at her, surprised.

She nodded. "The Porteries live over on Napoleon Avenue between Prytania and Magazine. You must know her grandmother…she's one of Mama Bradley's friends. Grace Porterie? You don't remember her? She's short, kind of solidly built? Always wears her pearls?" When I shook my head, she went on, "You'd know her if you saw her. I used to babysit Hope sometimes—she's always been a sweet little girl, and smart as a whip. Nothing at all like that mother of hers…I suppose I shouldn't be disrespectful now that she's dead, but I can't imagine abandoning my child like that." She reached down and scratched one of the dogs' heads. "I wouldn't abandon the dogs, let alone a kid. What kind of mother does that?" She took another sip of her coffee. "I suppose Hope was lucky her grandparents were willing to take her. Can you imagine having a mother like that? Who killed someone?"

"No." Mom had been arrested any number of times, but the charges were usually dropped or suspended. Mom's arrests had something to do with some kind of protest or an act of civil disobedience, like the time she chained herself to the gates of a nuclear power plant in Oklahoma.

Before the Troy Dufresne incident on Monday, she'd only once been arrested for assault.

Of course, she'd slugged a cop, but videotape showed she was provoked and the charges had been thrown out.

But murder? I couldn't imagine Mom ever killing anyone.

"And you might have known better than to go out there with Mom—that's always a recipe for trouble." Her eyes twinkled. "You just can't get away from stumbling over bodies, can you?"

I gave her a dirty look. "You make it sound like it happens all the time."

"It happens to you a lot more than it does to normal people," she retorted, but her smile took the sting out of the words.

Much as I hated to concede, she did have a point. "Seriously." I thought back to the first time it had happened, that same Southern Decadence weekend when I'd met both Frank and Colin. Since then, it had happened a lot more often than I'd like to admit, or remember. "But it's been a while."

She rolled her eyes. "Not even twenty-four hours, baby brother."

"Har har." I looked back into the kitchen. Taylor and Frank were sitting at the island, talking intensely. "What do you think of Taylor?"

Her face darkened a bit, and she scowled. "He's a good kid, a really smart, sweet kid with good manners. What is wrong with his parents? I mean, look at him." She wiped at her eyes. "They should be proud they raised such a good kid. So what if he's gay? I swear to God, I want to drive up there and knock their idiot heads together. It's all so stupid, and to claim religion as a basis for throwing out their child? No thank you. You'd think they'd turn their backs on a religion that would tell them they need to treat their kid like garbage. What kind of God, what kind of religion would ask that of a parent? Where's the compassion? Where's the Christian love?" Her eyebrows came together. "I just hope someday I get the chance to tell his dad exactly what I think of him. I'm so glad you and Frank are taking him in."

"Yeah." I looked down at my hands.

"What's wrong with you? Is there something more you're not telling me?" She looked at me shrewdly. "Mom said you were nervous about having him around. You do know that's stupid, right?" She narrowed her eyes.

"Yeah, yeah, I know." I shrugged. "I just don't know, Rain. Am I the right person to be around an eighteen-year-old?"

"Listen to me." She reached over and grabbed my hands. "You're a good person, Milton Scott Bradley, and you know it. You have a big heart, and you always put others ahead of yourself. Mom and Dad raised us all right, and who better?" She giggled. "I remember when *you* were eighteen." She rolled her eyes. "Constantly horny and going out all the time—he'll be much the same, I would imagine."

"I suppose," I said dubiously. "Did he say anything about his plans? For after the summer?"

"Scotty." She leaned forward and grabbed both of my hands. "We are all going to do everything we can to make him a part of the family—because he *is* family. Don't *ever* forget that he's family, okay? If he wants to go back to school at Alabama, we support him. If he wants to stay here and go to Tulane, we support that choice. If he wants to go to Paris to live with Jean-Michel, we support that decision."

The door slid open, and I stood up as Frank and a red-faced Taylor came out onto the porch. "Taylor, I want you to meet my partner, Scotty. Scotty, this is *our* nephew, Taylor."

I held out my hand and took his, shaking it. "I'm glad to

finally meet you, Taylor. Welcome to New Orleans, and welcome to the family."

"Thanks for putting me up," he mumbled, looking down at his shoes again. "Sorry you have to."

He was so adorable my heart melted. I threw my arms around him and gave him a big hug. He stiffened at first, but relaxed and hugged me back. "You're family, Taylor. You're welcome to stay with us as long as you like. You always have a home with us. I hope you know that."

Frank beamed at me. "Go get your stuff, Taylor, and we'll take you home."

Without a word and still blushing, Taylor disappeared back into the house.

"Thanks, Rain." Frank kissed the top of her head. "Taylor's crazy about you."

"What's not to be crazy about?" she asked, one eyebrow arching upward. She stood and linked arms with us, walking us back to the foyer. "Frank, you were amazing last night. As soon as I burn the DVD, I'll bring it over so you can see for yourself." She punched him lightly in the arm. "I was so proud of you!"

Frank's face turned just as red as Taylor's had. Before he had a chance to say anything, Taylor was coming down the hall with a big green duffel bag slung over his shoulder. Rain hugged him. "Don't be a stranger," she said with a big smile. "I mean it!"

"Here." I took his duffel bag, which was surprisingly heavy, and carried it out to the Explorer. I tossed it into the back and closed the hatch door.

"You all have to come over for dinner. Soon. I mean it!" Rain called from the front steps as we climbed into the Explorer. She waved as Frank backed out of her driveway.

"So, what do you think of New Orleans so far?" I asked, turning in my seat.

Taylor blushed furiously but grinned in a way that was so like Frank my heart almost skipped a beat. "I haven't really seen much of it," he confessed. "Rain just picked me up at the airport and we rushed home so we could see Uncle Frank's match." His eyes got wider. "That was *awesome*, Uncle Frank. I never knew you were a professional wrestler." His face clouded. "Mom didn't tell me anything about you."

"Well, for one thing, you don't have to call me *uncle*." Frank smiled at him in the rearview mirror. "I told you, Frank's fine."

"And I'm Scotty," I insisted. "No formality, okay?"

Frank headed up to Claiborne Avenue. "This isn't quite the scenic route, but it's quicker, Taylor," he explained as he stopped at the light at Nashville.

"I think this is the way we came last night." He looked out the window.

"Probably," I replied as we started heading down Claiborne. "This way doesn't really show the city off at its best, but we have all summer to show you around."

"Thanks again," he replied. "I'll try not to be much of a bother."

My heart broke a little at the sad tone in his voice. *What kind of parents do you have?* I wondered. Aloud I said, "You're no bother, Taylor, really. You're *family*." I glanced over at Frank, who smiled back at me, reaching over to pat my leg with his big hand.

No one really spoke again until we reached Esplanade—although I did look into the back when we drove past the Superdome to see the starry-eyed look on Taylor's face, and again when Claiborne passed behind St. Louis Cemetery Number One. He looked like an excited little boy, absolutely adorable. I felt some of my worry about having him around start to slip away. One of the things I loved about being a native was showing the city off to strangers—and how much fun would it be to show off New Orleans to an eighteen-year-old from rural Alabama? The food, the music, the gay bars, the architecture—I could easily spend the entire summer being a tourist with him. I started making a list in my head of all the places I needed to take him when we made the turn down Esplanade Avenue toward the river.

"Wow," he said as we drove past the big beautiful old houses. "It's so beautiful here."

"What was Corinth like?" I asked.

"Ugly," he mumbled. "Everything about Corinth was ugly. Especially the people."

And my heart ached a little bit more, and I vowed to make sure he had the time of his life while he was staying with us. *You never have to go back there*, I thought determinedly. *This is your home now. Fuck your parents.*

Frank dropped us off on Decatur in front of the house and headed off to the parking lot.

"There used to be a coffee shop here," I explained as Taylor stared at the boarded-over windows on the first floor of our building, unable to mask the shock on his face.

"Was this because of Katrina?" he asked solemnly.

I laughed. "No, the owners got divorced and they shut down, so our landladies boarded over the windows to prevent break-ins. Millie and Velma own the building, and they live on the second floor," I explained as I unlocked the gate and opened the door. "We live on the third and fourth floors." I led him down the dark passageway to the back courtyard, remembering how weird this must all seem to him, especially when we reached the sunlight again. Millie and Velma had done an excellent job with the courtyard. In the center a fountain bubbled with koi darting around in the water. Millie, in fact, was trimming back the roses as we entered the courtyard. "Millie! This is Frank's nephew, Taylor. He's going to be staying with us awhile."

Millie straightened up and grinned at us. She was wearing a pair of cut-off blue jeans and a white T-shirt with Frank's picture in full wrestling drag on the front. Millie was a retired gym teacher in her early sixties. She wore her iron-gray hair down to her shoulders, and she jogged along the levee every morning to keep herself in shape. She wiped at her forehead. "Nice to meet you, Taylor." She pulled a joint from her shorts pocket, lighting it up and taking a deep inhale. "You smoke, Taylor?" she asked, offering it to him.

He gave me a panicked look.

"It's okay, Taylor," I said, thinking, *He's eighteen and in college. I started smoking when I was thirteen.* "We all smoke—even your uncle. You're not in Alabama anymore." But as I watched him take it from her I couldn't help but feel like I was being a bad parent.

I felt a little better as I watched him take a long hit and hold it in expertly. *Clearly he's smoked pot before.*

The smoke exploded out of him in a coughing fit.

"Yeah, we only get good stuff, Taylor, so if you're used to dorm pot, you might want to take it a bit easy," I said as I took it from him and inhaled, handing it back to Millie.

She waved it off. "Nah—you boys keep it. Scotty's right, Taylor, that's good shit. Primo. Another hit and I'll go to sleep, and I promised Velma I'd get these roses trimmed today. You know how she gets." She winked at us and picked up her shears.

As we climbed the back steps, I asked, "Is that duffel bag all you have?"

"Yeah." He sighed. "Mom said she'd ship the rest of my stuff here, but this should do me until then."

My heart broke just a little bit again as I fit my key into the lock of the third-floor apartment and opened the door. "You'll be staying upstairs," I said, standing aside so he could walk inside. "But this is where Frank and I live. The upstairs apartment has the same layout as this one, but we keep all the food and stuff down here. We primarily use the upstairs for guests and storage. Colin's—" I bit my tongue.

Had Frank told him about Colin?

I expelled my breath. If Taylor was going to be with us a while, he was going to eventually meet Colin, and why not get all of the questions out of the way to begin with?

"Do you know about Colin?" I led him into the living room

and flipped on the light switch. The chandelier flooded the room with light.

He blushed again and nodded. "Rain told me everything." He took a deep breath and the next thing I knew he was giving me a big hug. "Thank you so much for everything! I'm so glad you're letting me stay here! It's so awesome! I'm so lucky! And how cool that you guys have a ménage with a hot international spy!"

Rain apparently told him everything. But then again, he is family.

"I'm just glad we can help out," I said, extricating myself from his grasp with a big smile.

"Sorry." He stepped back from me, a sheepish look on his face. "That really is some good pot. I feel pretty stoned."

"Have a seat and let me get you something to drink," I said. "What would you like?"

"Water's fine." He sat down on the couch. "This is a really nice place."

"Thanks," I said, going into the kitchen as the back door opened and Frank came into the apartment.

"Where's Taylor?" he asked.

"In the living room, he's a little stoned," I called as I got a glass down from the cabinet and added ice to it.

"What?" Frank stormed into the living room, his face red and his jaw clenched.

"I've smoked pot before," Taylor replied, his hands going onto his hips, his jaw clenching just like Frank's. "It's not a big deal."

Frank's face relaxed a little bit, and finally he laughed. "I suppose there's no way around it," he said, sitting down on the couch next to his nephew and putting his arm around him. "The Bradleys are all pot smokers, so it's going to be around. When did you start smoking?"

"In high school."

I filled up the glass with water out of the gallon jug in the refrigerator and carried it into the living room just as my cell phone started ringing. I excused myself and went out onto the balcony. It was Mom.

"Hey, Mom," I said. "What's up? How are you feeling?"

Her voice sounded shaky. "Have you talked to your father today, by any chance?"

"No. Why?"

"I think you and Frank need to come over here. Pronto."

CHAPTER SIX

NINE OF PENTACLES, REVERSED

Possible loss, danger from thieves

Anyone who thinks New Orleans tourism hasn't recovered from Katrina is someone who clearly has not set foot in the Quarter in a while.

One of the weird aftereffects of the disaster that I've noticed involves my memory—everyone I know has the same problem. It probably has to do with PTSD—there was an article about it in the paper back when the *Times-Picayune* was still a daily newspaper. Some memories of my life before Katrina are sketchy and not very clear. I swear I have no memory of the Quarter being as crowded back then as it often is now, but I wouldn't be able to swear to it. It's entirely possible I'm wrong, of course. It's very likely that I view life *before* through the rosy glasses of nostalgia—everything was better *before*. For example, I don't remember there ever being lines at Café du Monde stretching almost all the way to Jax Brewery. I don't remember Decatur Street's sidewalks being so packed with slow-moving window-shopping tourists that I had to detour out and walk in the street.

Despite my sketchy memory, I am certain the Quarter was always deserted during the heat of summer.

Maybe as I've gotten older my tolerance for crowds has decreased.

When I walked out through the front gate, Decatur Street was swarming with people. Café Envie at the corner had a line out the door, and all of its tables—both inside and out—were occupied. As far as the eye could see, the sidewalk was packed full of people, and the air had gotten hotter and thicker while I was inside. People heading into the Quarter swarmed past me, and I could hear music playing on the neutral ground on Esplanade Avenue. I took a deep breath and dove into the crowd, wondering if this was how a salmon felt on its way upstream to spawn. By the time I got to the corner I was already sick to death of ducking around people walking at a snail's pace.

So when I reached the corner, I turned and headed up Barracks to avoid it all. It was the right decision—Barracks was practically abandoned, and I walked up to Royal.

Frank had stayed behind to help Taylor get settled. That surprised me a little at first, but then I realized he wanted some private time with Taylor to get to know him a little better. It made sense—Frank hadn't seen him since he was a little boy, and they were practically strangers to each other. I couldn't imagine that— as awful as some of my close relatives were, we were still *family.* Both of my grandfathers had refused to release my trusts to me when I turned twenty-five, but that was more about me dropping out of college than the gay thing.

Taylor seemed like a sweet kid, and I was glad we were able to give him a home while his parents sorted things out. It was probably too much to hope they'd see the light by the end of the summer, buy PROUD OF MY GAY SON T-shirts, and march with PFLAG in Pride parades—but stranger things have happened. I hoped they'd at least come to realize that Taylor was still their son, no matter who he was attracted to, and they'd want to be a part of his life.

I thanked the Goddess again that I have such amazing parents.

❖

Mom and Dad's place is on the corner of Royal and Dumaine, on the second floor of a corner building. Mom had inherited the place from her maternal grandmother, who was apparently quite a pistol. On the first floor was their tobacco shop, the Devil's Weed. The store specialized in cigars, pipe tobacco, and all the assorted paraphernalia that goes with it, and also does a bang-up mail order business through their website. (Of course they also sell bongs—which they legally have to call "water pipes.") Before Katrina, they'd also sold specialty coffee, bagels, and muffins—but there was so much competition now they'd discontinued it.

Like I said, the Quarter is booming.

They'd opened their shop when they were first married, converting the upper floor to a spacious apartment where they raised Storm, Rain, and me. I'd lived there until I was about twenty-two, when I moved into my current apartment. There's a staircase from the storage room that leads upstairs, but the main way up is hidden behind a wooden door right behind the building. Behind the door and the razor wire above it is a wrought iron staircase leading up to the second floor. At the top is a door that opens into the kitchen. There's also a balcony that runs around the two street sides of the building, but the only access to it is French doors in the living room.

I put my key in the lock and took the stairs two at a time. I hadn't liked the way Mom sounded on the phone. She hadn't sounded like herself, and that probably had something to do with my lack of patience for the gawking tourists I'd had to dodge on my way over. I was also drenched in sweat, and my socks were soaked through. When I reached the top of the stairs, I inhaled sharply. The back door was open, and I could feel cold air escaping. This was unusual—Mom and Dad rarely, if ever, left the back door unlocked, let alone open.

"Mom?" I called, stepping inside and pulling the door closed behind me. The kitchen was dark—all the lights were off and the shutters were closed. I switched on the overhead lights and walked through the kitchen. "Mom? You're scaring me."

"I'm in the living room," was her response.

I crossed the kitchen and walked through the doorway into

the darkened living room. The shutters in here were also closed. The only light was from a table lamp Mom had turned on. I could see in the light she was wearing a ratty old pair of black Saints sweatpants and a Drew Brees jersey. She was sitting at the end of the couch, holding a joint in one hand while she examined a piece of paper she was holding in the other hand.

She took another hit and offered it to me. When I waved it off, she pinched it out and carefully placed it in a Mason jar about half-filled with roaches. She resealed the jar and placed it back on the coffee table. She waved me over and exhaled, filling the room with pungent smoke. She coughed and took a drink of water, passing me the piece of paper. I sat down in an easy chair and stared at it.

We have your husband. Notify the police and we'll kill him. Further instructions to follow.

I stared at Mom. "What the hell is this, some kind of sick joke?" I could feel all of my nerve endings coming alert, and I swallowed as panic rose up inside me. *Stay calm, stay calm,* I reminded myself. *Panicking won't make anything better or solve anything.*

"That's what I came home to." She rubbed her eyes and took another drink of water. "It was thumbtacked to the back door, Scotty." She shook her head. "Of course I looked everywhere, and there's no sign of him. Emily hasn't seen him since last night."

Emily Hunter was a lesbian in her late twenties who managed the Devil's Weed for Mom and Dad. She'd come down for Mardi Gras after grad school and just stayed. She shaved her head and had an amazing singing voice—the main reason she hadn't become an international superstar was because she just didn't care about things like that. She'd become a member of the family during the eight years or so she'd been working for Mom and Dad.

"I don't get it." I stared at the ransom note in my hands.

"Why would someone kidnap Dad? Is there something going on around here I don't know about?"

She bit her lower lip. "No." Her eyes were watery and bloodshot, and her voice shook a little. "It doesn't make any sense."

"I don't understand." I took a deep breath to calm myself and control the panic trying to take over my mind. *You can't panic, you have to stay calm, panicking is the worst thing you can do.* "Is anything else missing?"

She shook her head. "Believe me, I've gone through the whole place. Everything's exactly the way it was when I left for Baton Rouge."

"But how did they get in here?" I got up and walked over to one of the windows. I turned the bolt and pushed it up. I unlatched the shutters and swung them open, flooding the room with light. "Dad had to have let them in, right?"

Mom and Dad had always been big on security—hence the razor wire over the door to the back steps. The door at the foot of the indoor staircase, which opened into the storage room of the Devil's Weed, was always locked and dead-bolted. Only once had someone broken into Mom and Dad's—and they had been thoroughly trained agents who'd gone over the roofs.

But how could they have gotten Dad out without anyone on the street noticing?

"Scotty, it doesn't make any sense." She shook her head, the long braid swinging. "Believe me, I've tried to figure this out. I can't think of anything."

"You and Dad haven't gotten into anything weird with the drugs, have you?"

My parents had always been stoners. Some of my earliest memories were of Mom and Dad smoking joints in the living room with their friends. They always had an enormous supply they kept locked in a private closet, which they were more than happy to share with everyone they knew. They've always believed that marijuana should be legal and the laws prohibiting it were ridiculous. Mom and Dad never restricted any of their kids from using it, but were always very clear about the laws and penalties so we could make an informed choice. Storm and Rain don't smoke that much anymore, but I generally smoke a little every day. It took a while for Frank—those years with the FBI—to get comfortable enough to indulge, but eventually he came around. Mom and Dad usually buy it by the pound and always get the really good stuff. I get mine from them—but I don't go through it as quickly as they do. They hope it will someday be approved for medicinal purposes in Louisiana, and the Devil's Weed can become a dispensary.

Of course, the odds of deeply conservative Louisiana legalizing medicinal marijuana any time soon were around the same as hitting the Powerball.

"Of course not." She waved her hand. "We use the same source we always have, and you know we don't deal—that's just asking for trouble. You know the house rules—anyone who wants some can have it."

"You think they want a ransom?"

"What else could they want?" She bit her lower lip again, and I could see she was close to tears. I sat down next to her and put my arm around her shoulders. She put her head down on mine.

It was possible, I reflected. Dad and Mom were sitting on a pile of cash—they had inherited trusts, like all of their kids and my cousins and everyone in the family on both sides—but why kidnap *Dad* for ransom? And while the Diderots and the Bradleys both had money, there were far richer people in New Orleans. "We must have *something* they want, Mom."

"But what?" Mom shook her head again. "What could we possibly have anyone would want?"

"Maybe…" I hesitated. "Maybe this has something to do with Veronica's murder."

"Veronica?" She goggled at me. "But…" She paused. She opened the coffee table drawer and pulled out a baggie of weed.

She rolled another joint. "It's possible, I suppose." She put the joint into her mouth and lit the end, taking a deep inhale.

"It's the only thing that makes sense." My mind was leaping from thought to thought. I shouldn't have smoked the joint with Millie; I wasn't sure if what I was thinking made any kind of logical sense or if it was what Frank always called *stoner thinking*—that sense of wonder that's a by-product of smoking pot. "Well, you're a lifelong friend of hers, and yesterday we stumbled on her body. And now Dad's been kidnapped with some kind of weird ransom note left behind. You think that's a coincidence?"

"'I don't know what to think, to be honest," she replied, taking another drag on the joint. "None of this makes any sense to me. None at all. I thought Veronica's murder had something to do with stealing the tiger."

"Well, that's what I thought." My mind kept racing. "But there has to be some kind of connection, Mom." The reality of it hit me. "You don't think they'll hurt Dad, do you?" I felt a sob rise in my throat that I quickly choked back down.

"I refuse to even entertain that idea." Mom said, her voice trembling a little bit. "If they harm him in any way—"

The phone started ringing.

We stared at each other for a moment before Mom grabbed it. "Hello? Yes, this is she…I'm listening…no, I want to hear his voice, do you understand me? Hello? Hello?" She put the phone back down. She stared at me for a moment before saying, "I don't know what to do." Her hand went to her throat as her face drained of color. "It didn't seem—it didn't seem real before." She swallowed. "Like it was some kind of joke, you know, like he was playing a trick on me and was going to laugh about it, you know?" A tear slipped out of her left eye. "But someone's really *taken your father!*" She started sobbing.

Stay strong, Scotty, I told myself. "What did they say?" All of my life Mom had been a rock of strength for everyone who knew her. Sure, she had a bit of a temper and always spoke her mind no matter the consequences, and she was passionate about her beliefs. But one thing anyone who knew her could always be sure of was that Mom would always have your back, and she was a tough cookie. I'd never seen her like this before, and it was kind of scary.

"They have him," she repeated. "But I don't understand what they want, Scotty. They don't want money." Her voice sounded empty and hollow, and her body was trembling a little. "We're not supposed to call the police, obviously, but for some reason they seem to think I know something about the weirdest thing." She shook her head. "They said, *we know you know where the deduct box is. That's what we want. If you don't give it to us within seventy-two hours, you'll never see your husband again.*"

"Deduct box?" I stared at her, confused. "What the hell is a *deduct box?*"

"I haven't the slightest idea, Scotty." She pushed herself up to her feet, swaying a little. "I—I think maybe I need to go lie down for a bit." She paused when she reached the hallway, and looked back at me. "Scotty, do you think—do you think you could read the cards for me?"

It was the first time Mom had ever asked me. "Yes, of course, Mom, when I get home I'll do a reading."

She gave me a weak smile. "Thanks, baby." She turned and walked down the hallway. I watched her go into her bedroom. The door shut behind her.

Deduct box? Where have I heard of that before?

Then it came to me—I'd heard about it in my Louisiana History class at Jesuit High School. It had something to do with Huey Long.

I went back into the kitchen. In the corner opposite the back door was the little desk where Mom kept her laptop computer and paid the bills. She never logged out of the computer—Storm lectured her fairly regularly about that. I sat down and touched the mouse pad. The screen sprang to life. I opened an Internet search engine on her web browser and typed "deduct box" into the blank space.

A series of links came up, and I stared at the list in surprise. Most of them were newspaper or magazine archives, and all of them were links to articles on Huey Long.

That triggered a bit of memory, but it eluded me as I clicked on the top one, which was from a recent issue of *Crescent City* magazine.

The article popped up, with a picture I recognized as Huey Long. It was written by someone named Paige Tourneur, whose name was vaguely familiar. I scanned the opening paragraphs, which seemed to contradict what I'd learned about Huey Long.

Huey P. Long has a long-enduring reputation for being a corrupt demagogue, for running Louisiana as a dictator and treating the state as his own personal fiefdom. Yet this is very simplistic, and as with anything to do with political history, skips over a lot of nuance. The truth about Huey Long is a lot more complex than the histories written and/or influenced by his enemies. As Barney Fleming, professor of history at Tulane University and an expert on Huey Long's career, said, "Think of it this way: imagine that the only histories and biographies of George Washington available to us in modern times were ones that had been written by British historians. Our modern perception of Washington would be considerably different, wouldn't it? Almost everything we know about Huey Long today has come from the newspapers of the time—and they were conservative papers, and they were violently opposed to what they called Longism. The conservatives called him every name in the book, and after he was assassinated, they continued to blacken his name."

One cannot simply look at the negatives when it

comes to the most colorful and famous politician to ever come out of Louisiana. Governor Long accomplished a lot during his short political career; one has to wonder had he never existed how backward Louisiana would be! He took LSU from a sleepy, backward and underfunded little military college into a major university of national repute. He was absolutely dedicated to educating the population; few American politicians have done so much for education. He provided all schoolchildren in Louisiana with free textbooks, made sure all children, black or white, had bus transportation to school, improved curricula, and raised standards for teachers. He worked tirelessly to abolish the poll tax, which was keeping the poor and blacks disenfranchised. He paved most of the roads, built bridges, brought natural gas to New Orleans, created the Homestead Exemption, expanded the Charity Hospital system, created the LSU School of Medicine, and a lot more—far more than any other three governors combined. Yet these accomplishments are frequently ignored or overlooked; all that is remembered of this remarkable leader are the labels of demagogue and dictator...but clearly, "demagogue" is inaccurate.

So what about the charges of corruption that are so casually attached to Governor Long? In a state with a long history of corrupt governors and corrupt legislatures, where there has never been a decade in over a hundred years without some elected official being convicted of some kind of corruption in office, what sins did Governor Long commit to make him stand out from the rest?

Much of his reputation as "corrupt" has come about because of the way he funded his campaigns. Anyone who had a state job was, of course, in the governor's debt, and Governor Long had no compunction about deducting money from the salaries of the state employees for his campaign finances—since they owed their jobs to him, saying no to his request was simply not an option. Governor Long believed cash was the best way to go— whether this was because paying in cash ensured there would be no accurate accounting and no record of how much money was being spent is a matter for debate. Others besides state employees contributed to the fund, which was kept in a large strong box everyone in the Long organization called the "deduct box," which was usually kept in the safe at the Roosevelt Hotel, where Governor Long kept a suite of rooms (the owner of the hotel at the time, Seymour Weiss, was a vital part of the Long organization). The box was moved shortly before then–Senator Long was assassinated in Baton Rouge, and no one knew where he had moved the box. Some of his men asked him for its location as he lay dying, and his only response was "Later, later." The location of the famed box, rumored to contain over a million dollars in cash as well as damaging information about his political enemies—which included, at the time of his death, President Franklin Delano Roosevelt—remains a mystery to this very day. A replica of the box is currently on display at the Roosevelt Hotel.

I leaned back in my chair and stared at the computer screen.

It made absolutely no sense.

How on earth would Mom know where Huey Long's deduct box was?

But scrolling through all the other links that had come up in my search, it was pretty clear that the only "deduct box" was Huey Long's.

I went back to the article and read it over again. Paige Tourneur was right—all I knew about Huey Long was that he'd been a corrupt demagogue. I'd had no idea he'd accomplished so much, had done so much for Louisiana.

But what was the connection between Huey Long and my parents?

I couldn't think of one. As far I could remember, I'd never heard either of my parents mention his name.

Maybe the connection is Veronica Porterie somehow. Maybe her murder has to do with this deduct box, and for some reason they think Mom knows more than she does.

Veronica met with Mom over the weekend. If someone was watching Veronica, following her...

The more I thought about it, the more sure I was that I was right.

I walked down the hall to ask her more, but when I stuck my head in through the door, she was sound asleep. Not wanting to wake her, I shut the door carefully.

I walked out onto the balcony and pulled out my cell phone. "Hey, Frank." I filled him in quickly. Once I finished it all hit me, like an anvil landing on my head. I started to tremble and had to grab on to the railing as my knees buckled a little.

Someone had kidnapped my father because they thought my mother knew where Huey Long had hidden the deduct box—and she not only didn't know its location, she didn't even know what the deduct box *was.*

They weren't above kidnapping—so why wouldn't they stoop to murder?

It was highly likely they'd already killed Veronica.

"Frank, think we should call Venus and Blaine?" I said, managing somehow to keep my voice from shaking. Sure, they'd said not to call in the police—but they couldn't possibly know *everything.* They might have Mom's place under surveillance, may have even tapped her phone, but they couldn't have my phone tapped and they couldn't have my place watched, too.

Or Frank's phone either, for that matter.

"Just to ask them what they think we should do," I went on, leaning on the black iron railing and watching the people walking around below me. "Obviously, we can't do anything overt with the police—they may be watching the apartment—but I don't think they could have tapped her phone or anything. As long as Venus and Blaine don't come anywhere near here, we should be okay." I exhaled. "No, honey, it just doesn't really seem real to me yet. I don't want to leave her here alone—do you think you could call Rain and see if she'll come sit with her? I think we should be doing everything we can to look for Dad, you know?" Just saying it made me feel a lot better, and I could feel adrenaline starting to surge through me as the despair faded. "Okay, call me back and let me know what Rain says."

I hung up and put my phone back in my shorts pocket.

The more I thought about it, the more I liked it.

We were investigators. We could investigate. We could find him.

I went back inside, feeling even better about everything.

I sat down at the computer again and entered "Huey P. Long" in the search engine. There was actually a website for him: hueylong.com. I clicked on the search function and typed "deduct box" into it. It brought up a page titled *Governor*, and I quickly scanned through the text. There was nothing in it about the deduct box, but I was startled to read he'd been impeached while governor, and he'd accomplished a lot more than what Tourneur had said in her article. A column on the right side of the page listed: 9,700 miles of new roads, 111 new toll-free bridges, free textbooks, free schools, statewide school bussing, adult literacy programs, reformed mental institutions, abolished poll tax, built a new state capital and governor's mansion, built the New Orleans airport and sea wall, reduced bank failures... I whistled.

His enemies, I reflected, had done a great job of smearing his memory and legacy.

I was about to search again when I noticed a small box of text further down on the right of the page, under the words *People Are Asking*:

What Was the Deduct Box?

Most state employees who received a job from Long were expected to contribute to his campaign fund, which was kept in a locked "deduct box" at his Roosevelt Hotel headquarters in New Orleans.

Without a base of wealthy political contributors, Huey reasoned that this was an appropriate source of funds for his political activities. He refused to take the usual bribes offered by business in exchange for their support, and he was frequently in need of cash to print circulars and travel the state to advocate for his programs and combat negative press.

According to historian T. Harry Williams, Long collected between $50,000 to $75,000 each election cycle from state employees, contrary to exaggerated reports that he collected a million dollars per year.

Few employees complained about the deducts, because jobs were scarce. They knew they would lose their jobs if Long lost his.

Huey did not personally enrich himself with these funds and had surprisingly little money to his name when he was killed. The deduct box was never found and is believed to have been stolen by one of his associates.

That's weird, I thought. *Hardly seems like there's enough money in there for anyone to care about now. Maybe a hundred thousand or so dollars?*

It was a lot of money, but not enough to justify kidnapping and murder.

I did some more searching but didn't find anything new that I hadn't already found.

I was about to go check on Mom again when my cell phone started vibrating in my pocket. I pulled it out and Frank's promotional photo for GSWA was on the screen. I couldn't help but smile—he looks so hot in that picture—before touching the screen to take the call. "Hey, Frank, what's up?"

"Rain is on her way over, and I called Storm as well," Frank said. "Taylor's unpacking and is out of the way. I decided not to call Venus and Blaine just yet, not until we know a little bit more about what's going on. When do you think you'll be heading back over here?"

"As soon as Rain gets here," I replied. "Frank, I've been doing some checking on this 'deduct box' thing—it's Huey Long related." I remembered something. "Didn't we meet someone at a party at Papa Diderot's who's an expert on Long?"

"That Tulane professor who wanted to get in Colin's pants," Frank replied. "Remember?"

That was the trigger I needed.

My maternal grandparents lived on Third Street in the Garden, and every year on the Sunday before Fat Tuesday they had an open house for anyone who wanted to come by and watch the parades that day—five parades were regularly scheduled for that Sunday, including two of my favorites, Bacchus and Thoth. This past year was the first year we'd actually made it to the party. In previous years we were either too worn out from dancing till dawn or hungover from drinking till dawn or some combination of the two to make it uptown. But there had been a horrific thunderstorm on Saturday night. That night's major parade, Endymion, had been postponed until Sunday night to follow Bacchus. The weather had been so horrible we hadn't been in the mood to brave the elements. (Primarily because our costumes were flimsy and revealing, and getting soaked to the skin wasn't any of our idea of a good time.) So, when Sunday morning dawned sunny and bright, we decided to head to the Diderot manse and drink for free on my grandparents.

The Tulane professor in question was actually more interested in getting into my uncle Misha's pants when we arrived—Misha has an amazing body—but soon switched his attentions to Colin. Being loyal lovers, Frank and I left him to get away from him on his own—while pointing and laughing the entire time, of course.

It might seem mean, but we enjoyed it.

And he'd do the same to either one of us.

The professor's name was Barney Fleming, and he was a Louisiana history expert. I just remembered him drunkenly going on and on about how Huey Long had been a great man whose reputation had been blackened by his enemies after his death. I told Frank his name and asked him to look him up.

I hung up and took a deep breath. It might not be much, but at least we were doing *something*.

I heard footsteps coming up the back staircase. A moment later my sister Rain, a grim look on her face, came through the back door.

"Oh, Scotty." She gave me a big hug. She shuddered. "What are we going to do?"

"Don't worry," I whispered. "Frank and I will find Dad."

And I pity the bastards who took him.

CHAPTER SEVEN
FOUR OF CUPS
A time for reevaluation

I managed to make it to the bottom of the stairs before I lost it. I sat down hard on the steps and buried my face in my hands.

My mind was spiraling out of control, but I knew better than to try to stop it. That was futile and a waste of energy. Instead, I gave in to it, allowing my fears and worries to take over. I leaned down with my head between my knees and took deep breaths. My eyes overflowed and the sobs racked my body as my brain raced from thought to thought, each one a little bit scarier and worse than the one before.

After what seemed like forever, my mind calmed down. I wiped my face off with my T-shirt and stood up. I took a few more deep breaths before opening the door and stepping out onto the sidewalk.

Dad would be fine. We'd find what the kidnappers wanted or we'd find him.

I started walking back to my apartment.

The sky had clouded over a bit while I was at Mom's, so it wasn't as bright out as I hurried down Royal Street, dodging around window shoppers and other pedestrians. The air felt like a hot wet cloth, and sweat ran down the sides of my face. It felt like it was going to rain at any moment. Every once in a while my mind started going to the bad place again, but I quickly pushed those thoughts out of my head. *Everything will be fine*, I would remind myself.

But I still couldn't wrap my mind around Dad being kidnapped.

My father was one of the kindest, gentlest people on the planet.

I'd been kidnapped a couple of times. It's really not a pleasant experience, to say the least. I could easily go the rest of my life without it ever happening again. Both times it worked out for the best—well, I'm still alive, at any rate—and as worried as I was about Dad, I felt pretty damned confident we'd be able to find and rescue him. It's not like we were your typical kidnap victim's family—if there is such a thing. Frank was a retired FBI special agent, and we were both licensed private investigators. And I had the perspective of someone who'd been kidnapped before. However, I was really sorry Colin was out of the country on a job. His access to Blackledge assets and their sophisticated technology would be a huge help to us.

I wiped sweat off my forehead as I unlocked the gate and slipped through, pulling it shut behind me. As I climbed the back steps to my apartment, I wondered if the mysterious Angela Blackledge would help us—or could somehow get a message to Colin.

Not likely, I thought as I opened my apartment door. *She wouldn't want him to get distracted.*

"Distractions can get you killed," Colin had told us once when I'd asked about getting in touch with him when he was on a job. "So there's no telling when Angela would get the message to me."

Needless to say, the last thing I would ever do is distract him from the job at hand. His work was too dangerous—he needed to be able to focus on what he was doing.

But I couldn't help but feel he'd want to know about Dad.

"Frank?" I called as I walked in the door. I could hear the television in the living room, but the entire apartment was dark.

The shower in the master bathroom was running, and I walked down the dark hallway to the living room. *What the hell?* I thought as I recognized the sounds coming from the television as grunts and groans—and finally a male voice was saying, "Oh, yeah, baby, that's what I like—"

I flipped the light switch and the chandelier flooded the room with light.

There's nothing like coming home worrying about your kidnapped father and walking in on a gay teenager pleasuring himself to *The Squirt Locker.*

The absurdity of it all!

"You're watching *porn?*" I gasped out as Taylor leaped up, pulling up his shorts and underwear while I looked away, trying hard not to laugh.

Taylor's face was beet red as he fumbled with the DVD player's remote and the television screen returned to *Judge Judy.* "I—uh—"

I knew I had to handle this the proper way—I didn't want to scar him or make him feel unwelcome or uncomfortable in our home. I also knew laughing was one of the worst things I could do, so I did everything I could to control it—to no avail. I doubled over and gave in to it, managing to hold the sound in while my entire body rocked with it. After a few moments, I got myself back under control and took some deep breaths, straightening up and forcing myself to look him squarely in the face.

"I'm sorry, really, I am, but when I was going through the DVDs I found some porn and I—" He broke off, sounding completely mortified and embarrassed. He was staring at the floor, shifting his weight from one foot to the other. "Uncle Frank was taking a shower, so I figured..."

I took a deep breath and walked into the living room, gesturing for him to sit back down. *He's just a kid*, I reminded myself, *and remember what you were like at eighteen? You were a walking, talking hard-on, that's what you were.*

"Seriously, Taylor, it's okay," I said, managing to keep my

voice even. "It was a bit of a shock, you know? I just wasn't expecting to walk in on that, you know." I smiled. "You weren't doing anything wrong, so don't be embarrassed. It's normal, and it's healthy—believe it or not, I was your age once, and I can remember what it was like. But in the future, let's just try to make sure that when you're, um, pleasuring yourself, no one is going to walk in on you, okay? Make sure you have some privacy. I hope I didn't embarrass you too badly." Looking at his face, I could tell it was going to be a long time before he got over this mortification. So I brightly added, "Did you get all settled upstairs?"

He nodded, his face still red.

I heard the shower water stop running. "Okay, then. Do you mind running upstairs? I need to talk to your uncle Frank privately."

"You're not going to mention *this*?" His voice cracked.

"Of course not." I patted him on the leg. "We'll just keep this between us, okay?"

He nodded and fled down the hall. I heard the door slam behind him, then his running footsteps going up the back stairs. I rubbed my eyes. Having an eighteen-year-old around was going to take some getting used to, apparently.

I reached under the couch and retrieved the worn cigar box where I kept my old deck of tarot cards. I opened it and caressed the deck.

The cards had been a gift from a friend of my mother's when I was a teenager. Madame Xena, a friend of my parents' who was a psychic, had given them to me. She'd come to dinner one night and when she met me, her eyes got really wide and she proclaimed, "But, Cecile, he has the gift!" I didn't know what she was talking about at first, but a few days later the cards arrived with a note from her. She told me that I was a psychic, just as she was, and she had found when she was first trying to master her own gift that she used the tarot cards to focus and refine it. I just thought they were cool—I'd never seen a deck of them before. Mom bought me a copy of Eden Gray's book *Mastering the Tarot*, and I started studying the cards, learning the different layouts for readings and practicing. I got pretty good at it pretty fast, and I also began communing with the Goddess.

I wasn't sure who the Goddess really was, I just knew the entity who sometimes spoke to me in dreams and visions was a strong feminine force.

I held the deck in my hands and closed my eyes, focusing on the question, *Who has my father, and will we be able to save him?*

I shuffled the deck, spread the cards out, and peered at them.

A dangerous man from your past.

Growth through effort and hard work.

New conditions confront the seeker, courage and hard work are required to meet these new conditions.

Unforeseen perils, deception.

Love is always stronger than hate.

I stared at the cards for another few moments. It wasn't completely clear—it never really was, and sometimes it took the benefit of hindsight to understand the readings, but this seemed like a good one to me. Basically, the cards were telling me that as long as we met the challenge with courage, we would be able to overcome it.

Feeling better, I swept them back into a pile, carefully wrapped them up in their blue silk, and slid the box back under the couch.

I went into the kitchen and poured a glass of iced tea before walking back into the master bedroom. Frank was toweling off in the bathroom and smiled at me when I sat down on the edge of the bed. "Taylor's a good kid, isn't he?" Frank slid his underwear on and hung the towel over the shower curtain rod to dry. "I think it's going to be good for him to be around us, don't you?"

You have no idea, I thought.

"I didn't tell him about Dad," Frank went on. "I figured that could wait. What exactly happened?"

I took a deep breath and filled him in on everything. The smile faded from his face as I spoke, and that muscle in his jaw started twitching the way it always did when Frank got angry.

"We're not going to sit still for this, are we?" Frank said, his voice disturbingly even—never a good sign. Frank always sounds calmer as he gets angrier.

"Of course not—but we have to be careful," I cautioned as Frank pulled on a pair of cargo shorts. Once he zipped them up and fastened them they slid down a bit so the waistband and about an inch of underwear showed. He pulled on a dark-green *Archer* T-shirt. "We don't know who these people are, or how many of them there are." I rubbed my eyes, suddenly very tired. "We don't even know why they think we have this deduct box or can find it."

"You think they might have bugged the apartment, or Mom's?" He sat down next to me and kissed me on the cheek, putting a strong arm around my shoulders. "They had plenty of time to get in here. Maybe we should get the scanner?"

I knew immediately what he meant. Colin, being an international agent for hire, kept a shitload of what I always referred to as "superspy equipment" in one of the closets in the upstairs apartment. One of the first things he did when he got home from a job was use the scanner to check both apartments for listening devices—and he always checked every few days when he was here. I always thought it was a bit paranoid, but better safe than sorry. "Oh my God." I stared at Frank. "We sent Taylor up there—"

Frank shook his head. "He wouldn't know what any of that stuff is, even if he finds it," he pointed out. "And we keep the guns down here." They were locked away in our bedroom closet.

"Well, the scanner should be in the spare bedroom closet upstairs with everything else," I said, keeping my voice down just in case the place was bugged. I stood up. "You finish getting dressed. I'll go have a look."

I kissed the top of his head before heading up the stairs.

Going up to the top floor of our building has never been one of my favorite things to do. I get vertigo sometimes—it's nothing bad, and I have to be pretty high up for it to kick in. Usually when I climb the stairs up to our floor, I stick close to the inside railing and don't look out much at the landings. They also aren't out in the open—the only place where you can see out is at each floor. There's a big landing outside each apartment door, and the wall is open at the end opposite the doors.

But the steps up from our apartment to the top floor are completely open air. And no matter how many times I do it, I can't help but glance out at the dizzying drop down to the courtyard below. There's also a pretty great view out there of the Quarter—Colin and Frank both absolutely love to sit on the steps, smoking a joint and enjoying the view. Not me—I am safely inside our apartment on the third floor, more than happy to wait for them to stop being bored and come on down. Once you get up to the landing on the fourth floor, there's also an iron ladder attached to the wall so you can climb up to the roof—something I've done only when forced, and I still sometimes have nightmares about the damned thing. I took a deep breath and closed my eyes, my hand firmly on the inside rail as I climbed up. The weather had changed in the short time I'd been inside, the way it is wont to do in the late spring in New Orleans—the wind was picking up, dark clouds were coming in, and there was a damp chill to the air that meant a thunderstorm was going to hit at any moment. I hurried up the last few steps, not wanting to be outside when the sky opened.

The door was unlocked—we always leave the door to the upper apartment unlocked—and I stepped in just as there was a crack of thunder in the distance and some raindrops started coming down. It was getting darker, and there were no lights on in the apartment. I didn't hear anything, either, which was weird. "Taylor?" I called out tentatively, wondering where he was.

I walked down the hall and was just outside the master bedroom when I heard the unmistakable sounds of a porn video coming from the television set inside the spare bedroom.

Great, I thought, *I'm going to interrupt him watching porn twice in less than an hour?*

I cleared my throat and called out, "Taylor? Everything okay?"

The sound stopped in mid-moan, and I heard some thumping around in the spare bedroom while I waited patiently in the hallway. After a few moments, he stuck his reddened face out of the door. "Hey," he said, his voice cracking nervously.

"I'm sorry," I said. I exhaled. "We're going to have to come up with some protocols around here to protect your privacy, I think." I gave him a halfhearted smile. "We're used to running back and forth between the two apartments—but you need some privacy. You'll have to forgive me, I'm not used to having you around yet."

"Do you want me to go?" His voice was so miserable that my heart broke just a little bit.

He had his shirt off, and his shorts were hanging down low enough for me to tell he hadn't bothered to put his underwear back on. His hair was messy, and his skin had that rosy glow I remembered from when I was his age (and liked to think mine still had). He was lean and defined, just like his uncle, but his muscles weren't as thick and developed as Frank's. There was a patch of dark blond hair in the center of his chest, and wiry hairs leading from his navel down to the thicker patch the low-slung shorts didn't cover. He avoided my eyes as I walked into the bedroom, pulled out the rolling desk chair, and plopped down in it. I gestured for him to have a seat on the bed.

Once he sat down, I said, in as kind a voice as I could muster, "First off, Taylor, I want you to know you're welcome to stay with us as long as you want or need, okay? This is your home, and I mean that—you are always welcome here. That's never going to change. Both your uncle and I are really glad you're here, but this is kind of an awkward time for us." I gestured toward the television. "Obviously, you need privacy—so from now on the rule is Frank and I will call before we come upstairs, and you can consider this apartment *your* apartment—which means you can lock the door, and we'll always knock if the door is locked. I'm sorry to have caught you twice today—but no more in the living room downstairs. You're more than welcome to watch porn DVDs or watch it online, anything you want—we aren't going to judge you. Hell, it's our porn you've been watching." As the words left my mouth I remembered that we had actually recorded ourselves several times having sex, and made a mental note to hide all the homemade porn in the house.

Better safe than sorry is a mantra I fully believe in.

He cleared his throat, his face reddening yet again. "Uncle Scotty—"

"And none of that, just call me Scotty." I went on, looking him directly in the eye. "If your uncle wants you to call him Uncle Frank, that's between the two of you—but I'm not that formal, okay? You can also call my parents Mom and Dad, if you like—but that's also up to them—you all can work that out amongst yourselves. But you're part of the family now—" In spite of myself I started to choke up. The stress of everything was finally catching up to me. I took a deep breath and gathered myself. "I am also not one of those people who believe in lying to young people, so I'm always going to be honest with you. Right now, my father has been kidnapped, and we're not entirely sure why."

The color faded from his face and his eyes widened. "Kidnapped?" He goggled at me. "Seriously?"

"Seriously," I replied. "How much do you know about your uncle and me? What we do?"

"We-ell," he paused, licking his bottom lip, "Rhonda told me that you actually have a third—Mom didn't know about *that*." He gave me a big smile at that, his eyes twinkling. "We might want to keep that from her, you know. She's pretty uptight about sex—

which is why the whole gay thing kind of threw her for a loop. She's not a bad person," he added quickly. "I mean, she goes to church and everything, but I don't think she really believes everything she's supposed to." His face darkened. "Dad's the one. He's a true believer."

"I can't even imagine what that must be like for you." I closed my eyes and quickly said a prayer for my father. "My parents have always been really supportive. So what did else did Rain tell you about Colin?"

"He works for some kind of international company, so he's gone a lot—Colin. I know Uncle Frank is retired from the FBI, but other than that, not really a whole lot."

"That's all true, to some degree or another." I sighed. "But if you're going to be around here, you might as well know everything. For one thing, Frank and I have our own business, we're licensed private eyes." I chose not to mention that we didn't really get a lot of cases. Storm and some of his lawyer friends threw us some work every once in a while, but that had kind of dried up lately. Fortunately, between Frank's FBI retirement and my trust fund, we pretty much had enough money to live comfortably anyway. "And yes, Colin works for an international company called Blackledge. Blackledge is kind of an independent version of the CIA." As I spoke, his eyes got wider and wider and his smile grew wider in excitement. I gave him a quick overview of some of the cases we'd been involved in, and finished with Mom and I finding Veronica Porterie's body. "So, that's where we are right now, Taylor. Dad's been taken—we're not really sure why, so we have to find this deduct box in order to get him back. Don't get me wrong—we're also going to be trying to find Dad, but we don't have any clues as to who took him or where they are keeping him, so we're going to focus on the deduct box for now. Mom's pretty shaken up, understandably. We can't contact the authorities, but Colin has a lot of really great equipment here in the spare bedroom closet that we're going to have to move if you're going to use this room, but we'll worry about that later.

I'm going to scan both apartments for bugs, and then we're going to head back over to my mom's and do the same thing there. Once we know if they're listening to us or not, we can make some plans about how to proceed."

Once I finished talking, the enormity of it all overwhelmed me, and I felt really tired. I *was* tired. I don't sleep well in beds other than my own, so the last few nights I'd been restless and hadn't gotten much sleep. What I really wanted to do was curl up in bed with Frank and sleep for at least a week. But with Dad in danger, I wasn't going to be able to do that any time soon.

Not that I'd be able to sleep all that well under the circumstances anyway.

"What can I do?" Taylor asked. "I want to help. I mean, you've taken me in and given me a place to stay. It's the least I can do, right? There has to be something I can do."

I looked back at him. His eyes were dancing with excitement. "Taylor—just stay here until your uncle and I get back from my mom's." I got up and walked over to the closet. I opened the door and smiled to myself. I'd never had to come into Colin's equipment closet before, but should have known that it would be organized to within an inch of its life. Everything was in a box, and each box was carefully labeled in a very neat script. A quick glance showed that they were all organized alphabetically. I could hear Colin saying in my head, "Organization is the key. The last thing you want to waste time doing when an assignment goes bad or your cover is blown is to try to find some piece of equipment you need because you didn't organize everything properly. That's a good way to get yourself killed."

I found the scanner and removed the box. I opened the box and lifted it out. It was small, had a handle that fit easily into my hand, and looked kind of like a price gun. There was a little screen on the top. I remembered seeing Colin use it—you just turned it on and made large sweeping motions throughout the entire area being searched. I switched it on—it had a rechargeable battery, and the charging cord was looped into a figure 8, with twist ties keeping it in that shape so it wouldn't tangle. "We're definitely going to have do something about this closet if this is going to be your room." Another thought came to me. "And you need to stay out of this closet until we move this stuff out of here. These aren't toys—it's dangerous and expensive equipment, and Colin wouldn't be too thrilled to need something and have it be broken." As soon as I said it, I could have slapped myself senseless. I'd pretty much guaranteed Taylor was going to go through everything in the closet by saying that—telling a teenager not to do something was like waving a red flag in front of a bull.

The first minute he was alone, he was getting in there.

As though he could read my mind, he said, "Of course not. No worries."

I made a mental note to get everything out of the closet as soon as possible.

"Want to see how this works?" I asked.

If his eyes opened any farther, they'd pop right out of their sockets. He nodded excitedly.

"Come on downstairs with me, then."

He followed me down the hall. I opened the outside door. The air was even thicker and heavier, and it had gotten even darker. The air was so damp it might as well be raining already. I mumbled a little prayer to the Goddess and stepped outside. I took a deep breath and grabbed the railing, starting down. Taylor, of course, was completely fearless and went clattering down the stairs so quickly he was down to the landing in a matter of seconds, smiling up at me expectantly. I resisted the urge to slap the grin right off his face, and focused on making it down to the landing and around the second flight to the third floor. I breathed a sigh of relief when I was finally standing in front of my apartment door. I opened it and stood aside so he could go inside first. I shut the door just as the rain started coming down. There was a flash of lightning followed by an immediate clap of thunder so loud and close the entire building shook.

Thank you, Goddess, for letting me get down the stairs before THAT happened.

I locked the dead bolt and smiled at Taylor. I switched the scanner on and passed it to him. "You want to do the honors?" I asked with a big grin.

"Oh hell to the yes!" He grabbed it out of my hands and stared at it. "What do I do?"

"You hear that beeping?" It was low and regular, with maybe a three-second interval between beeps.

"Yeah." He nodded vigorously.

"That's a normal reading. It'll beep a lot louder and a lot faster when it finds something it deems not normal," I said. "The easiest way to use it is to go along the walls in a general sweeping motion, like this." I demonstrated, moving about five feet and then going down the wall in a waving motion. "Generally, it can be assumed bugs wouldn't be planted on an open wall like this—they usually try to hide them on picture frames or on lampshades—somewhere no one would notice it right away. That way they aren't readily noticeable."

We were finished with the hallway and were working on the cabinets in the kitchen when Frank came out of the bedroom and frowned. "What the hell?" He gave me a weird look. "What's going on here?"

Taylor's frown of concentration turned into a grin as he stopped what he was doing. "Scotty told me about Colin and his dad and everything!" He turned back to the open cabinet and started working his way back through the kitchen.

Frank grabbed me by the arm and dragged me into the living room. "Are you insane?" he hissed through clenched teeth.

"Sorry, we kind of told him to use the spare room upstairs, didn't we?" I whispered back. "And that's where Colin stores his equipment—in the spare room closet. Didn't have much choice, did I? Besides, it's not fair to him not to let him know what's going on. He's pretty bright—he'd figure it out for himself something was going on. And I don't want him to think *he's* the problem. Do you?"

Frank smacked his palm on his forehead. "Christ."

"Rain already kind of told him what we do—I don't see any reason to lie about what Colin does." I shook my head. "Who knows when Colin will be back, and I don't like the idea of lying to him, do you?"

"No, I don't." He looked worried. "Maybe having him come here wasn't the best idea. I didn't think this through, I guess."

"Don't be ridiculous." I rolled my eyes. "Don't be such a drama queen. You didn't create the situation, your asshole brother-in-law did. He's a good kid and we can't turn our backs on him. We just have to figure out how to make this all work."

"I just don't like the idea…" He paused. "That maybe we've put him into danger."

I shrugged. "Well, if the kidnappers are keeping tabs on us, it's too late to worry about that now—they've already seen him. We just have to make sure he's careful, until we have Dad back and the case is solved."

He grinned at me. "You're pretty amazing, you know that?"

I grinned back. "Yeah, I know. In the meantime, we just kind of need to figure out what to do with that stuff, or move Colin's clothes out of the master bedroom—"

The loud beeping of the scanner interrupted me.

I turned around to see Taylor standing next to the desk, an excited look on his face.

Frank crossed over quickly and started looking.

The bug was attached to the base station for the landline phone.

Frank pulled it off, a grim look on his face.

He gestured for Taylor to keep going.

CHAPTER EIGHT
THE HERMIT
The courage to do what is necessary and right

After another half hour or so of thorough scanning, that was the only bug we found in the entire apartment.

"What are we going to do with it?" Taylor asked. His eyes were glittering with excitement. He was bouncing on the balls of his feet, like a ball of nervous energy. With a grim look on his face, Frank dropped the bug down the garbage disposal, turned on the faucet, and flipped the switch. The grinding sound was loud, and after about twenty seconds, Frank flipped it off. "I hope," Frank said angrily, "someone was listening to that. And it burst their fucking eardrum." The muscle in his jaw was twitching the way it always did when he was angry.

"It doesn't make sense," I said as thunder shook the building again. "Why bug *us*? And why kidnap Dad in the first place? I just can't figure this out."

"We don't have much to go on," Frank replied, his voice tense and even. He leaned back against the counter. "All we know for sure is whoever took Dad for some reason thinks we either know where this deduct box thing is or can figure it out. Which means they've probably been looking for it without any luck."

I nodded. "Somehow Veronica Porterie must be connected to it."

Frank made a strange face. "How do you figure?"

"It's simple." Taylor interrupted me before I could say anything. "Unless you believe in coincidences, there has to be some connection. Ms. Porterie was an old friend of Scotty's mom, right? Didn't you say she came by your mom's this weekend? Maybe she was being followed, so whoever the bad guys are, they think maybe she told your mom something. And then she was murdered—the Porterie lady, I mean—and someone kidnapped Scotty's dad, probably around the same time she was murdered, right? It's not much of a stretch." We both stared at him. He turned red and shrugged. "I watch *Law and Order* and I love to read mysteries."

"Real life isn't like a TV show, Taylor," Frank replied. He exhaled. "Okay, say you're right. Wouldn't it make more sense for them to bug Mom's apartment rather than ours?"

"Well, whoever it is, they've done their homework," I said grimly, giving Taylor an approving look. "And how did whoever it was get in to plant the damned thing?" One of the great things about our apartment was no one could get in without a key or being buzzed through the door downstairs. Millie and Velma were extremely security conscious—one of the benefits of having an older lesbian couple as landladies—and their rules were very strict about who was allowed in.

"You know damned well anyone who wants to break in here can get in if they want to." Frank scowled. "They just have to come in over the roofs and drop down to the balcony. We never lock the French doors."

"That doesn't explain why, though," I replied, conceding the point. I mean, it was true, but it was also highly unlikely. To begin with, how would they get onto the roofs to cross them without being seen? They'd have to break in somewhere, unless they were the Ninja Lesbians. That was how I'd first met them—they came over the roofs and swung down onto our balcony before kicking the doors in. But they were highly trained operatives—they'd scaled a brick fence and then the back side of a building. Maybe that wasn't as difficult as it sounded, but I'd prefer to think it was pretty damned hard. I opened my mouth to point that out—but I could tell by the look on Frank's face that now was not the time to argue the point. "I mean, that's good thinking, Taylor, but it still doesn't make sense. It was just a coincidence that we found Veronica's body. If we hadn't gone out there…"

Frank didn't say anything, just looked from me to Taylor and back. "Well, maybe we should have another chat with Mom." He hesitated before continuing. "We need to go over there to sweep her place anyway, and I'd like to talk to Emily or whoever was on duty in the store when your dad was kidnapped."

"Well, we don't really know when they took him. And for another thing," I looked over at Taylor, "how did they get Dad out of there without attracting attention? There's always a lot of foot traffic on the streets around the Devil's Weed. I don't see how they could have done it." My head was starting to hurt.

"It's the Quarter," Frank replied darkly. "Nobody notices anything here."

He had a point, much as I hated to admit it. "But AFAR was behind stealing the tiger, right? Maybe her murder had something to do with that."

"It's probably all part of the same thing," Taylor said, his eyes widening even farther. "Don't you think? I mean, AFAR's never really done anything in Louisiana, have they? They aren't exactly popular in the South."

Another good point. Why all of a sudden was AFAR interested in Mike the Tiger? LSU had had a tiger living on campus since the 1930s, and the current habitat was state of the art, probably one of the best tiger habitats in the world. AFAR usually confined its activities to states where they had a donor base, like California and New York. In the Southern and more rural states, AFAR had never gotten any traction. Louisiana's nickname was "sportsmen's paradise" because the hunting and fishing was so good here.

"So, all of a sudden, AFAR decides to come to Louisiana and free Mike," Taylor went on. "And the president of AFAR's daughter just happens to be one of his caretakers. And said president is murdered, probably on the very day the tiger is stolen.

And your dad is kidnapped right around the same time." He had stars in his eyes as he looked back and forth between Frank and me. "It's got to be all connected. It does!"

"I think he's right, Frank." I waved my hand tiredly. "I think we should question Mom a little more thoroughly about what she and Veronica talked about the other day. And then we need to go talk to that Huey Long expert."

"Huey Long expert?" Frank's eyebrows went up.

Today had been so crazy, I wasn't surpsied Frank didn't remember our phone conversation. "I did a web search for *deduct box* on Mom's computer." I filled them in quickly on what I'd found at the Huey Long website. "You remember that drunk Tulane professor who wouldn't leave Colin alone at Papa Diderot's Thoth party? Turns out he's an expert on Louisiana history, with a specialty in Huey Long."

"Too bad Colin's not here—he'd be able to get any information he wanted out of that guy." Frank made a face. He sighed. "Okay, first we'll go over and sweep Mom's place," Frank went on. "Taylor, you just stay here until we get back, okay? And whatever you do, don't let anyone in."

"I want to go with you," Taylor said, folding his arms stubbornly. He looked so much like Frank right then it was almost scary.

"No, you need to stay here," Frank replied sternly. "Like I said, stay here and lock the doors and don't answer if someone rings the buzzer and most definitely don't let anyone in."

"I want to help," Taylor insisted, setting his jaw. A muscle started jumping in his lower cheek, the way Frank's always did when he was angry. It was positively spooky. "I know I can help. I'm not a baby. I've already helped, haven't I?" He turned to me with puppy-dog eyes. "Please?"

"He's you all over again," I said to Frank. "We'd better let him come with, anyway. I'd rather he stay at Mom's so he's not alone when we go uptown to talk to that professor." I looked at Taylor. "You can come help us sweep Mom's apartment—Rain's there staying with her, and when we go uptown you can stay there—I'd feel better and would worry less if you weren't alone." Frank started to protest but I held up my hand to cut him off. "Besides, if they got in here to plant a bug, they can get in here again, even if we lock the French doors. And by now they have to know we've found the bug and disabled it. It isn't safe for us to leave him here alone." For a brief second, I worried about warning Millie and Velma—but they were perfectly capable of defending themselves, as they'd proved over and over.

I walked into the living room and slipped the bolts on the shutters, then bolted the French doors, too. The rain was still coming down pretty hard, and there was a roar of thunder that shook the house and made the lights flicker briefly.

"All right," Frank said, slipping the scanner into a backpack, which he hoisted over his right shoulder. "Let's go."

We grabbed umbrellas and headed out the back door. I locked both the lock on the doorknob and the dead bolt. The rain was coming down in ridiculous amounts, so heavily that I could hardly see when I got to the bottom of the stairs. The courtyard, even with the drainage, was under about an inch of water as we splashed through it on our way to the passage to the front gate. Theoretically, both the roof of our building and the one next door covered the passageway, but it never really worked that way. Both roofs drained out to pipes that reached the sidewalk in the front, but in several places in the passageway it was coming down in a waterfall. My calves and ankles and feet were completely soaked by the time I got to the gate. I turned the dead bolt and opened it, letting Frank and Taylor out. Then I closed it and locked it just as a gust of wind almost ripped my umbrella out of my hands.

The sidewalks were pretty much deserted because of the rain, with people taking shelter under balconies or inside. The gutters were full and in some places were overflowing onto the sidewalk. The rain was relentless, battering at our umbrellas while gusts of wind tried to wrench them out of our hands. Cars were going slow since the water was rising and it was so dark. There was a bright flash of lightning before thunder roared so loudly that I jumped. I could smell burnt ozone when we reached the corner at Royal Street. I didn't think we were ever going to get to Mom's, but finally we crossed St. Philip Street and there was only another block to go. By the time we reached the door to her back stairs, my legs were soaked and I was shivering.

I unlocked the iron gate and the door behind it and let Frank and Taylor in before closing both and making sure they were locked again. Water was running down the steps like a gradated waterfall, and we splashed our way up, the rain beating steadily on our umbrellas. Frank and Taylor stepped out of my way when I got to the top and fumbled with my keys. Finally, I unlocked the back door and called out, "Rain? Mom?" as I shook the excess water off my umbrella before dumping it into the umbrella stand right beside the door.

My teeth started chattering immediately, because even though the temperature had dropped outside because of the rain, Mom still had her air-conditioning set at sixty-five.

The entire place reeked of pot smoke, and I walked through the kitchen to see Rain curled up under a blanket on the couch. She was holding a joint and watching *Grand Dames of Palm Springs*. She exhaled, a plume of smoke heading for the ceiling. She gave me a lazy grin. "Sorry. Didn't want to waste the hit. You know how it is."

I rolled my eyes as Frank came into the room, followed by Taylor, who had the scanner in his hands and was staring at it in fierce concentration. Frank didn't look very happy and gave me a frustrated look. I tried not to grin.

Taylor was really taking to being a private eye.

Rain watched him for a moment and looked at me, puzzled. I held a finger to my lips and shook my head. "How's Mom?" I asked in a pleasant, conversational tone, gesturing for her to play along.

"Still sleeping," Rain replied. *You think the place is bugged?*

She mouthed the words at me, her eyes following Taylor and Frank as they cleared the room and headed down the hallway.

I plopped down next to her on the couch. "We found one in our apartment," I whispered. "If *our* place was bugged, surely the kidnappers must have planted some bugs here."

"This is all so fucking crazy, Scotty." She took another hit from the joint. "Why would anyone kidnap Dad? It doesn't make any sense. I mean, no offense, but Dad's pretty harmless. I can see Mom pissing someone off enough to kidnap her and fit her with cement shoes." She rolled her eyes and held up her hand to cut me off as I started to speak. "You know I'm right. She's pissed off a lot of powerful people over the years. So have you, for that matter—but everyone you've pissed off is in jail."

That hadn't even occurred to me—but I immediately dismissed the thought. All the killers I've exposed were still doing time and would most likely never get out.

"But then again, nothing around here ever makes sense," Rain went on. "I know I shouldn't have rolled this"—she gestured with the joint—"but I was going crazy sitting around here waiting for the phone to ring, you know? And Mom's just a wreck." She shook her head. "I've never seen her like this, ever. Have you?"

I shook my head. "No, but you know, she's always had Dad as her rock." I could feel the fear and worry building up inside me again, so I closed my eyes and focused on my happy place until I was able to get myself under control. "I can't imagine what she would do if—no, I'm not going to go there." I choked myself off.

"Nothing's going to happen to Dad, Scotty." Rain put her arm around me and I put my head down on her shoulder.

You don't know that, I wanted to say, but if that was what she had to believe to keep from breaking down, I wasn't going to take that away from her.

Frank and Taylor came back into the living room, Frank

putting the scanner back in his backpack. He was frowning. "Nothing—nothing at all." He shook his head. "It doesn't make any sense, any sense at all. Why would they bug *our* apartment and not Mom's?"

Taylor looked like he was about to explode. "What is it, Taylor?" I asked, sitting up and wiping at my eyes so Frank couldn't see I'd been upset.

He gave Frank a dirty look. He took a deep breath. "You're *assuming* the kidnappers planted the bug. You don't *know* that's who did it."

Of course—he's absolutely right.

"He's right." I stood up. "We don't."

"For all you know, it might have something to do with Colin's work," Taylor went on, as Frank just gaped at his nephew. "And you told me, Scotty, that any number of people have issues with you—you've put a lot of people in jail, haven't you? And Uncle Frank, you worked for the FBI long enough to retire, right? You probably made a bunch of enemies, right?"

"My God," Frank breathed, the words barely audible.

"And you also don't know how long it's been there. It could have been there for months, years even." Taylor stood there, his arms folded, a smug look on his face.

"Good thinking, Taylor, but Colin scans the apartment every couple of days when he's home—and I know he scanned the place right before he left two days ago," I said, and when his face fell, I added, "But it was very good thinking, Taylor— you're a natural at this!" He preened, which broke my heart just a little bit. Clearly, praise wasn't something he was used to. *What is wrong with your parents?* I wondered for maybe the millionth time since I'd met him. *He's bright, smart, healthy, good-looking—everything a parent would want. Why is gay such a crime to people like that?*

"Well, we need a plan of attack," I said, standing up and starting to pace. I always think better when I'm in motion. "Rain, you want to do some Internet research, maybe find out if anyone who has a grudge against me might be out of jail?"

"I can do that," Taylor said, whipping his smartphone out of his pocket.

"Easier for Rain," I replied, shaking my head. "She knows who to look for. Frank, you're going to have to make a list of people with a grudge against you." Frank had never, in all the years we'd been together, told me anything about any of the cases he'd worked as a special agent. The only one I knew anything about was the one he was working when we met. Come to think of it, I didn't know much about Frank's past—but that was something to think about later, once we'd found Dad. "And see whatever you can find out about the deduct box, Rain—anything, fact, fiction, legend, rumor—anything." I looked over at Taylor. "You have a driver's license, right?" He nodded. "Taylor and I are going to go interview Dr. Fleming."

"What?" Frank exploded. "No way! He needs to stay here! I can—"

I cut Frank off. "No, baby, I want you to stay here with Mom, in case the kidnappers call again—you need to be here." I held up my hand as he started to bluster again. "You're trained to deal with kidnappers, aren't you? You're the best person for that job. Taylor and I will be fine."

"I can handle it."

We all turned to look at Mom. She was standing in the hallway, wiping her eyes. She looked terrible, the worse I've ever seen her look. It was like all the fighting spirit had been sapped right out of her. She looked haggard, worn, and tired. She was wearing a ratty old LSU football jersey and a pair of sweatpants that belonged in the garbage. Her hair, usually so tightly controlled in her long braid, had come loose and she hadn't bothered to rebraid it. As we watched, she walked into the room, picked up a dead joint out of the ashtray, and relit it, taking a long, deep, healthy drag. She closed her eyes and held the smoke in for so long I began to wonder if she'd stopped breathing, before she expelled it in a huge plume that seemed to fill the room. She opened her eyes and smiled at us all. Her face slowly came back into itself and her eyes came to life.

"Yeah, I'm ready for those fuckers." Her smile chilled me a little bit, and I hoped, for their sake, the kidnappers never came face-to-face with her. "Sorry." She shook her head, the braid swaying. "This kind of took the wind out of my sails a little bit, knocked me down. But I always get back up, and now I'm ready for action." She rubbed her hands together. "What's the first move?"

"Mom, when you saw Veronica this past weekend, what else did you talk about besides Hope?" I asked.

She frowned. "Why do you ask?" Her eyes narrowed. "You think that had something to do with why your father was kidnapped?" She scratched her forehead. "I didn't tell those cops about seeing Veronica—that was deliberate—but after finding the note and your father being gone…"

I understood her weird logic about not telling the cops—she didn't trust any cops other than Venus and Blaine. "Did she say anything else, Mom, anything that didn't have anything to do with Hope?" My voice was gentle. "There has to be a connection, Mom, think."

She took a deep breath. "Finding Veronica like that—I'm sorry, son, you remember how shook up *you* were when we found the body, and you've seen a lot more dead people than I have." She shuddered. "And she was one of my oldest friends. Nothing quite like facing your own mortality. Anyway, and then to come home to this?" She shrugged. "I was off my game. But I'm back, and we're going to get your father back." Her eyes took on a determined glint, one that I was used to seeing there. "And if they harm one hair on his head…"

"We get the idea, Mom," I said, Frank and Rain were both smiling—I assume in relief—and Taylor was just staring at her, his mouth open, clearly awed. Mom had made a new fan, that was for sure.

"And this must be Taylor." She crossed over to him and threw both of her arms around him. She was quite a bit shorter than he was, but she squeezed him so hard he gasped. At first he was stiff and rigid, but then he relaxed and hugged her back. She stepped back away from him and smiled. "You look just like your uncle." She glanced over at Frank. "I've always regretted that I never got to see him when he was a boy—now I don't have to anymore." She cupped Taylor's face in her hands. "Welcome to the family, son. You *always* will have a home here with us—you can take that to the bank, Taylor. You're a Bradley now, just like Frank is."

I choked up a little bit, and seeing Taylor's eyes swimming with tears didn't help matters. Frank put his arm around me, and I leaned into him a little.

"All right." Mom clapped her hands together and sat down on the couch. "Taylor, I'm sorry your entry into the family had to be in the middle of this mess, but it can't be helped and I'm not sorry you've entered the family. We're not normal, in case you hadn't noticed, so it's probably just as well you joined us in the middle of a crisis." She winked at him. "Yes, Veronica called me last week. I was shocked, to say the least. I hadn't heard from her in years—that wasn't a lie, Scotty. Your father and I sent her some money a few years ago—she said she was in trouble and you know we don't ask questions. We just help." She patted the couch next to her. "Sit, Taylor." When he did, she put her hand on his knee. "That's what you do when you love someone, son. You help and you don't ask questions, you don't judge. Judgment is for whatever higher power there is—if there even is one. When you love someone, you don't ask questions. You just do."

I tried not to roll my eyes. Taylor already worshipped her—and it had taken her less than five minutes. "She's going to want him to move in here," I muttered to Frank. "You just wait and see."

"He's going to want to," Frank muttered back.

"Anyway, when Veronica called me on Friday and wanted to see me, of course I assumed she wanted money," Mom went on. "Why else would she call me? I hadn't heard from her in years—she used to call me for news of Hope, but that stopped long ago. I took my checkbook with me—I met her Saturday afternoon down on the river walk."

"How much did she want?" I asked.

"Nothing. She didn't want any money from me—I felt terrible for even thinking it. But I only heard from her when she wanted money, what else was I supposed to think?" Mom looked at me. "But she just wanted to talk. She asked me a lot of questions about Hope, which I was really happy to answer. It was a really hot day, and she was sweating a lot, so I brought her back here." She stared off into space. "It was nice seeing her, but something was wrong, I could tell. I tried to get her to tell me what was going on, but she wouldn't." She looked at me. "That's why I really wanted to go to the fishing cabin, Scotty. She told me then she was staying there for a while, lying low. She was afraid, and that worried me. In all the years I knew her, I'd never known her to be afraid before, not even when they accidentally killed that security guard in that lab explosion. Then, she was defiant, proud. She's never been sorry about that man's death—and to be honest, because of that I wasn't sorry we drifted apart, you know? She changed over the years…" Her voice trailed off.

"Go on, Mom," Frank said softly. "So the two of you came back here?"

She nodded. "I tried to get her to tell me what she was so afraid of, but she didn't want me to know—didn't want me to be involved. All she would say was it was something from the past coming back to haunt the present, but she was sure she could handle it. She kept saying that, like she was trying to convince herself. I don't know, looking back now maybe she had a sense that she might wind up dead, you know?" She shivered a little. "Then, when Mike was kidnapped, I figured that must have been what had her so rattled and worried—that was a pretty major heist. I mean, a lot of planning had to go into that, and if one thing went wrong…" She whistled and shook her head. "I thought maybe if we went out there, Scotty, we could talk her into giving Mike back. I'm sorry, I should have told you the truth…but I was worried you'd want to just call the police."

"Like I would have done that if you didn't want me to," I replied crossly. "You do need to tell Storm, though, Mom—if you didn't tell those cops, you need to. You're obstructing justice otherwise."

Mom laughed derisively. "Tell bumbling Barney Fife and the rest of the Keystone Cops? Please. Besides," she narrowed her eyes, "didn't you tell me that the cop who talked to you was a Porterie?"

"He's engaged to a Porterie." I closed my eyes and tried to remember what else Donnie Ray had told me. "He said there were a lot of Porteries on the north shore, and they all were well aware of who Veronica was."

She waved her hand. "The deduct box—that must have been what she was talking about when she said 'something out of the past.'" She noticed loose hair on her shoulders and frowned, pulling her braid around and loosening it. "I just assumed she meant the security guard's death, but I must have been wrong." She started rebraiding her hair, and I was amazed at how fast she was at it.

"Taylor and I are going to go talk to Dr. Fleming, see what we can find out," I said. "Mom, maybe you could call Veronica's mother? See if either she or Hope is willing to talk to us? And you need to call Storm."

Rain stood up, her cell phone in hand. "I'll call Storm. I promise."

Frank leaned over and kissed me on the cheek. "I'm going to call one of the local feds, one of the locals I worked with on the Perkins case." He winked at me; that was the case he was working on when we first met, "and see what they can do to help us out on the down-low." Mom started to protest, but he cut her off. "There's no way the kidnappers can find out, Mom—I'll use my cell phone and I won't call from inside, okay? I'll ask unofficially." He handed me the car keys. "You and Taylor be careful out there, okay?"

I kissed him back with a big smile on my face. I'd forgotten how much I loved being in the thick of things. It had been a while.

I almost felt sorry for the kidnappers.

CHAPTER NINE

EIGHT OF PENTACLES, REVERSED

Intrigue and sharp dealing

I thought you wanted me to drive," Taylor said, puzzled, as I unlocked the driver's side door of the Explorer.

"It was an excuse to get you to come with me," I replied, climbing up in the seat and hitting the auto button to unlock all the doors. After Taylor climbed into the passenger seat and strapped himself in, I went on, "I just wanted to spend some time with you, okay?" I made a face at him, which made him smile. "You kind of got thrown into the middle of crazy, for one thing, so you need to know this isn't normal for us." I thought about it for a moment. "Well, it's not like this kind of thing hasn't happened to us before, it doesn't really happen very often." I pursed my lips. "Okay, I mean, when I first met your uncle, it was because I got involved in one of his cases and one of my friends wound up being murdered…" I let my voice trail off. "Same weekend we both met Colin, actually."

"So what does Colin look like?"

I pulled out my phone and touched the Pictures app, then swept through them with my finger until I found a particularly hot shot of Colin. He'd just gotten back from a job, and his white tank top was soaked through and stuck to his skin like a bandage. He was grinning at the camera, and I couldn't help but smile as I looked down at it. I turned it so Taylor could see him. "This is him."

Taylor's jaw dropped. "Oh. My. GOD."

"Right?" I smiled at him and took the phone back, putting it into one of the cup holders between the seats. "He looks better in person, if you can believe that."

"Wow." He ran a hand through his hair. "Jean-Paul wasn't even remotely close to being built like that."

"How serious is the thing with you and Jean-Paul?"

He shrugged. "I mean, it was fun while it lasted. But I knew I wasn't going to be moving to Paris, so it wasn't going anywhere. I'm kind of young to be getting serious about anyone yet, anyway."

"Smart boy."

"So, how are you doing?" he asked, pulling out his own phone. "I mean, about the whole dad-being-kidnapped thing."

I put the key into the ignition and started the Explorer. I leaned back and looked at him. "Something I've learned over the years is that life doesn't give you anything you can't handle—it's how you handle it that matters." I took another deep breath. "Yeah, I'm worried about my dad. He's a great guy, you'll be crazy about him—but worrying myself sick isn't going to change anything. But we can do something, right? And doing *something* is better than not doing *anything*." I shrugged. "Can you Google Barney Fleming's address for me?" I waited while he played with his phone, and finally he rattled off an address on Constance Street. "Punch it into the GPS." I frowned. The address sounded pretty far uptown—the 5500 block—but I wasn't exactly sure where it was.

Once he finished fiddling with the GPS, I grinned. Barney Fleming lived between Octavia and Joseph Streets, which meant it was just on the uptown side of Jefferson Avenue. The GPS instructed me to drive down Decatur Street.

"Forget the GPS," I said, reaching over and turning it off. "That's *not* the fastest way from the Quarter to get there."

Taylor gave me a quizzical look. The parking lot where we rented spaces was in the center of a block on Barracks, just around the corner from the apartment. A major secret of the French

Quarter is the hidden parking lots for the residents. Ours was hidden by an innocuous-looking garage door that blended in so well with the buildings on either side of it that it was unnoticeable. Parking is always a problem in the Quarter, and for me, it was well worth it to pay the ridiculous amount of money every month so we never had to find a parking place. The street in front of our apartment was metered, so that wasn't an option. "But—"

"GPS finds the shortest distance," I said, turning the key and starting the engine, "and in New Orleans, that's not necessarily the fastest way." We'd gotten pretty wet on our way back from Mom's, and it was still pouring outside. I backed out of the space carefully—the spaces are incredibly narrow, and the last thing in the world I wanted to do was scratch the side of Colin's spy Jaguar in the spot right next to the SUV. I clicked the remote and the garage door slid up. I pulled out onto Barracks Street and turned right on Chartres.

GPS was right—the most direct way to get uptown was to take Decatur Street, which turned into Tchoupitoulas after it crossed Canal Street. Tchoupitoulas ran along the river all the way to Audubon Park, and once you got past Jackson Avenue, you could fly at about forty miles per hour. There were only lights at Louisiana and Napoleon, and a stop sign at Jefferson. GPS didn't take into consideration that it was never quick to drive down Decatur Street through the Quarter. The street was always clogged with cars, donkey-drawn sightseeing carriages, pedal cabs, and of course, the tourists who simply walked across the street without looking to see if a car was coming.

Claiborne Avenue, also known as Highway 90, was much faster. The major streets of the city that run to and from the river are much closer to each other on Claiborne; they spread farther apart the closer they get to the river. There's also the added bonus of not losing your mind and screaming at the stupid pedestrians who are everywhere in the Quarter. I'm not the greatest driver to begin with, and any route that helps me keep my cool is greatly appreciated.

I turned left on Esplanade and headed up to Claiborne. From Esplanade to right around the Superdome Claiborne seems like a frontage road for I-10. Around the Superdome, I-10 makes a ninety degree turn north, while 90 West splits off and crosses the river. 90 East continues through New Orleans and runs to the river, eventually merging with Jefferson Highway to run alongside the river all the way to Baton Rouge.

Taylor didn't say anything until I'd successfully navigated the spaghetti-like snarl of on- and off-ramps to come down safely on the other side of I-10 and stopped at the light at Martin Luther King. "Wow, that was crazy." He turned to look out the back window. "They couldn't come up with an easier way to do that?"

"I've always just assumed the engineers who designed the highway system here were somehow related to an important politician," I commented as the light turned green. "It's a wonder there aren't more accidents here, especially the way people drive." I smiled at him and turned my eyes back to the road. It was still raining, and there was a lot of water on the road—probably a couple of inches, which made me even more glad we'd brought the SUV. The Jaguar was far too low to the ground for me to be comfortable driving it in the rain.

And I don't like driving the Jaguar. Blackledge had really souped it up for Colin, and I'm always afraid I'm going to launch a cruise missile by hitting the wrong switch.

"Louisiana is really corrupt, isn't it?" Taylor asked.

I sighed. "I don't know that Louisiana is any more corrupt than any other state," I replied with a slight shake of my head. "I think the primary difference between Louisiana and everywhere else is here, we *expect* our politicians to be crooks, and always have. We call it a banana republic for a reason. It's not a shock when one of them gets caught, and we all just shrug it off or laugh at them for being so stupid."

"Like the congressman who was keeping cash in his freezer?"

I nodded. "Exactly. And no one would have even known about that if he hadn't commandeered resources while the city was underwater to *get* the money. One of our senators was involved with a brothel on Canal Street and he's been reelected since that story broke. We even reelected a former governor who'd been convicted of taking bribes in office. Of course he was running against a former president of the Klan—and went right back to jail after that term in office for taking bribes again." I laughed. "The irony is if he ran again, he'd probably win. We do love a charming scoundrel down here."

I slowed down to turn left onto Jefferson. The rain was letting up, and the sun was trying to peek out from behind the clouds.

"You know, Taylor, I'm glad you're here," I went on as I drove down Jefferson Avenue toward the river. "I'm sorry you had to go through what you went through with your dad—I wouldn't wish that on anyone. But Frank is really delighted you're here, and so am I." I hesitated. "I think it's always bothered Frank to be distant from his family."

"Oh, dealing with my dad wasn't that bad," he said, pulling out his phone again. He started fiddling with it. "I mean, I knew how Dad was going to be—he wasn't as bad as I was afraid he would be, you know? We're Church of Christ—do you know anything about it?"

"No, can't say that I do."

"Church of Christ makes the Southern Baptists look like Methodists—at least in Corinth County, Alabama." He made a face. "Makeup on women is a sin, dancing is a sin, mixed swimming is a sin…" He sighed. "Some Church of Christ kids were excused from PE because they'd have to shower and change in front of other kids—show their nakedness."

"Are you fucking serious?" I took my eyes off the road for a moment to look at him. "That's nuts." *Thank you, Goddess, for not giving me parents like THAT.*

He nodded. "Yeah, but it was funny how you could pick and choose. They wanted me to be a jock—I played football, basketball, and baseball—and I couldn't be excused from PE and be able to play sports, you know? And my older sister was a cheerleader, and my younger brother…and some of the women, including my mom and my aunts and my sister and my cousins, they all wore makeup *to church*." He laughed, but it wasn't a happy sound. "When I started figuring out, you know, that I liked boys the way I was supposed to like girls…well, that was when I began thinking about the things they'd say in church, and what it said in the Bible, and it didn't match up, you know?" He scowled at his phone and started playing with it some more. "I couldn't wait to get away to school. They sure didn't want me going to Paris, either—but my grandmother wouldn't let them say no."

The light at St. Charles was red. "Wow."

"It is what it is." He shrugged. "They'll come around someday."

And what if they don't? I thought. *Why worry about it, though? That's just borrowing trouble. And he's here with us—we can help him grow into the person he's supposed to be.*

We drove the rest of the way in silence. I made a right turn onto Constance Street and started looking for house numbers after we went through the intersection at Octavia Street.

Barney Fleming's house was a double shotgun camelback in the middle of the block facing the river. It was painted fuchsia, with black trim. There was a black wrought iron fence running alongside the sidewalk, which was surprisingly level. The house, originally a two-family dwelling, had been converted into a single home at some point in its history. There was a battered red Chevrolet Cavalier parked in front. I parked behind the Cavalier and shut off the car.

"That's it," Taylor said in a hushed town.

I stared at it for a moment. Something was off about the place—I couldn't quite put my finger on it.

I opened my car door and slid down to the street. I walked over to the gate and put both hands on it, leaning on it for a bit. I couldn't shake the sense that something was wrong.

"What are we waiting for?" Taylor said behind me.

I pushed the gate open and walked up the sidewalk, which was made up of red bricks set into the ground. The neighborhood was really quiet other than an occasional car driving by on Jefferson Avenue a block away. I climbed the steps to the porch with Taylor right behind me. The sun had come out now, and it was starting to get hot again. A bee buzzed around one of the rose bushes in front of the porch. I rang the doorbell, but didn't hear any noise from inside. Thinking the bell might be broken, I opened the wrought iron screen door and knocked on the door, which swung open silently.

Okay, this is definitely not good, I thought, taking a step back "Hello? Is anyone here?" I called. There was no response, but I heard something—a sound of some sort from the back of the house. "Stay here," I hissed at Taylor and stepped inside the house, making sure to leave the front door open. I turned back to him. "If you don't hear from me in five minutes, get in the car and call the cops, okay? Lock yourself in."

He nodded, his eyes opened so wide they looked like they might pop out.

I turned back around.

The walls separating the front rooms on both sides had been removed to create one enormous room. The hardwood floor was polished so it shone. There was a black, red, and white Oriental rug underneath the gray sofa to my immediate left. An enormous flat-screen TV hung on the opposing wall, and a mahogany coffee table stood in front of the couch. Framed black-and-white artistic male nudes hung on the eggplant-painted walls. The lights of the chandelier over the coffee tablet were on, the blades of the ceiling fan turning slightly and making a faint squeaking noise. To my right was what appeared to be a sitting area, with another gray sofa and some matching gray reclining chairs gathered around a glass-topped table. There was a tall table with bottles of liquor, glasses, and an ice bucket set out on top.

I moved forward, trying to make as little noise as humanly

possible. I could hear my heart pounding in my ears, loud and rapid. Adrenaline surged through my body. I crept into the next room, which was a dining room. That day's paper was scattered all over it, and there was also a pile of mail—magazines and unopened envelopes—close to the far left corner. A coffee mug with a cigarette butt floating in it was next to the disheveled newspaper pages.

The door to the next room, which I presumed to be the kitchen, was closed.

"Hello?" I called again, my voice only slightly shaky. "Is anyone here? Dr. Fleming?"

I heard the slight thump again. It was coming from the other side of the door.

I crossed the room and put my hand on the door handle. I heard the slight thump again, and took a deep breath, twisting the knob at the same time.

I heard a muffled sound, like someone trying to talk through a gag.

I pushed the door open and gasped.

Dr. Fleming lay on the floor on his side, bound and gagged.

He thumped the floor again with his feet, his watery green eyes looking at me pleadingly.

"Oh my God!" I rushed to his side, yelling for Taylor at the same time. I loosened the gag, sliding it down over his chin. He gasped for air as I helped him up to a sitting position. "Are you all right?"

He nodded, his face red. "Can…you…untie…me…please."

The knots were too tight, so I had to get a butcher knife and saw through the ropes. When Taylor appeared in the doorway, I ordered him to call the police.

"No, no—please don't," Dr. Fleming begged as I finally managed to get the ropes off his wrists. He took the knife from me and cut through the ropes around his ankles. He stood up, breathing hard, and set the knife down on the kitchen counter. He rubbed his wrists, which were red where the ropes had bit into the skin. "I really don't want the police involved." He picked up a pair of wire-framed glasses off the floor beneath the kitchen table.

He wasn't very tall, maybe an inch or so taller than me. He was wearing khaki shorts that sagged underneath a round belly and stopped just above his knees. His calves were bony and covered in thick black hair. He was wearing a dark green Polo shirt with half-moons of sweat at the armpits, and his thinning dark hair was also slick with sweat. He got a glass from a cabinet and filled it with water from a plastic jug inside his refrigerator, gulping it down quickly.

"You were tied up in your kitchen," I objected with a frown. Why didn't he want to call the cops? What was going on here?

He goggled at me. "I know you, don't I?" He placed the glass in the sink. "You look familiar."

"We met at a party a few months ago, at my grandparents'— the Diderots?" I replied, sticking out my right hand. "Scotty Bradley. This is Taylor Rutledge."

"Yes." He took my hand. His was warm, soft, and moist. "Yes, of course. Your grandparents are wonderful people, and they certainly know how to throw a party." He smiled at me. His teeth were yellowed by nicotine, and not particularly straight. He hadn't shaved that morning, so there was salt-and-pepper stubble all over his chin and neck.

"That they do." I nodded, and he smiled at Taylor, looking him up and down in a way that kind of turned my stomach. I remembered him hitting on my uncle Misha and Colin at the Thoth party and bristled. He also seemed remarkably calm and collected for someone who'd been bound and gagged in his own kitchen just a few minutes earlier.

"I don't understand why you don't want me to call the police," I said again. "What happened, Dr. Fleming?"

"Please, call me Barney. I'm sorry, where are my manners? Would either of you like something to drink?" When we both declined, he got his own glass back from the sink and refilled it from the jug again. He leaned back against the counter. "That's right, you're a private investigator, aren't you?" His forehead creased. "Maybe *you* can help me. Why don't we all have a seat in the living room and talk?"

Taylor and I followed him into the living room and sat down in what I thought was the sitting area. "What's going on, Dr. Fleming?" I asked. "Who tied you up?"

"I'm afraid I may have gotten into something I shouldn't have gotten involved in," he said, removing his glasses and wiping the lenses on his T-shirt. "As you may know, my specialty is Louisiana history. I'm currently working on a history of the Huey Long organization, his years in power in Louisiana. He was a remarkable man, a most remarkable man."

"I'm afraid I don't know much about Huey Long," I replied. "Other than he was corrupt, of course."

He rolled his eyes. "Huey Long wasn't corrupt. A corrupt man enriches himself at the public trough. Huey didn't make himself rich." He shook his head. "Anyway, my work isn't going as quickly as it should, because—well, never mind why, that's irrelevant, isn't it? You're interested in what happened here today." He took his glasses off, wiped them with a chamois cloth sitting on the coffee table, and placed them back on his nose. He gave me a phony-looking smile that didn't quite reach his eyes. "A few months ago, a man came to see me in my office on campus and offered me a very generous grant to help me with my research." He got a dreamy look in his eye. "Enough money so that I could afford to hire not only a research assistant, but a fact checker for the manuscript, even so I could take an unpaid sabbatical from the university if I needed to. In exchange, he simply wanted me to let him know if I came across the Porterie diary in my research, or anything about it."

This got my attention. I leaned forward. "The Porterie diary? What exactly is that?" I gave Taylor a warning look I hoped he knew meant for him to keep his mouth shut and let me do the talking.

"It really is criminal how little the people in this state know about its history." He scowled, pointing an index finger at Taylor. "Make sure you learn Louisiana history, son. Make sure you know and understand it. There's a lot we can learn from history, if we study it and learn the lessons it has to teach us." He leaned back in his chair. "Those who do not study history are doomed to repeat it—and you'd be horrified to know how true that quote really is."

Taylor bit his lower lip and nodded.

Dr. Fleming cleared his throat. "When Huey Long was just getting started in politics, he befriended a New Orleans businessman who was also interested in political power. That man's name was Warren Porterie. Warren had been a big donor to the political machine controlling New Orleans at the time, but he was tired of them and thought it was time for things in both New Orleans and Louisiana to change. He really liked Huey and became involved in the machine he was building. Warren wasn't interested in kickbacks or a position for himself. He was primarily interested in making money through his businesses, and he believed that the best way for him to get more customers was to create them—and Huey was all about helping the poor." He shrugged. "No one really knows why Warren Porterie became so aligned with Huey, but it's a fact. Do you know the story of the deduct box?"

Taylor looked confused, but I said, "Yes. The deduct box was Huey's campaign war chest, and it was rumored to have a couple of million dollars in cash in it."

"A couple of million dollars was a lot of money back then," Dr. Fleming observed. "I doubt there was ever more than a hundred thousand dollars in it. I don't know how to adjust for inflation, but a hundred thousand dollars in the 1930s would probably be about ten million dollars in today's money, maybe? But Warren Porterie was the only person Huey ever trusted with the deduct box. After Huey was assassinated, the deduct box was missing. Huey had moved it out of the safe at the Roosevelt Hotel only a couple of days before he died, and he never told anyone what he had done with it. He died before he could say where he'd put it. Obviously, the logical conclusion at the time was he'd given it to Warren Porterie, the only person he'd ever trusted it with before. Unfortunately, the very same night Huey was shot and killed, Warren Porterie was also killed—he was in a car accident just outside of New Orleans—he was heading for the north shore. His car flipped over, killing him and his mistress instantly." He snorted. "Of course, that never got into the papers—that he was with his mistress, I mean—the Porteries were too powerful and too wealthy for *that*. But that's the true story. And his diaries were also missing—he was quite famous for keeping a diary. Huey always joked that Warren's diaries would ruin everyone in Louisiana some day." He smiled at me. "It's generally always been believed that his last diary, the missing one, has the location of where he hid the deduct box. And this millionaire who wanted to fund my research—he was very interested in the Porterie diary. What else could I conclude but he wanted to find the deduct box after all this time?"

"I don't understand," Taylor blurted out. "Why would anyone care today where the box is? That's not a lot of money. Especially if he's a millionaire."

"Ah, my young friend, that would be true if all that was in the box was cash." He folded his hands in his lap.

"There's something else in the box?" I asked, not quite sure I believed what he was saying.

"Huey believed there was a conspiracy against him—and he was probably right." Dr. Fleming went on. "The story is that right before he died, he took all the cash from the deduct box and bought state bonds with them. State bonds with the name left blank. Warren Porterie recorded the serial numbers of the bonds in his diary, and so if anyone stole one of the bonds and cashed them, there would be a record of who did it—that was Huey's fail-safe." Dr. Fleming smiled. "With compound interest, those bonds would be worth tens of millions today, my friends. Tens of millions of dollars owed to whoever possessed those bonds, owed by the taxpayers of the state of Louisiana." He smiled. "Huey also kept a lot of damaging information in there, in case he ever needed to strong-arm either friends or enemies. There were rumors he had affidavits on Franklin Roosevelt, evidence of wrongdoing by the president that would not only destroy his political career but could possibly land him in jail." He shrugged. "All those people are long dead now, of course, so that information would only be of interest to a historian like myself. But the bonds? Whoever had those bonds would have the power to possibly bankrupt the state. And that is not just financial power, but political power." He grinned at me. "Wouldn't you think the governor would do just about anything to stop someone from bankrupting Louisiana completely? Our governor has his eyes on a much higher prize than Baton Rouge, you know. Something like this could finish him politically."

"So, who was the millionaire who gave you money?" It was hard for me not to use the words "bought you."

"I never actually met the man—he sent an assistant to meet with me." He said the name.

I froze in my seat, hoping I didn't give myself away with a facial expression.

I knew the man all too well.

Rev Harper.

I bit my lower lip. Barney was still talking, but I was only vaguely aware of what he was saying. A chill when through my body, and I flashed back to a memory—

—I was strapped to Colin's back, and we swung out and away from the building, and the stars and the night sky over my head rotated as we dropped, and I felt my stomach jump into my throat as we dropped through space. Then we were moving back toward the building and I closed my eyes. There was a thud as Colin's feet hit against the side of the building—Jax Brewery, that's where we were, he was rescuing me and I'd been drugged, my mind was only vaguely aware of what was going on, and with

my eyes closed I could hear the traffic on Decatur Street and a band playing somewhere in the distance, and as Colin pushed off from the building yet again I heard the sound of the nylon rope zipping through the pulley he was controlling, and we were dropping again, and I realized it was better to have my eyes open—

"Scotty?"

I shook my head and came back to the present. "I'm sorry." Barney and Taylor were both staring at me. "So, it was Harper's men who did this to you?"

Barney gave me a funny look, but he nodded. "They wanted my notes—they took everything. I wasn't moving fast enough for Harper, so he decided to go after the diary himself." He wrung his hands. "So you can understand why I don't want the police involved. It would really look bad for me at the university, and—really, there wasn't any harm done, was there?" He gave me a phony smile.

"But if we hadn't shown up when we did, you could have—"

Fleming cut Taylor off abruptly. "I told you, they were starting to question me—there's no telling what would have happened, but we heard your car pull up. They gagged me and went out the back door when you knocked on the front door."

"But what if they come back?"

"They got what they came for." Fleming stood up. "For what good it will do them. If I couldn't figure out where the diary was, they don't have a chance. Now if you'll excuse me, I'd like to lie down for a while."

I nodded at Taylor, and we both stood. "You're sure…"

"Positive."

"Come on, Taylor." I shook Fleming's hand. "Thank you for your time, Dr. Fleming."

CHAPTER TEN

THE HIGH PRIESTESS, REVERSED

A selfish and ruthless woman

H e was lying, wasn't he?" Taylor said once we were back in the car.

I was impressed. I hadn't believed a word of what Fleming had said about getting tied up either. "Why do you say that?" I said, putting the keys in the ignition.

Taylor rolled his blue eyes dramatically. "Someone breaks into your house, ties you up, and threatens to torture you if you don't talk, but you don't want to call the police?" His eyebrows met over the bridge of his nose. "I call bullshit on that. Bullshit." He shrugged. "And then wants to be left alone in the house and isn't worried about them coming back? Uh-uh. No sense at all." He buckled his seat belt. "So, who is this Rev Harper person?"

"No one, really."

"I'm not blind, Scotty—I saw how you reacted when he said the name."

"He's a millionaire—made his money in oil, I think." I put both hands on the steering wheel. "He's a little on the unsavory side, and he's not above bending the law to get what he wants." *To say the least*, I said to myself.

When I'd first met Rev Harper, I was tied to a chair, much as Fleming was when we found him. I was investigating the murder of a tabloid reporter whose body I'd actually stumbled over— maybe it does happen a lot more than I was willing to admit— and I'd gotten my friend David to give me a ride to follow a lead.

Harper's men had followed us, forced off the highway, and pretty much caused us to have an accident. Within minutes, they'd whisked me out of David's car and into the trunk of theirs. That time, Harper was looking for the death mask of Napoleon, which had disappeared during the Cabildo fire in 1988. He'd drugged me with sodium pentothal to make sure I was telling the truth. Once he was satisfied that I didn't know where the death mask was, his men had locked me into a bedroom in his penthouse on top of Jax Brewery. Colin had rescued me while I was still stoned from the drug, and despite my fear of heights, had strapped me to his back and scaled down the side of the building.

I still had nightmares about that. Call it post-traumatic stress disorder.

"Wow." Taylor's eyes had widened again. "You live a pretty exciting life, don't you?"

"I don't know that I would call it *exciting*," I observed. "I would say it's not average, that's for sure. Although there have been times when I've wished for something a little more normal and boring." I grinned at him. "But boring and normal's not all it's cracked up to be, you know?"

"Yeah." He frowned. "Dr. Fleming didn't seem all that upset that Harper's men took his notes."

"Well, my guess is he has another set." I drummed my fingers on the steering wheel. "But didn't you think it was weird how neat and tidy his house was? I mean, other than the crap on his dining room table."

Taylor thought for a moment, and then smiled at me. "No signs of a struggle."

"Very astute of you." I smiled at him as I started the ignition. "So, he either didn't resist or try to get away from them, or they had other methods of persuading him to let them tie him up."

The one thing I didn't understand, though, was *why* put on such a show for us?

He couldn't have known we were stopping by.

I pulled away from the curb, drove two blocks, then turned

right and swung back around, heading back to Octavia Street, where I turned right again and parked right before the corner at Constance. I turned off the engine and turned to look through the passenger window.

"What are we doing?" Taylor looked out his window, following my gaze.

"We're going to watch the good doctor's house for a little while—not long, I promise."

"Why?"

I shrugged. "I have a hunch." I turned in the seat so I was looking right at him. "He seemed to be in a hurry to get rid of us—which is also suspicious. So we'll just sit here for a while and see if he is up to anything. We'll give it no more than ten minutes."

I set the stopwatch function on my phone and propped it up on the dashboard of the truck. A car drove by. A pair of sweat-drenched joggers ran past. It was starting to get hot inside the Explorer, so I turned the key to accessory to get some cold air moving.

The stopwatch beeped, and I was just about to ask Taylor if he thought we should give it another couple of minutes when the front door of Fleming's house opened. Fleming stepped out with a backpack slung over his left shoulder. He locked the door, got into the Cavalier, and started the engine. The tires squealed loudly as he pulled away from the curb.

"Here we go," I said, starting the SUV and slipping it into gear. I went around the corner and caught sight of his car about a block ahead of us. He turned on his signal when he reached the stop sign at Magazine Street. I pulled over to the curb, not wanting to come up behind him at the corner—the SUV was too big not to notice. He turned onto Magazine and I swung out again, flooring it and driving too fast. I hoped I wouldn't lose him on Magazine—it was a narrow, two-lane business street, and traffic was a nightmare under the best of circumstances. I stopped at the corner and looked to the right. He was stopped at the light at Jefferson. I had to wait for a few moments before I could turn, but I could see him clearly as he went through the intersection when the light changed and continued downtown on Magazine.

I've been a passenger with Colin and Frank enough times when they were following someone to figure out what I was doing. The key was to never lose sight of him while keeping enough distance between us so he didn't notice us behind him. I kept three cars between us, figuring that was good enough on the narrow street. He turned on his left turn signal when he got to the intersection at Napoleon. The oncoming lane was clear, so I turned left onto a one-way side street and headed up a couple of blocks before turning right again and heading toward Napoleon. I reached the stop sign just in time to see the red Cavalier drive past, away from the river. I had to wait for another couple of cars to go by before I could pull out to the neutral ground and make a left onto Napoleon. Napoleon was under construction between Prytania and St. Charles and narrowed to only one lane. I could see him ahead of us, three cars back from the red light. There were a couple of cars in between us, but I could easily lose him when the traffic merged when the light changed. I couldn't see if his signal was on. I cursed under my breath and hung a sharp right.

"What are you doing?" Taylor asked, surprised.

"I don't want to lose him—" I swore again as the SUV bumped over potholes on the side street. I turned left and drove up to Prytania and shot across the street, right in front of a gray Lexus, which slammed on its brakes and blared its horn at us.

When I got to St. Charles, I could see the light was red at Napoleon, so I drove across to the neutral ground and didn't slow, almost going up on two wheels as I turned left. I swung into the right turn lane and got to Napoleon in time to see the Cavalier heading toward Claiborne, still on Napoleon. The light finally changed, and I breathed a sigh of relief as I turned to follow him. There were about four or five cars between us now.

I relaxed.

"Where do you think he's going?" Taylor whispered.

"You don't have to whisper—he can't hear you," I said, suppressing a grin as his face turned red. "I'm hoping he's going to meet whomever he's either working for or with. Maybe we can figure out what he's up to once we know who that is." What I was really hoping was wherever it was he was leading us, was where they were keeping Dad.

But I didn't believe for a minute that Harper had Dad—that wasn't his style. Sure, he'd kidnapped and drugged me to find out what I knew all those years ago, but kidnapping Dad and holding him hostage was not his style. Harper was more direct—he didn't play Machiavellian games like that.

No, I didn't doubt Harper was looking for the deduct box for reasons of his own, but Dad's kidnapping was the work of someone else.

Which meant there were two opposing groups looking for the deduct box.

And us.

"Call Frank, let him know what we're doing, and find out what's going on around my mom's—see if the kidnappers have called since we left," I instructed, keeping my eyes on the back of the Cavalier as it continued toward Claiborne Avenue. I heard Taylor talking in a low voice.

Even though I was confident I was right that Harper wasn't behind Dad's kidnapping, I wasn't happy to know he was involved in any way in whatever it was that was going on. The big Texan firmly believed his wealth and power put him above the law and he was justified in doing whatever it took to get what he wanted. But Harper seemed to have a grudging respect for me. I had kept him from getting his hands on the death mask, but he'd given me the fifty-thousand-dollar reward he'd put up for its discovery since I had in fact found it.

No, Harper was more likely to deal with me directly than grab Dad.

The more I thought about it, the less sense it made. Whoever had kidnapped Dad seemed to think we either had the deduct box or knew where it was. The only way we could possibly know that was if Veronica had somehow known where it was and passed the information on to Mom. And unless Mom wasn't telling us everything, she didn't know either. The kidnappers were wrong.

I also wasn't sure if Fleming had lied about the bonds—it just seemed really weird to me that the state government would have issued what were essentially bearer bonds against state funds, even if Huey Long had wanted it to. None of that made sense. The Huey Long legacy website had been pretty clear that he'd always kept the money as cash, so why on earth would he have done something so out of character? No, Fleming *must* have been lying about that. He might be an expert on Long, but that didn't mean he wasn't a liar.

There had to be something else, more than the money, in that box that everyone wanted.

Fleming turned right onto Claiborne and headed downtown.

I bit my lower lip as I turned to follow him.

I didn't like having Taylor along with me. He was just a kid, and there was no telling how this might end up. But there was no way I could just dump him on the side of the road either. There was nothing to do but keep following Fleming and hope things didn't take a turn for the worse.

This is why I can't be a parent—why kids shouldn't be around me. I get into too much trouble, and I'd put the kid at risk. Frank will never forgive me if anything happens to Taylor. I shouldn't have brought him with me. I should have known this would turn into more than just a talk with Fleming. But if he can lead us to Dad—isn't it worth the risk?

Yeah, GREAT parenting skills there, Scotty.

I got even more nervous after we passed through the intersection at Martin Luther King and he got into the lane for the on-ramp to cross the river bridge.

"Fuck it," I told myself, following him up the long ramp

onto 90 West. Traffic wasn't as heavy as I'd thought it would be, but it was also still early in the day—during rush-hour traffic would come to a horrible stop-and-go, bumper-to-bumper halt. I still didn't think he'd noticed us following him, and I saw out of the corner of my eye that Taylor wasn't on his phone anymore and was just holding it loosely in his left hand. "What did Frank say?" I asked as we made the steady climb to cross the river.

"They haven't heard from the kidnappers," he replied. "But my mother called."

"Is that good or bad?" I asked as we went over the high point of the bridge and started down the other side to the West Bank. "What did she have to say?"

"She wants me to call her to let her know I'm all right." He made a face. "She wants to hear my voice. Well, *fuck* her!"

I glanced over as I braked to slow us down—the downward slope had gotten us to about ninety miles per hour. The Cavalier continued ahead of us on 90, going around the big turn at the bottom of the incline but not getting off at Charles de Gaulle Boulevard. In that quick glance I could see his lip was quivering and his eyes were filled with tears.

"Taylor, it's okay to be angry with your mother, but she's still your mother," I said, trying to keep my voice as soothing and consoling as I could. "You're going to have to talk to her sometime. I know—I can't imagine what it must be like to be so completely rejected by your parents, but your mom is doing the best she can, you know?"

He nodded, wiping at his eyes.

I didn't like sticking up for his mother—frankly, I thought she deserved to be boiled in oil—but saying that wasn't going to make him feel any better.

"You don't have to decide now anyway," I went on, turning my attention back to the highway and frowning. I didn't see the Cavalier anywhere—had he somehow gotten off the highway when I wasn't looking? "Do you see him?"

"He's in front of the eighteen-wheeler," Taylor said, his

voice hushed and a little shaky. "That's why you can't see him—oh, look—there he goes! He's taking that exit!"

Sure enough, Fleming was getting onto the Belle Chasse Highway.

Where the hell is he going? I wondered as I followed him through Belle Chasse and stayed back as he started driving along the river levee.

I stayed back as far as I could. There were no longer any cars between us, and I had to hope he hadn't noticed us following him before. *Where is he going?*

Farther and farther we drove; it became clearer we were heading into the marshes that eventually became the coastal wetlands.

"Do you know where we are?" Taylor asked.

"No, not really," I replied nervously, without taking my eyes off the back of the Cavalier.

Finally, after it seemed like we'd been driving long enough to be out in the middle of the Gulf of Mexico, he made a left turn and drove along a dirt road.

I hesitated for just a moment before following.

After about another ten minutes, he pulled off the road into a dirt parking lot and drove around behind a building made of rusty corrugated steel with a tin roof. All around us was marsh and water and towering live oak trees dripping with Spanish moss. I stopped on the road and let the truck idle for a while.

I didn't know what to do.

Every instinct in my body was screaming at me to turn the SUV around and head back to New Orleans. I knew I could find the place again, and I couldn't think of a single good reason we could give to whoever might be back there if I drove around to the back of that building. I was just about to put the car into reverse and turn around when three men materialized from the side of the road, pointing shotguns at us. A woman, short in stature and wearing cut-off jeans shorts beneath a Greenpeace T-shirt, came around my side of the SUV and gestured for me to roll down the window.

Starting to sweat, I rolled the window down and plastered a smile on my face. "Can I help you?"

"Turn off the engine and get out of the car," she said with a scowl. She had long black hair that hung limply around her face. Her forehead was covered by her greasy bangs. Her skin was pitted with acne scars, and she wasn't wearing any makeup. "Don't make us shoot you, because we will." She gestured over her shoulder. "There're plenty of gators out there that'll be more than happy to eat the two of you. No one would ever find you or know what happened to you."

I glanced over at Taylor, who looked absolutely terrified. I turned off the engine, mouthing the words *we'll be okay* to him as I opened my car door and stepped down onto the dirt road. "I'm Scotty, and this is Taylor. I'm not sure what you think we're doing out here, but we're lost and—"

She shook her head. "Don't make things worse by treating me like I'm stupid," she said. "I'm nobody's fool, Scotty. I don't know what you're doing out here, but you didn't get out here by getting lost, all right? So just drop the dumb act. Frisk them," she instructed, "and then drive the vehicle around back." When they finished patting us down, one of them climbed into the SUV and drove it around behind the building. "Come along, then," she said, and started walking.

One of the rifles pushed me in the center of my back, and I started walking, following her. I mumbled a quick prayer to the Goddess to watch over Taylor, and asked, "Won't you tell me your name?"

"I'm not feeling like making your acquaintance at the moment," she snapped, walking a little faster. She took a few more steps, then stopped and whirled around, a smile on her face. Her teeth were gray, and I noticed she had a rather sickly pallor to her skin. She stuck out her hand. Her arm was covered in mosquito bites. "My name's Diana. Diana Killeen. Pleased to meet you." Her voice was saccharine sweet and about as phony as her politeness.

I didn't take her hand. "Nice to meet you."

She scowled at me, her eyes narrowed momentarily, and she turned and started walking again.

Once we reached the building, she opened a side door and went inside. We followed. She pointed at two chairs. "Sit." She pulled some water from a cooler and held the dripping bottle up to her sweating face for a moment, her eyes closed. "Tie 'em up nice and tight," she instructed, and smiled as she watched her henchmen tie us to the chairs. I looked around but didn't see Fleming anywhere, cursing myself as an idiot.

This is what you get for thinking you can play hero and follow someone. He probably knew we were following him from the start and called ahead to make sure they caught us. I just hope they don't kill us.

Once they finished tying us to the chairs she walked over and stood in front of us. "Why were you following Doc Fleming?" she asked in a conversational tone. Her face was still completely blank and free of emotion. When I didn't answer, the corners of her lips twitched in what was probably an attempt at a smile. "If you don't talk, I can have one of the guys start breaking your little friend's fingers, one at a time." She sounded rather pleased with herself, and my palm itched to slap her right across her smug face. I promised myself if I got the chance I'd make it count. "Answer me! Why were you following Doc Fleming?"

I glared at her. "I knew he was lying to us, so I figured we'd hang out for a while and see what he was up to. When he got into the car, we followed and wound up here."

"Who are you?" Her eyes narrowed. "And what do you care about Doc Fleming?"

"Well, like I said, my name is Scotty Bradley, and I—"

"Wait a minute, did you say Bradley?" She interrupted me, her eyes widening momentarily, and she exchanged a look with one of the men. "Bradley? Did you say Bradley? As in Cecile Bradley?"

"She's my mother," I answered.

And just like that, I knew exactly who and what she and her friends were.

"You're AFAR, aren't you?" I tried to turn my head to give Taylor a reassuring glance. "You were working with Veronica Porterie. You're the ones who took the tiger. Is this where you have him hidden?"

"That's none of your business," Diana replied. Her face was expressionless, her eyes and voice cold. "Doc Fleming said you broke into his house and tied him up, and then when he escaped, you chased him out here."

"I don't know what you're doing with him, but he's playing you for a fool," I replied, over Taylor's gasp of indignation from somewhere to my left. I laughed. "He was tied up *when* we arrived. *We* untied *him.* He told us some bullshit story, like I said, and we followed him out here. He must have seen us following him, so he concocted this bullshit story to tell you." I rolled my eyes. "I don't care what you people are doing with the tiger. All I care about is—" I stopped myself.

They must not have Dad, so best not to say anything.

"What do you care about, Scotty Bradley?" she asked, a smile twitching the corners of her mouth. "And why should I believe you over Dr. Fleming?"

"It's true!" Taylor exploded. "He's a liar!"

She looked at him coldly. "Gag him." I heard movement behind me, and another grunt from Taylor—which probably meant he was now gagged.

I looked her straight in the eye. "If you know my mother's name, you know Veronica trusted her." I said. "They were friends since childhood. Veronica always turned to my mother when she needed help."

"Veronica's dead," she snapped, her face taking on a worried look. She rubbed her eyes. "Leave me alone with them." The three men vacated the room, shutting the door behind them. She walked over and knelt down in front of me. "Look, if you're telling the truth about Fleming, I'm sorry about this, I really am. I don't know what to do." Her voice rose in tone until the last few words sounded almost like a childish whine. What I'd taken for coldness I now recognized as worry and stress. I relaxed a little. *That* I could deal with.

"Let me guess," I said in a soft, gentle, understanding tone. "You've been thrust into a leadership position because someone murdered Veronica, and you don't know what to do."

She bit her lower lip. "I thought taking the tiger was a bad idea," she said, her voice barely above a whisper. "Now we're responsible for the damned animal, Veronica's dead, and we didn't kill her." She slammed her fist down onto her leg. "I know that's what they're going to try to pull, you know—that we killed her."

"What was the plan?" I asked. "Surely you had to plan for a long time if you were going to steal the tiger. Was Veronica's daughter involved in the plan?"

"Veronica's *daughter*?" She looked and sounded shocked, and was pretty convincing at that. "Veronica doesn't have a daughter."

"Yes, I'm afraid she does. Her name is Hope, and she is one of the veterinary students who work with Mike the Tiger." I could tell by the look on her face she was getting worried, and I know it was small of me, but I was enjoying it tremendously. Hey, I was tied up! They'd held guns on me! "The police think Hope had something to do with the tiger's theft because of who her mother is."

Her face hardened. "Good enough for her." She raised her chin defiantly, but her eyes still looked panicked. "Veterinarians are butchers." She went on at great length about how evil veterinary science was—since it primarily existed to continue the enslavement of animals by humans.

The obvious response to that was *So it's okay to let animals get sick and die or not help them with serious injuries?* But getting into an argument with her about AFAR's mission and positions on animal rights wouldn't get me—and Taylor—anywhere.

I couldn't believe I'd gotten Taylor into this. I'd put Frank's nephew into danger his first day living with us.

If this was what parenting was like, no thank you.

"Fine," I replied. "So, what happened with Veronica? Did you get into an argument about the tiger, and someone shot her?"

"I told you, we didn't kill her!" she insisted. "Look, the last thing in the world I or anyone else in our group wanted was to kill her. Sure, there were times when I wanted to—she was a rather exasperating woman, and there was just no arguing with her, she was always right—you have no idea how infuriating that can be."

Don't I? I thought, thinking about Mom.

"But the last thing we would have done was kill her, especially after we stole that fucking tiger!" She stood up and began pacing around. "She was the only one who knew what to do with the tiger. She wouldn't tell any of us what the plan was—said it was better we not know, in case we got caught, that way we couldn't talk. So we took the tiger and went out to the place in the swamp. We get there, and she's already dead." She shuddered. "Then what were we supposed to do? We couldn't give him back so he could live a life of slavery. But what was she going to do with him?" She ran her fingers through her short hair, gripping it with both hands and yanking until her eyes got watery.

She's fucking nuts, I thought. *Better not do or say anything that could set her off.* "So, if keeping him in his habitat on campus would be slavery, surely a zoo would be out?"

She narrowed her eyes and stared at me. "Zoos are an abomination."

"Well, then the only option would be to set him free in the wild." I would have shrugged, but I was tied too tightly to move at all. "Did Veronica know anyone with that kind of money, who could return him to the wild?"

She bit her lower lip. "No. There was no one like that."

"Then what could she have had planned?"

She swallowed. "She may have wanted to euthanize him."

I closed my eyes.

It very clearly stated on AFAR's website that they believed a noble death was better for animals than a lifetime of slavery to humans. There had been a bit of a scandal a few years earlier—not much, really, it was reported a few times but it didn't go viral and after a few days everyone forgot about it—that AFAR's unwanted animal shelters in various cities throughout the country were actually death camps. The story, released by a former employee, was that people would bring abandoned or unwanted animals to these shelters, thinking AFAR would find them good homes, when in fact they were all euthanized within twenty-four hours of being dropped off. He claimed that they honestly thought the animals were better off dead than in loving homes. I'd been absolutely horrified, but I was unable to find any corroborating evidence, and most of the news agencies, once the story didn't get any traction, dropped it as the ranting of a disgruntled ex-employee. AFAR's reputation for advocating for animal rights was pretty strong, so most people didn't think it was possible that they'd kill animals trusted to their care.

But if Veronica had planned on euthanizing Mike, then it was probably true about the shelters being death camps.

Someone needed to expose AFAR to the public. I took a deep breath and gave it another try.

"Look, just let us go," I said softly. "You can take Mike back. Just make an anonymous call to the police or the veterinary school in Baton Rouge. Seriously. You have no reason to keep us here. We won't rat you out or anything. You can trust me."

I could see she was wavering. "I'd like to believe that." But then her eyes clouded over and she shook her head. "Like I can believe anything you say?"

She walked over to me and swung the hand holding the gun.

The last thing I saw was the butt of the gun coming toward my eyes.

And then everything went black.

CHAPTER ELEVEN
THREE OF CUPS
Happy conclusion to an undertaking

I was floating through darkness with no sense of time or space. It had been a long time, I realized as I drifted downward, since the Goddess had summoned me to speak with her.

I'd never really understood where I was when I came here, but I did know that despite the endless physical sensations I was only here in spirit. My physical body always remained on the earthly plane.

I could hear some sounds, the way I always could when I came here, sounds that soothed my soul and made me relax even further than I already was. Coming here was like smoking a joint and taking a Xanax at the same time. No matter what concerns or worries I had in the real world, they no longer weighed on my mind when I was here.

And of course, just being in her presence was always a comfort.

I kept drifting, floating in a gentle free fall. I didn't know where the ground was, or if I was facing up or down. The darkness at first was confusing, but gradually I became aware of stars sparkling in the velvety darkness above me. It was warm, almost perfectly warm, with a soft, gentle breeze ruffling my hair and making me feel like I was enveloped in peace and love. I could smell flowers: roses and daffodils and honeysuckle and lilac. I was at peace, blissful, wonderful peace, and I never wanted this *feeling to ever go away. I didn't want anything to change. I didn't want to go back to the real world.*

And then I felt the ground beneath my feet, warm sand between my toes as water lapped over them. The darkness began to brighten, and the black velvet sky overhead gradually transformed into a beautiful, bright azure blue as the sun began to materialize. The water was brownish-blue, and I could smell the sea, that odd smell of salt and water and fish. I knew I was standing on the shore of the gulf somewhere, and I could see her a few yards away from me. She was facing out to sea, but as always her face and form continually shifted and changed. She has many names and appears to different people in different ways. But she is always love and peace and hope—unless she is angered.

And you do not want to see her angry.

She beckoned to me, her long, silky white sleeves flowing through the air "Come to me, Scotty, we have to talk and there isn't much time."

The white sand scrunched under my feet as I walked over to her side, keeping my eyes down.

"What they have done to the beautiful world I created," she said softly. There was no anger in voice, only sadness. "This great big beautiful world, full of wonders and life, and it is being destroyed, killing my innocent creatures, poisoning the water and everything around it in the obscene quest for wealth." She shook her head gently. "Why must man be so destructive?"

I bowed my head. There was nothing I could say to contradict her, and I had no words to say in defense of my own kind. It was true. The long-term damage to the gulf from the Deepwater Horizon disaster couldn't be measured or estimated for years— we would still be finding its effects for generations to come. Globs of oil were still washing up on shore from Lake Charles to Pensacola. I kept hearing dire stories about mutated shrimp and fish, and that the oyster beds weren't producing the way they did before the oil slick.

"You are in danger," she said simply, turning and walking

*along the shoreline, her feet in the water. I walked along side her,
unable to find the words to say anything to her. "But you must be
brave, and if you do not falter, you will be a great hero."*

"I'm no hero," I replied, my heart sinking.

*"You will find that being a hero sometimes simply means
doing the right thing, no matter how badly you don't want to.
Now go, and may your heart be brave."*

Everything began to fade away before my eyes.

I opened my eyes and winced almost immediately, blinded
by bright light directly above me. I blinked a few times, and as my
eyes started adjusting to the brightness above, my first coherent
thought was *where the hell am I?*

My head ached a bit, and my throat was dry. My tongue felt
like it had swollen to the point where it had filled my mouth.

I sat up, rubbing my eyes, and groggily took in my
surroundings.

I was in a very small room. The bright light was coming
in through a round window about three feet above where I was
laying. As the fog started clearing, I realized I was in a twin bed,
and not a very comfortable one at that. The mattress was hard,
and the blanket I was lying on top of was scratchy and coarse.
There was a tiny table right next to the narrow bed, and there
was a door on the opposite wall from the window. The room was
swaying a bit—rising on one side before leveling and then rising
on the other side, and the air smelled a little funny—

Like the sea.

That thought did the trick—I was now wide awake and
adrenaline was pumping through my veins. I somehow managed
to get up on my knees and pulled myself up to the window. I
looked out, and my heart sank when I realized I was right—I
couldn't see anything but dark-blue water in every direction. I
felt for my cell phone in my pocket and yanked it out. The battery
was almost dead—there was a picture of it on the screen with a
little bit of red colored in, along with a little note saying *Low*

Battery, Less than 10% charged. I touched the little Ignore button below the message and my phone screen went back to normal… but it didn't matter—in the upper left-hand corner were the words *No Signal.*

"Fuck, fuck, *fuck,*" I muttered.

I was at sea with no phone signal.

But they hadn't taken my phone away—that was weird.

I pushed myself up to my feet and headed over to the door, which wasn't as easy as you might think it would be, the way the room kept rolling and moving. I lost my balance and fell into the door, shoulder first, and wasn't able to stop the side of my head from bouncing off it.

"Damn it!" I screamed as stars danced in front of my eyes. My head started throbbing, and as I felt my forehead I could feel a lump starting to form. *Terrific, way to go, clumsy ass.*

I turned the knob and was surprised that it not only turned in my hand but the door itself opened. I didn't pause to think about what that implied other than I wasn't a prisoner in the little room. I stepped out into a dim hallway. There were a few more doors on either side of the hallway but at the end of the hallway was a staircase. Holding on to the wall to keep my balance, I made my way over to the landing. There was a door at the bottom of the flight and two closed doors at the top. Obviously, the smart thing to do was go up, so I did. I turned the handle on the right door and pushed. It swung up and outward, landing with a loud crash. Bright light flooded the staircase, blinding me for just a moment, and a wave of hot, damp, fishy-smelling air slapped me in the face. I was just about to climb up and out when a loud roar from below me triggered some atavistic reaction in my DNA.

I froze in absolute terror as my heart sank into the pit of my stomach, my entire body went cold, and my stomach clenched into a knot.

Every hair on my body stood up.

The roar sounded like—like a *tiger.*

Did they set me adrift at sea with Mike the Tiger?

I climbed out onto the deck as quickly as I could and shut the doors behind me with trembling hands. Once my eyes adjusted to the bright light, I looked around to get my bearings. It was a big boat, one of those commercial deep-water fishing boats people hire out for a few hours to go try to catch marlin or whatever big fish there were out in the gulf. With the belowdecks quarters (and enough room for a tiger on a lower level), it might even be able to stay out overnight. A ladder led up to where the captain could drive the boat—I could see two swivel chairs, a steering wheel, and all kind of dials and gauges on the dashboard.

None of which would do me any good—I hadn't the slightest clue on how to operate the damned thing.

But I could figure it out if I had to.

The gulf—the water was too blue to be Lake Pontchartrain—stretched as far as I could see in every direction. There were only a few wisps of white clouds in the sky above, and it was hot. The air was heavy and wet, and I was sweating. I could smell my armpits. I pulled my phone back out and looked at the screen. It was now about 6 percent charged and was going to die on me in just a few minutes. It still read *No Signal*.

And according to the clock in the upper left corner, I'd been unconscious for well over three hours.

I climbed up the ladder and sat down heavily in the pilot's chair. *They must have drugged me somehow*, I thought tiredly. There was no way hitting me on the head with a gun would have put me out that long.

I sighed.

The ignition was right there next to the steering wheel, but the keys weren't there.

Of course not, that would have been too easy.

I was so thirsty.

And it was hot. Every bead of perspiration rolling down my face or down my sides was more water leeching out of me.

There were another three or four hours to go before the sun went down and made things a bit cooler, but that wasn't going to do me any good now.

But it was cooler downstairs and out of the sun.

I went back to the stairs and got a strong whiff of ammonia that made my eyes water, and I almost retched.

There's a tiger belowdecks. Of course there's going to be a strong smell. You think he's going to hold it?

My stomach also growled—and I remembered I hadn't really eaten much before Diana and her AFAR cohorts had taken us prisoner.

I hope the bitch spends the rest of her fucking life behind bars.

I knew I shouldn't send such negativity out into the universe, but at this point I was beyond caring.

I climbed down the stairs. I figured if there were little rooms for sleeping, there might be a kitchen—well, a *galley*—behind one of the doors.

I opened the first door to find a very small bathroom, with a little sink, a shower stall, and a toilet. I turned the faucet, but nothing happened. I sighed and went back out into the hall. The next door opened into a little galley. There were cabinets, another sink, a little table for two, and a full-sized refrigerator. My stomach growled again as I opened the refrigerator door. It was empty and the light didn't come on; there were several bottles of water on the shelves in the door, but other than that, it was empty.

Gratefully, I uncapped one of the large bottles. It was lukewarm, but I didn't care. I gulped down half the bottle, wiped my mouth, and put the cap back on. Much as I wanted to drink it all, my rational side warned me I might need to ration the water out.

Behind the third and final door in the hallway was another little cabin, with Taylor in the bed. He was curled up in a ball and out cold. I walked over to make sure he was breathing— and sighed in relief when he groaned and rolled over onto his stomach. The back of his T-shirt was drenched in sweat, and his thick blond hair was also damp.

I bit my lip and sat down on the edge of his bunk. *At least he's alive*, I thought, my entire body relaxing. *Some parent you are—the first day he's with you and you put his life at risk. Nicely done, Scotty!* Frank was probably going out of his mind with worry.

I never should have followed Fleming with Taylor in the car with me. I should have known better. *What were you thinking, Scotty? That's just it, you weren't thinking. How many times have you put people you care about in danger because you don't THINK?*

Stop it, that's not going to help matters any. He's alive, and you're alive, and even if you are marooned out in the middle of the gulf, as long as we're alive there's a chance we can get out of this mess.

I couldn't help but smile down at him as he shifted again, rolling over onto his back. He started snoring softly. He looked so peaceful. I reached down and brushed a lock of hair away from his forehead. A surge of affection for him swept through my mind.

He really was a sweet kid.

How could his father throw him away like he was yesterday's garbage?

As long as I live, I'll never understand how some people's minds work.

I crept back out of the little room as quietly as I could and softly shut the door behind me. *Might as well let him sleep until I have some kind of idea what we can do to save ourselves.*

I went back up and onto the deck, taking another swig of water from the bottle. I swished it around in my dry mouth a few times before swallowing. I sat down in the shaded captain's chair and looked out over the vast expanse of water. I hadn't the slightest idea where we were. We could be out in the middle of the gulf, or we could just be a mile offshore. But we were drifting without power. No one would ever think to come looking for us out here—and it was a pretty safe bet AFAR had gotten rid of the Explorer somehow—probably sank it in the bayou or the salt marsh.

At least it was insured, I thought bitterly. *Burn in hell, you fucking bastards.*

I tried to remember the entire conversation I'd had with that bitch Diana Killeen. Despite the fact that she and her cohorts had basically set Taylor and me adrift at sea with a tiger in the hold of the boat, I believed her when she said they hadn't killed Veronica. They hadn't known what to do with the tiger— Veronica's murder had put them into an extremely bad position, so much as I would've liked to believe the worst of the bitch and her buddies, I had to believe they were innocent in that regard. Whatever the reason behind someone shooting Veronica, it didn't have anything to do with stealing the tiger or AFAR.

I leaned back in the chair, putting my feet up on the dashboard. More importantly, what kind of game was Barney Fleming playing? I didn't believe for one moment Rev Harper had sent goons to beat information out of him. If they had, they sure as hell wouldn't have been scared off when Taylor and I got there. I knew from bitter experience that Harper only hired the best. No, if Harper's men had been the ones to tie up Fleming, they would have taken Taylor and me prisoner as well.

They certainly wouldn't have been scared off and left without the information they were being paid to get.

So he lied about that.

He'd also led us straight into the arms of Diana Killeen and AFAR. He'd lied to them about us, which was why we were adrift at sea with a tiger.

Yes, good old Dr. Fleming had some serious explaining to do once we got back to shore.

Mom and Frank must be going crazy with worry, I thought, which made me want to get my hands on Barney Fleming all the more. It was bad enough that *Dad* was missing, but now Taylor and me, too?

I sighed in relief as I remembered I'd had Taylor call Frank to tell him we were following Fleming. Frank knew that much at least—and while he might not think to look for us at sea, maybe he'd get it out of Fleming.

I knew it was wrong, but I actually kind of hoped Frank beat it out of him.

He certainly deserved whatever he got.

But Dad was still missing, on top of everything else. Fleming—and AFAR—clearly didn't have anything to do with Dad being taken.

Fleming was the connection between Dad and AFAR?

Okay, Scotty, reason it out, I told myself as I took another slug of water and wiped sweat from my forehead. I slipped my T-shirt over my head and started thinking.

This whole thing had started because of Veronica Porterie. She was the common denominator for everything that was going on. She masterminded stealing the tiger. She'd been murdered. And through her family, she was also a link to the deduct box.

I thought about that for a moment. Okay, her grandfather had been a cohort of Huey Long's, one of the governor's closest friends and advisers. Dr. Fleming claimed Governor Long had passed the deduct box along to Porterie for safekeeping, but he was killed in a car accident the same night Governor Long was shot to death in the state capital, and had never told anyone where he'd hidden it. The people who'd kidnapped Dad—and there was no reason to believe Rev Harper wasn't behind that—were looking for Porterie's long-lost diary, in which he recorded the location where he hid the box.

I sighed and took another swig of water.

None of it made any sense to me, quite frankly—I didn't see why the deduct box, some eighty years later, would be of any value to anyone.

Certainly it didn't have enough value to make finding it worth the risk of kidnapping someone.

And why, of all people, *Dad*?

Even if they believed Veronica had told Mom something last weekend, wouldn't it make more sense to kidnap *Mom*?

No, what made the most sense was for them to kidnap VERONICA.

Whoever had killed her clearly wasn't looking for the deduct box.

I took another swig of the water.

Maybe the problem with figuring all this out is I'm assuming everything is all part and parcel of the same thing, when maybe it's separate things.

Maybe Dad's kidnapping had nothing to do with Veronica's murder.

The kidnappers didn't mention the diary when they called—they mentioned the deduct box.

They wouldn't have killed Veronica before they got the diary from her, and if they had the diary, there was no need to kidnap Dad.

My head was starting to hurt. I was almost there—but the answer was just out of reach in my head. It was so fucking frustrating.

I took a deep breath, stood up, and started pacing.

It was only logical to conclude whoever killed Veronica was not the same person—or persons—who'd kidnapped Dad.

I really wanted to talk to Barney Fleming again.

If AFAR wasn't interested in the deduct box and hadn't been involved in Veronica's murder, why were they involved with the leading Huey Long scholar in the country? What was the connection there?

How had he come into contact with Veronica and AFAR?

The deduct box—he had to be involved in that part of the story.

Another unexpected roar from below made me almost jump

out of my skin, and I had to grab the dashboard for balance as the boat went up a large swell.

The sea was getting rougher, and I'd noticed too that the wind was picking up.

I went down the stairs to the second level and heard another noise—a low moan—coming from Taylor's cabin. Remembering how thirsty I'd been, I went into the little kitchen, grabbed a bottle of water, and carried it back to his cabin. As my eyes adjusted to the dimness, I saw him sitting up and rubbing his eyes.

"Scotty?" he said faintly. "Where are we? What happened?"

I sat down next to him on the bunk and pressed the water bottle into his hand. "Here, take a drink. Are you okay?"

"Yeah, I think so. I'm a little confused and groggy. How long have I been asleep?" He downed half the bottle in a couple of quick gulps before belching loudly. "Where are we?" he asked again. "What happened? The last thing I remember was those people had tied us up and were asking you some questions."

No sense in sugarcoating anything, I figured. "We're adrift in the gulf in a boat with no power," I said. "And no way of calling for help."

Almost on cue, Mike roared so loudly it seemed like the boat shook.

"Oh, yes, Mike the Tiger is belowdecks."

He shook his head. "We're adrift at sea with a tiger?" He surprised me by starting to laugh. "How *Life of Pi*."

I stared at him, worried that he'd lost his mind. "Life of pie?"

"It's a book, by Yann Martel?" He stared at me. "We read it in my lit class last fall. It's a great book, about a young kid stranded at sea in a lifeboat with a tiger after a shipwreck. It's a great metaphor about—oh, never mind, it doesn't matter." He stood up and wobbled a bit, putting his hand on my shoulder to steady himself. "Wow, what a headache I've got. What are we going to do, Scotty?"

"I wish I knew." I stood up. "Come on, let's go up and get you some fresh air." I walked alongside him to the hallway and up the stairs to the deck.

"There's a storm coming." He pointed off into the distance.

I followed his finger and felt a chill go down my spine. Dark clouds and that misty-looking sky surely meant not only a storm, but a bad one. I could see lightning flashing—no wonder the sea was getting rougher.

This was most definitely not good.

"I don't suppose your cell phone has service?" I asked, turning my back on the storm.

He pulled out his phone and looked at it. "No, no bars. And it's almost dead anyway." He looked at the compass on the dashboard. "We're pointed south—I wonder…" He grabbed hold of the wheel and fought with it, slowly getting it to start turning. "Can you help me with this?"

I obliged, grabbing hold and yanking in the same direction he was. "What are we doing?"

"If that storm is coming toward us, we're better off if the front of the boat is facing the direction we need to go to get ashore," he replied. "The storm is going to drive water in front of it, so hopefully it'll push us that way, too. It makes more sense to be pointing in the same direction the storm will be moving us, don't you think?" He shrugged and frowned. "I don't know, to be honest. My only experience with boats is going waterskiing or fishing on lakes—not the open sea. But I don't suppose it can hurt, right?"

The front of the boat slowly started coming around, and the muscles in my shoulders were starting to ache as we kept fighting the wheel. But finally, we were facing north according to the compass, and we both let go of the wheel with a sigh of relief. Taylor started rooting around, opening cabinets and compartments. I didn't ask him what he was looking for—he'd tell me when he was ready. I closed my eyes and let my mind wander.

I must have still been groggy from the drug because I dozed off, not waking until Taylor's excited shout jolted me awake.

"What?"

He grinned at me, holding up a gun of some sort. "I knew there had to be an emergency flare gun on the boat somewhere." He gestured to the little cabinet that was open. "There's a first aid kit, too—I took some aspirin, you might want to if you have a headache from whatever it was they shot us up with." He tossed me a packet and walked to the rear end of the boat. He pointed the gun straight up in the air and pulled the trigger. A red flare shot up into the clear blue sky, floating in a slow arc when it reached its full height, trailing a tail of red smoke. He grinned back at me. "There's a shitload of flares. Every half hour or so we can fire off another one. Someone is eventually bound to see one and come rescue us."

"Pretty smart," I said. "I would have never thought of looking for a flare gun."

He shrugged off the praise like it was nothing. "Why would you? If you've never been on a boat before."

"But you've never—"

"My dad always taught me you never go out on a boat without a flare gun, in case you get into distress—that way you can always signal for help." His face colored at the mention of his father. "So I figured there was probably one on board somewhere." His face screwed up. "I don't think they meant for us to die out here, you know?"

"You don't?"

He shook his head. "Well, sure, it could happen—you never know what's going to happen when you're at sea—but they left water for us in the refrigerator, enough to last us for a few days, if we're careful with it. They didn't get rid of the flare gun or the flares. They just took the keys so we couldn't use the engine, and they disabled the radio. Besides, if they wanted to kill us, they could have just killed us back on land and fed us to the alligators in the bayou."

Much as I didn't want to give Diana Killeen credit for anything, he *did* have a point. As long as we kept our heads and didn't panic, eventually we would have found the flare gun—and we had. Now it was just a matter of firing off the flares and hoping someone saw them before the storm arrived.

I glanced off into the distance. The storm was coming closer, and it looked even nastier than it had when Taylor had first pointed it out to me.

And, of course, there was a thousand-pound tiger down belowdecks.

When was the last time he'd been fed? The way the boat was moving up and down with the swells couldn't be doing much for his nerves. If the storm scared him enough, he could probably break down that door with ease.

And without a weapon of some sort, there wasn't any way we could protect ourselves from him.

They couldn't have known how any of this would turn out when they cast us adrift.

How could anyone claim to be for animal rights yet abandon a beautiful animal like that at sea? No matter what Taylor said, there wasn't any guarantee that we'd be rescued or would have figured out a way to save ourselves. And had Mike not roared, I wouldn't have even known he was down in the hold. I could have just as easily walked down the stairs, opened the door, and found myself staring at a live, hungry, angry, and frightened tiger.

And no matter how used he was to people, that was a combination that might have added up to one dead Scotty.

Diana Killeen just better hope she never comes face-to-face with me again, I thought angrily. *I hope they throw the book at that bitch.*

"Scotty!" Taylor shouted excitedly. "Look!"

In the distance in the east, a boat was heading our way rather quickly.

It was a Coast Guard cutter.

Thank you, Goddess, I prayed with gratitude, and the sense of relief that swept through me was instantaneous and staggering.

Oh, thank you, Universe, for the United States Coast Guard!

CHAPTER TWELVE

THE DEVIL

Temptation

I opened my eyes and stared at the ceiling.

I had probably the worst cottonmouth ever, and I also had to go to the bathroom.

Frank was lying next to me in the bed, gently snoring. He was lying on his side with his back to me, and I could feel warmth radiating off his skin. *Is there anything nicer than being in bed with Frank?* I thought, a smile creeping across my face. I didn't want to get up. I turned my head to look at the clock and was startled to see it was already after noon.

I sat straight up and hurried to the bathroom.

As I brushed my teeth, I stared at my face in the mirror. I was a little sunburned from yesterday, and my lips were still chapped. I'd sweated out a lot of water while out on that boat, and I definitely needed to rehydrate.

I hadn't gotten back to the apartment until around three in the morning and had barely been able to get my clothes off before collapsing into bed and going to sleep.

The Coast Guard had been wonderful to Taylor and me. We hadn't just gotten lucky that they'd seen the flare—they'd received an anonymous tip about a boat in distress, with our approximate location. So the cutter had already been out looking when Taylor fired the flare. Diana Killeen or one of her gang must have phoned it in, but it didn't soften the way I felt about them. Sure, they'd called in a tip, but the gulf is big and there was no way they could guarantee the Coast Guard would find us.

Not to mention what might have happened had they not found us before that storm hit.

The Coast Guard gave us sandwiches and water, and a medic they had on board had checked us both out as the cutter headed toward shore, towing the boat behind us. I kind of wished my phone's battery hadn't died, because the look on their faces when I told them there was a tiger belowdecks was priceless. They'd originally considered riding out the storm at sea until I told them about Mike. Instead, they secured a towrope to the boat we'd been on—after checking first to make sure I wasn't bullshitting about the tiger—and then made a beeline for shore.

They also radioed ahead, and somehow managed to arrange for the veterinary school at LSU to bring his traveling cage down to the Coast Guard station at the Port of Baton Rouge.

Taylor and I didn't make it all the way upriver to Baton Rouge, though. They dropped us off in New Orleans and in fact delivered us right into the waiting hands of the New Orleans Police Department. Detectives Venus Casanova and Blaine Tujague, to be exact—both of whom I have already become well acquainted with over the years. I used to get on their nerves, I think, but I've proven myself to them over the years and they've become, if not friends, at least more tolerant of me.

Venus is a tall black woman probably in her late forties who is always dressed to kill and clearly spends time in the gym keeping her body in top physical condition. She's very pretty, and she wears her hair buzzed down close to her scalp. Her face is very hard to read, and when Taylor and I were escorted ashore by two uniformed Coast Guard men (who looked sexy as hell in their uniforms) she shook her head. "You know," she said with no facial expression, "when the Coast Guard called in, I just had a feeling it was you."

"That's not totally true," her partner said with a grin. "They told us who you were."

Blaine Tujague is about my age, give or take a few years, and is just as gay as me. We're about the same height, but he's a little more thickly muscled than I am. He has bluish-black curly hair and bright-blue eyes. He's pretty attractive, to be honest, and I saw Taylor gaping at him with that *I'd like to tap that* facial expression I've seen on so many other gay men's faces over the years. I grinned to myself, but would have to warn Taylor about Detective Tujague. He lives with his long-term boyfriend in the lower Garden District. Blaine always wears dress slacks and a blazer, but his shirts are always a little small for his bulging muscles.

I couldn't blame Taylor, really. If I didn't already have the two most perfect boyfriends on the planet, Blaine would turn *my* head.

❖

They took us straight down to the Eighth District police station on Royal Street, putting us into the back of Venus's black SUV. I asked about my Explorer on the way, and Venus radioed in, asking someone to get ahold of the Placquemines Parish sheriff's department and have them go out and look for the Explorer, as well as to check out the place where AFAR had held us hostage. She also put out an APB for that bitch Diana Killeen, without really asking a lot of questions.

It is nice to have a good relationship with the police.

Before the questioning started, I asked for permission to call Frank and also for a phone charger. Venus passed me her cell phone and rolled her eyes before going to get me the phone charger. He answered his cell phone on the second ring. "Venus? What's up?"

"Hey, Frank, it's me, Scotty," I replied. "My phone's dead, and Venus is letting me use hers."

"Where are you?" He sounded relieved but still a little panicked. "I've been worried sick about you and Taylor. Are you both okay?"

"Yeah, we're fine, it's a long story, though, and I'm going

to have to answer some questions." I smiled at Venus as she returned to the interrogation room with an iPhone charger in her hand. "I'm at the Eighth District station house, Taylor's here, too, and there's nothing to worry about right now. Thanks, Venus, for the charger."

"Still no word on Dad," Frank said. "And no word from the kidnappers, either."

"Okay, I'll call you as soon as I can." I disconnected the call and passed her phone back to Venus. "Thanks, I appreciate that."

She smiled. "No problem. Now, do you want to explain to me how the hell you and that kid and Mike ended up on that boat needing rescuing by the Coast Guard?"

I spent the next three hours being grilled by Venus—I assumed Blaine was interrogating Taylor. I hoped Taylor had the presence of mind to not spill the news about Dad being kidnapped—while it was pretty safe to assume the kidnappers wouldn't know if we told the cops, I didn't want to take that risk. We went over everything, over and over again. She knew I wasn't telling her everything—she's pretty sharp—but as much as I wanted her help in finding Dad, I couldn't tell her.

Finally, she leaned across the table, that look I've come to know so well on her face. "Scotty, I know you're lying to me about why you went over to Barney Fleming's in the first place." She peered at me, her gaze intent. "Why all the sudden interest in Huey Long?"

I just shrugged. "It was just a hunch that didn't pan out."

"It didn't pan out, but you decided to follow him out to Placquemines Parish and put Frank's nephew's life in danger." She leaned back in her chair, a suspicious look on her face. "And somehow I'm supposed to believe all of this?"

I sighed. "I told you, Venus, Frank and I are looking into Veronica Porterie's murder. You know the Baton Rouge cops think her daughter was involved in stealing Mike. We're trying to help her clear her name, and I told you, Mom had known Veronica her whole life. I thought it might have something to do with Huey Long—the deduct box thing has come up a couple of times. Why wouldn't we check with an expert on Long?"

"And you just decided to watch his house and follow him?"

I hadn't mentioned Rev Harper because I wasn't entirely certain he wasn't behind kidnapping Dad—and I knew it sounded lame. "Venus, both Taylor and I got the sense he wasn't telling us the truth, and he was trying to get us out of there as fast as he could." A little white lie never hurt anyone, after all. "And so we figured it couldn't hurt to watch his place. And sure enough, less than ten minutes after we left he took off. We followed him, and he led us right to AFAR's hideout, where they took us prisoner, and well, you know the rest. They set us adrift at sea with a tiger on the boat and no way of calling for help." I shrugged. "Sounds to me like they had more than a little to hide besides stealing Mike. Why wouldn't they have killed Veronica?" I didn't think Diana Killeen and her posse *had* killed Veronica—but Taylor and I could have easily died at sea. Payback's a bitch, Diana— and so are you. "Probably a falling-out over the tiger-napping, who knows? But clearly they don't have any respect for human life. Or animal life, for that matter. And Barney Fleming was clearly working with them—he led us right into their hands. So what was he doing out there? What's the connection?" I ran my fingers through my dirty hair. I really needed a long, hot shower. "Veronica's grandfather was a close associate of Huey Long's. Barney Fleming is an expert on Huey Long. You do the math."

"We're checking into Barney Fleming." She shook her head. "You'll be interested to know that the place AFAR held you burned to the ground this afternoon. It was definitely arson—I suspect they burned it to destroy any evidence that they were behind kidnapping Mike." She leaned back in her chair. "We've issued warrants for their arrest, for kidnapping and grand larceny, but I'm sure they're long gone. If it were up to me, they'd be charged with two counts of attempted murder, too." Her eyes hardened. "Probably couldn't make that stick in court, though. I'm pretty sure they were the ones who tipped off the Coast Guard. No one else knew you were out there."

"Yeah." I could hear Storm's voice: *You never charge people with anything you aren't positive you can convict them on. That's just asking for a hung jury or an acquittal. That call to the Coast Guard could very well be seen by the jurors as remorse, and any lawyer worth a shit would keep hammering that point home to the jury. We can convict them on kidnapping for sure, so why muddy the water?* "I'll be more than happy to swear out a complaint, if you need one. And I'll be more than happy to testify against them." The thought of being on the stand while Diana Killeen was sitting in the courtroom next to her defense attorney brought a smile to my face.

It was really amazing how much I hated her.

"I'll have your statement typed up." Venus pushed her chair back and stood up, her face unreadable. "And for the record, even if they did make the call to the Coast Guard, they also couldn't be sure they would get there before you both died. Or that the tiger didn't get loose and eat the two of you." Her lips narrowed into a tight line. "Not to mention the bomb threat to the LSU campus—Homeland Security wants in on that one. Domestic terrorism." She clicked her tongue. "I sure wouldn't want to be Diana Killeen when they catch her ass."

It was around two thirty when she gave Taylor and me a ride back home in her black SUV. Taylor looked like he was barely able to keep his eyes open, poor thing. Seeing him stagger with sleepiness when we got out of the SUV made me realize that he was the reason I wanted to fry Diana Killeen so badly—not because of what she'd done to me, but because she'd put *his* life in danger. *This is what it feels like to be a parent*, I mused as I unlocked the gate, and the thought made me even angrier at Taylor's parents.

How could you just turn off your feelings for your child like that?

What kind of people can *do* that? And call themselves Christians?

As we climbed the back stairs, I wished for a moment that the Christian afterlife would turn out to be true—but only if I could be there when his wretched excuse for parents tried to get into heaven so I could see the looks on their faces when St. Peter denied them entry and sent them to hell for eternity.

And I'm not proud to say it brought a grim smile to my face.

Once Frank let go of him, Taylor collapsed onto the couch and was asleep within a matter of minutes. I got a blanket and gently covered him with it, and watched him sleep for a few minutes before going back to our bedroom with Frank—who had the decency to let me shower before peppering me with questions about what had happened.

I was up for another good hour until I could finally collapse into bed and sleep.

And now I'd slept in, while every second that passed made it more and more unlikely we'd find Dad.

I pulled on a pair of Saints sweatpants and walked down the hall into the kitchen. I started a pot of coffee and checked to see if Taylor was still sleeping on the couch. He wasn't there, so I had to assume Frank got him upstairs after I fell asleep. I logged into the computer while the coffee brewed and checked some of the local news sites…and sure enough, Mike the Tiger's rescue was the big lead story on every one of them. There were some pictures of me and Taylor, but they'd been taken from a distance and were fuzzy, and unless you knew it was us, you'd never guess. None of the articles carried our names—which was an enormous relief. I didn't want to have to deal with the press.

But every article clearly stated that AFAR was behind everything, including kidnapping us and setting us adrift at sea. They also stated that both Homeland Security and the FBI were now investigating AFAR, and probably the IRS would get involved, as well.

Which was good enough for them—as far as I was concerned, they all deserved much, much worse. Veronica was obviously the brains behind the entire operation. I had no doubt that without her running the show, AFAR would crumble and they'd be caught soon enough.

Likewise, AFAR was off the hook for kidnapping Dad. They had no reason to take him. I was also pretty sure Barney Fleming was a lot more involved than just working with AFAR.

Whoever had taken Dad thought we had Eugene Porterie's diary, which meant they thought we knew where the deduct box had been hidden all these years. But I still couldn't understand why the damned deduct box was so fucking important eighty years later—important enough to kill Veronica and kidnap Dad.

If Fleming hadn't lied about everything, Governor Long had converted the money inside the box into state bearer bonds.

If that was true, wouldn't there have been a record somewhere of the bonds being issued?

I pulled up a search engine, and typed in "Louisiana State Bearer Bonds."

None of the links that came up had anything to do with what I was looking for—they were all explanations of bearer bonds.

So, if what Fleming had said was actually true, it would have been next to impossible to keep such a thing a secret for almost eighty years. From everything I knew about Huey Long—which, granted, wasn't that much—this was completely out of character for him. Why would he do it? It didn't make any sense. He was all about cash and not leaving records—so why the bearer bonds?

No, Fleming had to be lying.

But someone *had* tied him up—there was no way he could have tied himself up so tightly, and he'd had no idea we were coming by.

I got up and poured myself some coffee, leaning back

against the counter and thinking. We could rule out AFAR from the deduct box; the only link between them and it was Veronica Porterie. She was the key to everything—but why now?

We had to talk to her mother.

I woke Frank up with a cup of coffee and a kiss, and while he took a shower, I got dressed. I called Hope's grandmother. Mrs. Porterie didn't sound too thrilled about the idea, but she agreed to talk to us—after I reminded her Frank and I were working to clear Hope's name for the tiger theft.

I stuck a note for Taylor on the door, and we left.

Since the SUV had been impounded as evidence by the police, we had to take the spy Jaguar. Frank didn't say anything as we walked to the car, and it wasn't until we were heading up Esplanade that he finally said, "Honey, I know it wasn't your intent, but you put Taylor into danger yesterday, and I don't know how I feel about that."

It was so incredibly unfair I didn't know what to say, so I didn't say anything and merely sputtered in my head.

He glanced over at me. "I know it wasn't your fault—but I've been beating myself up over it ever since you two disappeared yesterday afternoon. And yes, I know, there was no way of preventing it. But given our lives—and what Colin does for a living—I'm not so sure it's such a great idea to have a kid around us." He held up a hand when I started sputtering out loud. "We never know when something's going to happen. At any moment, someone Colin has pissed off could come after him here in New Orleans, and we'd all be in the line of fire. I know Colin keeps his personal life very separate from his professional life—but the Ninjas found him. If they could find him, anyone can."

I took a deep breath and counted to ten as he made a left turn onto Claiborne Avenue. "First of all, the Ninjas found him quite by accident. They weren't looking for him when they came here, it was all just an amazing coincidence."

"Was it?" Frank tilted his head to one side. "A pretty big one, don't you think?"

I started to answer but stopped myself. It *was* a pretty big coincidence. I leaned my head against the window. "Frank, don't say things like that. It's really important to me to think that Colin doesn't lie to us that often, and if that wasn't a coincidence, it means Rhoda and Lindy lie to us, too. I don't want to believe that."

He patted my leg. "I know, I know, I'm sorry. But you have to admit, this may not be the best place for Taylor to live."

"Well, what are you suggesting?"

"I don't know." He bit his lower lip. "Maybe we could send him to LSU? Or find him an apartment closer to campus if he wants to go to Tulane here. I just can't imagine what I'd say to my sister if anything ever happened to him."

"I'd say *that's what you get for throwing him out*," I replied sourly. "I mean, I appreciate the sentiment—she is your sister—but as far as I'm concerned she and her husband have lost whatever rights they had to worry or be concerned about him. If they gave a shit about him, he wouldn't be in New Orleans in the first place."

"I know, I know, I know you're right." He exhaled with an enormous sigh. "You know, I never knew what it was like to be a parent...but when you two disappeared yesterday and weren't answering your phones, it was horrible. Absolutely horrible." He shuddered as he turned left onto Napoleon Avenue. "I mean, I thought I used to worry about *you*."

"Thanks, I think," I replied sarcastically. He winked at me, and I put my hand on his thigh.

The Porterie house was just below Prytania on Napoleon, past St. Elizabeth's and Sophie Wright Middle School. It was a classic Gothic revival house, probably built in the late nineteenth century. It was three stories tall, flanked by live oaks, with a big gable peak in the center of a slanted roof. Red brick chimneys rose from the roof on either side of the gable's peak. The front gallery ran the width of the front of the house, and a short wrought iron railing ran on its top, turning the gallery's roof into an uncovered balcony. The house was painted coral, with black trim. All the shutters on the second-floor windows were closed, but the ones on the first floor windows were open. The steps up to the gallery led to a beautiful set of double doors with diamond-shaped glass lights above them. The lawn was immaculately trimmed, and a statue of an angel stood to the left of the front walk with its wings spread and its hands clasped in front, the head turned up to face the heavens.

Frank pulled over next to the curb and we both got out. "Nice," he whistled. "Hope wasn't doing too badly."

I opened the gate and went inside. Other than the cars passing by on Napoleon, it was weirdly silent. Frank's opinion notwithstanding, the house wasn't that big or spectacular; if anything, it was understated. Given how wealthy Eugene Porterie had been—and how politically connected—I had assumed the place would be much more grand and pretentious. I rang the buzzer. On the other side of the beveled glass I could see a form approaching. The door swung open, and an older woman glared at me through her tortoiseshell glasses. "Scotty Bradley?" she said with a well-bred sniff.

I gave her my warmest smile, the one that always used to get the guys in the bars to open their wallets and stuff money in my G-string. "Yes, and this is my partner, Frank Sobieski. We really appreciate your taking the time to see us, Mrs. Porterie. May we come in?"

She nodded and stepped to one side, indicating with her hand that we were to go into the first door to the left.

She was older, probably in her seventies, but she looked older than both of my grandmothers. She was wearing a pair of sensibly heeled black leather shoes and a silk flowered print dress that reached her knees. She was slender, and her skin seemed fragile. Her hair was completely white and pulled back from her face into a tightly secured bun in the back. She was wrinkled and had a bit of wattle hanging from her chin—but I respected that she hadn't had any work done, unlike so many of her peers.

She wasn't wearing any jewelry other than an enormous diamond ring attached to her gold wedding band.

The room was tastefully decorated with heavy Victorian furniture. An enormous mirror in a gilt frame hung over the fireplace. The shutters on the side windows were shut, so the only light came from the front window. On the antique table next to her chair a rather large martini glass rested on a coaster, a couple of olives sunk to the bottom. She took a drink from it before sitting down again.

She didn't offer us a drink, but sat down in a wingback chair that looked sort of throne-like. She crossed her right leg over the left at the ankles and folded her hands primly in her lap. She blinked balefully at us until I cleared my throat and said, as politely as I could, "I'm really sorry about your daughter."

"As far as I am concerned, Mr. Bradley, my daughter died a long time ago," she replied stiffly, a vein in her neck twitching. "That woman who was murdered several days ago was most definitely not my child. No child of mine would ever callously murder an innocent man or commit the crimes that creature did." The corners of her mouth were turned down so far they almost reached her chin. "I wondered for years what we did wrong to turn out such a *monster*," she spat the words out at me, "but finally realized that sometimes it's just not the parents' fault. She was just born bad. Once I came to terms with that, I was able to live with myself again." She took a drink from the martini glass. Her hand shook a little, but her face remained set and grim.

Frank can turn on the charm when he wants to—probably partly why he'd been such a great field agent for the feds—and he gave her his most winning smile. But when he spoke his voice was cold and professionally polite. "We're not so concerned about Veronica, frankly, Mrs. Porterie, and I don't want to waste any more of your time than we need to. It's Hope we're primarily concerned with."

Her face visibly softened at the mention of her granddaughter.

"Why didn't you say so?" She leaned forward in her chair. "It's ridiculous that the police think she had anything to do with stealing that tiger! She would never do such a thing." She turned back to me. "You were the one who found Mike, weren't you?" She peered at me over the tops of her glasses. "Yes, you look a little the worse for sun exposure…you probably don't remember me, but I remember when you were a little boy." She relaxed back into her seat and recrossed her legs at the ankles. "The great irony was we always thought your mother was the one who'd turn out to be a lawbreaker."

Given Mom's arrest record, she wasn't that far off the mark. "You raised Hope, right? You won custody of her when she was a little girl?"

She nodded. "Hope was only three when that security guard was killed. We'd never seen her…we never even knew that Veronica had been involved with someone and had a child until she was arrested, and once we knew about the child, obviously there was nothing else to do. We took her in—even though Veronica didn't want us to, my daughter would have preferred the child become a ward of the state, can you imagine such a thing? She didn't even fight us for custody after the trial…she tossed that child away like she was a pair of worn-out shoes. What kind of woman does that to her child?"

I resisted the urge to point out how she'd turned her back on her own daughter.

She wiped at her eyes. "Hope is a good girl, she's never been a bit of trouble, not a bit. She's been a joy to raise—top of her class at Sacred Heart, straight A's at LSU—and you know you have to be a top-notch student to be selected to take care of Mike. She loves animals…for a while I worried she might become a fanatic like her mother, but no, she's a sensible girl."

"Did you know that Veronica had been in touch with Hope?"

Her eyes hardened. "That's absurd."

"I'm sorry to be the one to tell you this, Mrs. Porterie," Frank's voice was very gentle, "but Hope herself told us she'd been in touch with her mother."

She didn't say anything. The only sound in the room was the loud ticking of the grandfather clock in the corner.

Frank cleared his throat. "Mrs. Porterie, do you know anything about a family connection the Porteries might have to Huey Long's deduct box?"

She stared at him, her mouth open, and after a moment started laughing raucously. "Don't tell me someone's told you that silly old story?" She shook her head. "Yes, my husband's grandfather was a close associate of Huey's. My husband, Woody"—she glanced over at the enormous portrait over the fireplace—"never believed that ridiculous story about Huey giving his grandfather custody of the box. Anyone who knows anything about Huey Long knows that man never let that box out of his own custody and didn't trust anyone. That ridiculous Fleming man came around so many times, trying to get into the family papers and prove his story." She made a dismissive noise, pursing her lips. "When Woody was alive, he gave that idiot a piece of his mind but good. But after Woody died last year, he started sniffing around here again." She raised her chin. "I may have only married into this family, but I won't have my granddaughter's legacy tarnished by such idiocy."

"The Porterie family—it's pretty big, isn't it?"

She peered at him through her glasses. "Woody had a lot of aunts and uncles—old Gene Porterie and his wife Frances had eight or nine children. Woody also had three sisters. Why do you ask?"

"We were just wondering who else might know the family legends."

She snorted. "Anyone who believes that story…" She got up and walked over to a painting of an older man and stared up at it for a moment. She turned back to us. "Woody didn't believe it for a minute, he thought it was just a silly story his father used to tell him when he was a little boy, you know, to impress him on how important the family was." She barked out a laugh. "Woody thought—and so did I—that the box was destroyed or lost right around the time Long was assassinated."

"Well, we thank you for your time," Frank said, standing up and offering her his hand. She shook it, smiling up at him. "We can show ourselves out."

Once we were sitting in the car again, Frank looked at me. "She doesn't believe the story. But that doesn't mean it wasn't true."

"This is so damned complicated." I shook my head. "Frank—this was a colossal waste of time and hasn't helped us at all."

He patted my leg. "We'll find him, Scotty, don't you worry about that. Nothing's going to happen to Dad."

I wished I shared his belief.

He started the car and I leaned my forehead against the passenger window and closed my eyes. "Frank—"

"What?"

"Oh, nothing, was just a feeling I had." I rubbed my eyes.

Just a feeling that Mrs. Porterie might have shot her own daughter—there was certainly no love lost there.

CHAPTER THIRTEEN
THE WORLD, REVERSED
Success yet to be won

We hadn't gotten far when my cell phone started ringing. I looked at the screen: *Unknown Caller.* I usually don't answer those kinds of calls, but given my father had been kidnapped, I figured it was a good time to make an exception. "Hello?" I said cautiously.

"You're not an easy fella to track down," a voice drawled in a thick Texas accent.

Rev Harper.

I signaled to Frank to pull over again, and he gave me an odd look as he pulled the car back over to the curb. "Hello, Rev. I heard you were back in town," I replied, keeping my voice even as Frank's eyes bugged out. "In fact, there are some people who think you may have been the one to kidnap my father."

"Now, Scotty, you know me better than that." He chuckled. "What would it gain me to kidnap your daddy? That's not how I operate."

"Why should I believe you?"

"I don't suppose there's any reason why you should," he went on, still chuckling in that deep-throated way I remembered so vividly. "And I don't suppose my word is worth two shits to you, either. Why don't you and your boyfriend stop by and chew the fat for a while with me? I think we're both trying to find the same thing, and if we pool our resources, we might just get somewhere."

"Okay, where are you?"

He gave me an address on Harmony Street. "I'll expect the two of you soon." He hung up.

"Was that really Rev Harper?" Frank breathed the words out. "Does he have Dad?"

"He says he doesn't, but he wants to talk to us." I closed my eyes. "I don't think he would kidnap Dad—it's really not his style, Frank."

His lips tightened. "He kidnapped and drugged you, if I recall correctly. So why wouldn't he do the same to Dad?"

"He didn't seem too surprised to hear that someone had taken Dad," I mused. "But like I said, Frank, it's really not his style. Sure, he might take Dad and drug him, see what he knew—but he wouldn't try to keep him, you know, try to get us to find stuff for him. I mean, yeah, he's a son of a bitch, but I don't think he's *that* son of a bitch." I gave him the address. "Let's go."

Frank pulled back out onto Napoleon Avenue, heading toward the river, but made a U-turn at the first turnabout he came to. He took the U-turn a little too fast, slamming me into the side door, but I didn't say anything. He had a very grim look on his face, one that I knew all too well. Frank was slow to anger, but when he snapped, the best thing to do was just get the hell out of the way until it passed. The scar on his cheek even looked angrier than it usually did.

Honestly, though, I was glad Harper had called me—we needed to talk to him, and tracking him down wasn't going to be that easy. It was rather nice that he'd gotten in touch with us, and if it made sense to pool our resources and work together, I was all for it. I wasn't sure how Frank would feel about it, but I was fairly confident I could convince him it was for the best if it came to that. I put my left hand on his right leg and was a little reassured when he put his hand on top of mine and squeezed. When we stopped at the light at Prytania, he looked over at me. "Don't worry," he said, his voice barely above a whisper. "I won't do anything to put Dad in danger."

I took a breath and smiled back at him. "I wasn't too worried," I replied. "It's just so weird that they haven't called again."

"Amateurs," Frank said, turning onto Prytania Street when the light changed. "That's why I'm worried, Scotty. We deal with kidnappers a lot at the Bureau, and it's not like there's such a thing as *professional* kidnappers. Usually, it's amateur criminals that are desperate—and desperate, scared people who've already broken the law..." His voice trailed off, which was just as well.

I couldn't imagine what else he could have said to scare me any more than I already was.

The address Rev Harper had given me was between Camp and Coliseum Streets on Harmony. Harmony was one of those streets of indeterminate neighborhood; some people considered it to be Garden District, others said it was Uptown. But it was a nice, quiet street full of nice-sized houses with rather nice cars parked in their driveways or on the street in front. The address itself was an enormous Victorian-style three-story house on a large lot behind a tall black wrought iron fence with sharp-looking stakes at the top of each post. The lawn was in need of mowing, and a forest of bamboo ran along the riverside edge of the property, completely blocking the neighbors on that side from seeing anything in the yard. Weeds choked out the flower beds directly in front of the porch, and the house itself was in need of painting. All the shutters were closed, which made the house seem closed off and insular.

Frank parked in front—there were some black town cars parked in the driveway behind a closed gate. "Stay calm," I cautioned him as we closed the front gate and walked up to the porch. "He can be a bit smug and infuriating, but we need to know what he knows, okay?"

He gave me a look. "Scotty, I was trained on how to keep my cool with suspects when you were in diapers," he hissed at me as went up the front steps.

I resisted the urge to give him the finger and instead pressed the doorbell. I could hear it booming inside—it was a loud fucking bell. We heard footsteps approaching, and then the door swung open and I gasped out loud.

The man who opened the door was enormous, but none of it was fat. I don't think I've ever seen a man so huge and solid in my life. He was several inches taller than Frank and was wearing a very tight black turtleneck that hugged his torso so tightly it would probably have to be peeled off. His stomach was completely flat, and his pecs looked bigger than my head. His arms and shoulders were also thick and hard, and his tight black slacks left very little to the imagination. He was wearing dark sunglasses, his hair was cut short in a military style, and he was dark-skinned. He had an earpiece with a coiled wire hanging down from it that went down past his shoulder and down the back. He looked like he could have been a Hall of Fame NFL linebacker. "Bradley and Sobieski?" he asked in a voice that was so deep my ears almost didn't register what he was saying. When we nodded, he gestured with a massive hand for us to follow him.

He led us through the darkened house into a room filled with bookcases. Seriously, everywhere I looked there were books. The walls were lined with bookshelves, going from the floor to eighteen-foot-high ceilings. There were some easy chairs, and a desk in the center of the room. Seated at the desk was an all-too-familiar face, frowning down at a book he had opened wide on the desktop. When the enormous man cleared his throat, the seated man looked up and beamed. He shoved the chair back and jumped to his feet, crossing the room to where we were standing just inside the door in no time flat, his hand outstretched.

"Scotty!" He grabbed my hand and wrung it up and down so vigorously I was worried it might snap off at the shoulder. "And you must be Frank!" He turned to Frank, the big grin never wavering, and gave him the same vigorous handshake. "A pleasure to meet you at last! I've heard a lot about you!" He then turned to his enormous employee. "Bring us a bottle of my best Scotch." The big man bowed his head and walked out, shutting the door behind us. Rev gestured at two chairs in front of his desk. "Sit, my good men, sit!"

He jaunted back around his desk as we sat down. Rev wasn't a big man, maybe an inch or two taller than I was, but he had one of those weird bodies with an enormous torso straining the mother-of-pearl buttons on his western-style shirt over narrow hips and skinny legs. He was wearing tight Wrangler jeans over snakeskin cowboy boots and had an enormous gold Rolex on his left wrist. The ubiquitous cowboy hat was perched on a corner of the desk. He leaned back in his chair and spread his hands wide, a big smile on his leathery face. He had a flat nose that looked like he'd broken it a few times and it finally gave up. His eyes were brown and small, and his eyebrows were thick and long and graying. His lips were thin, his teeth were yellowed by nicotine. His big strong hands were manicured, and the fingertips also were nicotine stained.

The big man brought in an large bottle of Scotch and three cut-glass tumblers. He poured a couple of fingers of amber liquid into each glass and then silently disappeared, shutting the door behind him.

Rev picked up a glass and took a sip. "Drink up, boys, there're people who'd sell their mothers into white slavery to taste this hooch." When neither one of us made a move to pick up our glasses, he shook his head. "Now, I'm trying to be friendly here, boys. I think it's in our best interests to work together on this little matter."

"What exactly did you have in mind, Rev?" I asked, reaching for my glass and sniffing the Scotch. I wasn't much of a connoisseur of Scotch—it's an acquired taste, and I haven't acquired it yet—but my Papa Diderot was, and I could tell this was indeed a very good brand. I took a little sip, and it burned a bit but was also very smooth.

"I know about your dad, Scotty," Rev replied soberly. "I didn't have nothing to do with that, you know, and I don't know who took him—I mean, I do know where he is, and I've got a man on the inside, but I don't know who's behind it. But I do know why." He leaned forward. "And I know you boys know about the deduct box."

"Where is my dad?" I demanded, feeling an adrenaline surge as I leaned forward and put the glass of whiskey back down on the desk.

"He's safe." He held up his hands in a gesture of submission. "Like I said, I got a man on the inside who's been keeping me posted on what's going on with your dad. He's fine. They haven't hurt him, they haven't done anything to him, and they're not going to." He smirked. "And I've got plenty of other men stationed in place. All I have to do is make one phone call and my men will move in and get your dad out of there." He folded his hands on his chest and leaned back in his chair again.

"How do we know you don't have him yourself?" Frank's voice was very calm, but I wasn't fooled by it. He was barely controlling himself. Every muscle in his body was coiled into a knot, ready to spring across the desk and start beating the truth out of Rev.

Rev's eyes narrowed. "I don't kidnap people, Frank."

"You kidnapped Scotty, almost killed him, in fact." Frank's voice shook with controlled rage. "Forced him off the road— your thugs didn't know he wouldn't be killed when they wrecked his car. And then you drugged him and—"

"Those men fucked up," Rev replied evenly. "They weren't supposed to hurt anyone, and believe you me, they regretted causing that accident. Believe. You. Me." His voice was cold, and I felt a chill go up my spine at the look in his eyes when he said the words. "All I wanted was to have a little chat with Scotty. My men misunderstood my instructions. It won't happen again." There was silence for a few moments, and then his face warmed up again. "Scotty's dad didn't have any information I needed, so why would I take him? No reason at all for me to get involved in that. But someone pretty damned powerful here in Louisiana is the one who did take your daddy, Scotty. I don't know who he is, but he's got some pull in this state."

"But you said you have a man on the inside?" I shook my head. "Then you have to know who he is."

He shook his own head. "My guy's been doing his damnedest to find out, but this organization is pretty damned secretive."

This wasn't going anywhere. "So why do *you* want the deduct box, Rev? What's in it for you?"

He grinned at me. "You know me, Scotty. I'm interested in history, and I'm a collector. I just want it for my collection. I don't give a shit what's inside of it." He picked up the book on his desk and waved it at us. "This is supposed to tell me where it is, you know, but it don't. Old Eugene Porterie was a pretty tricky bastard."

Frank and I exchanged a look. "Is that—is that Eugene Porterie's diary?" I asked, stunned.

He nodded. "Yes, and I know you want to know where I got it from." He beamed at me. "I bought it from Veronica Porterie almost twenty years ago." He put it back down on the desktop again. "She came to me, you know, with this story about how the diary was the key to finding the deduct box. She wanted money to start her organization, some legal advice, all of that. I was more than happy to set her up." His face darkened. "Of course, I didn't know what she wanted was to start an animal rights terrorist group. Stupid bitch. Everybody knows animals were put on this earth by the good Lord to serve man, not for us to serve the animals." He clicked his tongue against his front teeth. "Still would have given her the money, though, even if I had known." He laughed. "I've been looking for that goddamned deduct box ever since." He closed his eyes and leaned back, putting his booted feet up on the edge of the desk. He put his hands behind his head and winked at me. "But you're a smart one, Scotty, you found that goddamned Napoleon death mask when people had been looking for it for decades, and you found it only a couple of days after you started looking for it. So I figured, maybe it was time to bring you in, see what you could find."

"Why now?" I barely choked the words out. "Why did you wait until now?"

"When those men took your daddy out of his apartment—oh, yes, I was having them watched, you know—like I said, I knew there was someone else looking for the box and managed to get a man inside, and then when they took your daddy, well…" He spread his hands wide. "I figured to myself, well, Rev, you're in a pickle now." His voice hardened. "I knew damned well you wouldn't want to work for me or with me—you might be holding a grudge from the last time we met. I don't hold a grudge, and I could have—hell, I paid you for finding that mask even though I didn't get to keep it, didn't I?"

He had—fifty thousand dollars.

He jerked a thumb at Frank. "And seeing how he came in here with a big old chip on his shoulders about old news, I figure I was right about that, too." He laughed. "Never you mind how I knew someone else was on the trail of the deduct box—I won't tell you anyway. But hell, with Veronica murdered and your daddy kidnapped, and all this shit about that damned tiger, I figured now was the time for the two of us to start working together. I didn't take your daddy, I didn't have nothing to do with that tiger being hijacked, and I sure as hell didn't have that woman murdered." He scowled. "Crazy as she was, it was just a matter of time anyway." He picked up his cell phone. "And just to show you how cooperative I'm willing to be…" He punched some numbers into his phone and listened to it for a few moments. "Hey. Get Bradley out of there. Now. And bring him to my place in the city." He disconnected the call and tossed the phone back onto his desk. "Your daddy will be here in less than an hour."

"May I see that diary?" I asked before Frank could say anything. I gave him a warning look as I took the diary from

Rev and opened it to the back. The last third of the book was blank, but I thumbed through until I found the faded, spidery handwriting on the last entry.

September 10, 1935

> *Huey just called me and wants me to come up to the capital tonight. I didn't want to leave New Orleans tonight, but I don't see as I have a choice. Enid won't be happy that I won't have dinner with her and the children tonight, but she knows I have to go whenever Huey wants me, and I am the only one he trusts. He wants me to bring it with me, and I know he must need it for something. This was the responsibility I agreed to when I took it from him, and I must not let him down.*

That was all there was to the entry. I turned back and read the last few days' entries before it, but there wasn't any other mention of Huey Long or whatever "it" was that Porterie was talking about on September 10.

"There's nothing in here about the deduct box," I said, closing the book and putting it back on the desk. "Just some 'it' that Governor Long wanted him to bring back up to Baton Rouge that day."

Rev smiled wickedly. "Don't you think that's what he was talking about? What else could 'it' have been?"

"Where did Veronica get this diary?" I asked, thumping it with my hand. "The story says it's been missing ever since her grandfather died. Isn't it kind of weird that she was the one to find it when she needed money?"

"It's authentic," Rev replied. "I had it authenticated before I gave her any money. The handwriting is Gene Porterie's, the age of the book is pretty accurate, so I had no reason not to believe her. She didn't tell me where she found it."

"Gene Porterie died on his way to Baton Rouge, didn't he?" I asked. "A car accident?"

Rev nodded.

I pulled out my phone and opened the web browser. I typed "Eugene Porterie obituary" into a search engine and stared at the phone as the little rainbow-colored wheel spun and spun until finally a list of links popped up. The first was from the Louisiana State Archives and was a PDF from the old *New Orleans States-Item.* I read through it quickly, and there it was.

Mr. Porterie lost control of his car on his way to Baton Rouge, and it flipped into a ditch on Highway 20.

In 1935, Highway 20 was *not* on the way from New Orleans to Baton Rouge.

The causeway bridge across Lake Pontchartrain wasn't built until the 1950s. For that matter, in 1935 not only hadn't I-10 been built yet, but neither had I-59.

For Gene Porterie to drive to Baton Rouge from New Orleans via Highway 20 in 1935, he'd have had to cross Lake Pontchartrain at the Rigolets Bridge—a good seventy miles out of the way.

Gene Porterie wasn't in New Orleans when he got the summons from Huey.

He'd been at the hunting cabin on the north shore near Lake Maurepas.

And really, what better place to hide something than a hunting cabin out in the marshes on the north shore? No one would ever think to look there. Now it was just a matter of figuring out where.

I felt an adrenaline rush.

I got up and started pacing. The more I thought about it, the more sense it made. But why wouldn't someone have found it before now?

I remembered Mom saying that Veronica had spent a lot of time at the cabin when she was younger. It was a place of refuge for her—even after she'd masterminded the ridiculous idea to steal Mike the Tiger, that's where she went to run the plan and hide out. She'd even died there.

Maybe she'd found the diary out there when she was younger.

And if Rev hadn't kidnapped my father—he'd said there was someone else looking for the deduct box.

I heard Donnie Ray's voice in my head again. *There are a lot of Porteries on the north shore, believe you me, and not many of them want people to know they're related to Veronica.*

"Rev," I said slowly. "I believe you. I believe you didn't take my dad, and I also don't believe you killed Veronica or had her killed."

Frank was staring at me, his mouth open.

"But this is all starting to make sense to me now," I went on. "I think I may know where to find the deduct box—or at least where to start looking. But the longer we sit here, the harder it's going to be to find it—the other people looking for it might be just as close to figuring it out as I am." I rather doubted that, but I didn't have to believe it—I just had to make Rev believe so he'd let us go. "You say your men are rescuing my dad right now?" He nodded. "Then we don't need to be here when they bring him here, do we? I think Frank and I should go and see if we can find the deduct box." I picked up the diary. "And we'll need to take this."

"All right, Scotty." Rev stood up. "I know I can trust you. I'll have your daddy call you once he's here."

"Come on, Frank." I started walking toward the door. "Let's get out of here."

Frank didn't say anything until we were safely in the car. Once he started the engine, and had pulled away from the curb, he said, "Do you really know what you're talking about, Scotty?"

I shook my head as my phone started ringing again. I pulled it out, holding up one finger to Frank, and answered. "Scotty Bradley."

"Scotty, hey! This is Taylor. Where are you and Frank?"

"Taylor!" I said out loud with a glance at Frank. "Your uncle and I are out doing some investigating, trying to find my dad. Did you sleep well? Are you okay?"

"I'm fine." He sounded irritated. "I'm not really happy you two took off and left me behind, for one thing. I think I deserve better than that, especially after yesterday." He sounded more than a little bit pouty, and I reminded myself that he was only eighteen. "I think I proved myself pretty well. Anyway, I just wanted to let you know something I found out online." He sounded a little dubious. "It might just be a weird coincidence, but it's interesting."

"I'm sorry we left you behind," I said, rolling my eyes at Frank. "What did you find out?"

"Well, you remember all that talk about how big the Porterie family was? I thought I'd look them up, you know, on ancestry.com? I mean, after I figured out you guys were gone, I thought I'd find a way to help, and if it didn't help, well, it would help me kill some time, especially since your note said for me not to leave the house." His voice got a little whinier on the last few words.

I was beginning to understand why people got so impatient with me when I was telling a story. "Get to the point, Taylor."

"Oh! Yes, sorry about that. Anyway, I looked up the Porteries, and you'll never guess who I found out is a Porterie. Just like Hope, his great-grandfather was Eugene Porterie. And when I saw it, I laughed, you know, because it's just so weird—"

I sighed. "Get to the point, please."

"Troy Dufresne!" He laughed. "Isn't that weird? The guy your mom got arrested for slugging on Monday, he's a Porterie, too! His grandmother was Eugene Porterie's oldest daughter! Isn't that a funny coincidence?"

"Yes, yes it is," I said absently, my mind racing. "Look, Taylor, I have to go, okay? Stay inside until we get home." I hung up the phone and put it back in my pocket.

Troy Dufresne was a Porterie.

Troy Dufresne was from the north shore.

I heard Rev saying, *Someone pretty damned powerful here in Louisiana is the one who did take your daddy. I don't know who he is, but he's got some pull in this state.*

The state's attorney general would certainly fit that description.

And while we were busy finding Veronica Porterie's body at the hunting cabin, Troy Dufresne was busy having Dad kidnapped.

I was exactly sure how that all worked, but the attorney general was really in charge of enforcing the law in the courts for the state, so didn't that mean he was in charge of the police?

How could someone kidnap Dad in broad daylight and get him out of the apartment in the middle of the French Quarter without anyone noticing?

If the people taking him were from the state police, Dad wouldn't have made a scene. He would have gone quietly. Mom would have screamed and yelled and been dragged kicking all the way down the back steps and into the police car—

And the state police also have access to unmarked cars.

I was starting to feel a little sick to my stomach.

"Frank, can you step on it?" I said in a very small voice.

"Are you okay?" He glanced over at me as we headed up Calliope to the on-ramp for I-10.

"I don't know." I took a few deep, cleansing breaths, but somehow, I *knew* I was right. I filled Frank in on what I was thinking and what Taylor had found. Frank listened, without saying anything, but I noticed that muscle jumping in his jaw as I kept reasoning it all out for him.

I finally finished talking after we passed the causeway exit on our way out of town. "So, do you think I'm crazy?"

"No, it makes sense." The corners of his mouth twitched a little bit. "In a crazy sort of way, of course, but it makes sense. Now, how do we get out to this place?"

"We have to take I-55 north to Jackson when we get over the lake estuary," I said. "And then once we're on dry land again, we take the Highway 20 exit. I'm pretty sure I can find it again once we're on 20."

I held on to my phone for dear life as we passed the last few exits for New Orleans and were out over the lake marshes again. I had no reason to trust Rev Harper, but then again he'd proven himself to be a man of his word back when I dealt with him the last time. I had to believe his men could rescue my dad, and that Dad was going to call me. Frank was speeding, expertly weaving his way in and out of traffic, sometimes getting so close to cars before passing them that my heart leaped up into my throat. I didn't bother looking at the speedometer because I really didn't want to know how fast we were going. As we sped along the bridge, I flipped the diary open again to read that last entry again—

—and that was when I noticed something.

The last entry was on the back side of a page, but Porterie had never started a new date and entry on a new page. He'd always simply written the date below the last entry and started the new one.

The last entry seemed...*incomplete*.

I held up the book and looked carefully at the binding between the last entry and the next page.

A page was missing.

It wasn't that noticeable, actually. If you didn't look closely, you'd never notice it was gone.

Frank hurtled onto the on-ramp for I-55, shooting around an eighteen-wheeler like it was standing still.

The question was, had Veronica removed the page before selling it to Rev, or had Rev removed it before giving it to me?

Or did Eugene Porterie himself tear it out before he died?

I looked at the blank page that came next, and remembered something I'd learned in a forensics course I'd taken.

I reached into the glove box, pulled out a pencil, and lightly ran it over the next page in the journal.

And words began to take shape.

CHAPTER FOURTEEN
TWO OF SWORDS, REVERSED
Movement in one's affairs

So, I have taken the papers Huey wants out of the box—I don't know what they are, they are sealed in envelopes and it is not for me to open them or question what they are. The box remains hidden, of course, Huey is right—his enemies, who are also the enemies of progress and the future, who want to drag Louisiana back into the old ways of the oligarchs who cheat and rape the poor every day, are everywhere, and if they could get their hands on the box and its contents, they would be unstoppable.

The bearer bonds must always be safe. But the box is safe, for now—even if I were to die right now, the box would be safe from wind and rain, from hurricanes and flood waters.

I know that it is bad luck, as my grandmother always used to say, to talk about your own death; but I have been dreaming a lot about death lately, so I have to believe that my own time on this planet is drawing to a close. This diary is the only record of where the deduct box has been hidden; if I should die before I am able to return it to Huey's custody, Huey must be given this diary, for he is the only one who will be able to decipher it and find what it is his.

And that was all it said.

I couldn't believe it.

Huey must be given this diary, for he is the only one who will be able to decipher it and find what is his.

"Motherfucker!" I swore, slamming the book shut.

"What?" Frank asked, looking over at me in concern.

"Just keep your eyes on the road," I said, unable to conceal my irritation. "How's this—I figured out that not only was a page missing from this stupid book, and how to read what was written on it, but good ole Gene Porterie's only clue to where he hid the fucking deduct box—well, the only person who could figure it out would be Huey Long himself." I counted to ten and took some deep, cleansing breaths. "So, if Rev was wrong and he can't get Dad away from the kidnappers…"

"Don't even go there," Frank said as we left the bridge and hit dry land again. "He didn't strike me as the kind of person who would say he could do something and then not be able to do it."

"He isn't." I concurred. "Mom should be calling at any moment to tell us Dad's home, in fact." I sighed and leaned back in the seat. "The exit for Highway 20 is coming up—we want to go west."

Frank slowed down for the exit, and I slumped down farther in the seat, putting my knees up on the dashboard while I thought some more.

Who'd torn the page out of the diary? Rev hadn't noticed it was gone—he certainly would have never paid for the diary had he been aware it wasn't complete. The other question, and perhaps the most important one, was *why* was the page torn out? If that was all it said, it was completely useless to anyone besides Huey Long himself, and Huey had been dead for almost eighty years. The secret of where the deduct box was hidden had gone into the grave with Eugene Porterie.

So why was Troy Dufresne so determined to find it? To the point where he'd kidnap Dad?

Of course, I had no proof, but I knew in my heart I was

right. Troy Dufresne was the leader of the other gang looking for the deduct box, and undoubtedly, he or one of his men had murdered Veronica. But why? That didn't make any sense—then again, Veronica was the person most likely to have torn the page out of the diary. She'd had an interesting sense of morality, after all—thinking it was more humane, for example, to kill dogs and cats rather than find them homes. She'd think nothing of selling the diary after removing the only thing of value in it.

It was a wonder someone hadn't killed her years earlier.

"Turn here," I instructed Frank as we approached the dirt road into the swamp. It all seemed kind of familiar to me now—the places where reeds and flowers grew out of stagnant water, the clouds of gnats swarming over something dead and rotting, the massive live oaks with Spanish moss hanging down from the branches. The sounds were much the same, too—the cicadas and crickets, the occasional squawk of a diving bird, the splash from a fish jumping. At one point I saw the beady eyes and round dark-green head of an alligator floating in the murky water alongside the dirt road. The way its yellowish eyes didn't blink made it look like it was dead, stuffed by some taxidermist and set afloat in the water to scare off birds or something. Yet it was beautiful out there in the marsh, a wild, stark kind of beauty with the blue sky above and the rays of the sun beating down relentlessly. Deeper and deeper we went into the marsh, Frank driving slowly so we didn't miss the driveway to the Porterie cabin.

"It's coming up here, on the left," I finally said as we went around the last curve I remembered, and sure enough, just ahead was the driveway—but this time there was a chain stretched across it from two metal poles that had been driven into the ground on either side. Frank turned into the driveway and stopped just outside the chain.

"Let me check it out," I said, opening my car door and climbing out. I walked over to the chain, which hung loosely between the two poles. It had been looped around both, and the ends pulled together and attached with a shiny new silvery padlock. I rolled my eyes. The Tangipahoa Parish sheriff's department meant well, but this was ridiculous. I shook my head at Frank as I walked over to one of the poles. I grasped the chain and with one swift yank was able to put it up and over the top. I took a big swing and tossed the chain to the other side of the driveway, where with a slinking sound it slid down into the ditch. I climbed back into the car. "I guess it was just for show," I said as I fastened my seat belt again. "Do you think I should put it back up after we go in?"

Frank thought for a moment before putting the car in drive. "I don't think it much matters—I can't imagine there's much traffic out here, do you? And like you said, that chain's not going to stop anyone else who wants in any more than it stopped us."

The Jag crept slowly forward along the narrow drive, and I found myself holding my breath with anticipation until we came out into the clearing where the cabin stood on its cinderblock columns.

The same old rusty car was still sitting where it was when Mom and I had been here. Yellow crime scene tape fluttered around the door to the screen porch. I got a weird feeling as Frank put the car into neutral.

"Pull the car around back, Frank," I suggested. I didn't know what the weird feeling was about, but the thought of leaving the Jaguar out in the open in front of the house just seemed wrong somehow.

Frank didn't argue with me, just put the car into gear. He drove even more slowly around the side of the cabin. When we reached the back corner of the cabin, I gasped in surprise. We'd not had time or reason to look behind the house the day Mom and I had found Veronica's body, so I was seeing it for the first time. There was no grass, just dirt and a big silver propane tank. About ten yards beyond the cabin's back door was a wide bayou, maybe six feet across, with a little pier jutting out a couple of yards. A rusty little fishing boat with an outboard motor was tied up to it.

Frank pulled the Jag around so that the front faced the back door of the cabin, and turned the engine off. "Now what?" he said in a whisper, which made me smother a laugh.

I got out of the car again and had to admit, it was weirdly quiet. I walked up the steps to the back door and tried to open it, but it was locked. I motioned for Frank to come with me and headed around for the front. I ignored the crime scene tape, opened the warped screen door, and stepped into the shaded porch. The body was gone, but the chalk outline of the body remained, and no one had bothered to clean up the blood. It had now dried, but there was a sickly sweet smell hanging in the air. I gagged and stepped across the porch as quickly as I could, hearing Frank's footsteps behind me. The front door was closed, but when I turned the knob and pushed, it opened.

The window unit was still running, so there was a blast of cold air as I stepped inside. I flipped on the light switch, and flinched at the bright light cast from the chandelier/ceiling fan, which was attached directly to the ceiling. The room smelled dank, and it looked like there was black mold on the walls in the corners near the ceiling. The walls had faux-wood paneling, and the floor was covered in old linoleum that in some places was curling up in the corners. A brown corduroy couch was pushed up against one wall, and the little coffee table in front of it was slanted to one side. A rusty coffee can sat on it, with cigarette butts floating in the murky water inside. I shook my head. It didn't look like the sheriffs had bothered searching for evidence inside the house—no fingerprint dust anywhere, and they never clean up after themselves.

I walked over to a door on the left wall, figuring it led into a bedroom, and was right. There was another window unit running there. The bed was old, the frame dark wood that looked like it had seen better days; it may have been new during the Eisenhower administration. But the bed wasn't made, so I had to assume this was the room where Veronica had been sleeping. I walked over to the bed and looked at the nightstand. There was a half-empty plastic cup with water in it, and next to that, a pill bottle. I picked it up. *Alprazolam .5 mg tablets, Veronica Porterie.*

I knew what alprazolam was—I'd had a prescription for it after Katrina.

I whistled. I waved the bottle at Frank, who was standing in the doorway. "Veronica was taking Xanax," I said. "I wonder how long she was taking it?"

Frank shrugged. "Probably ever since they killed that security guard twenty years ago."

I opened the closet door. Three pairs of jeans and a floral print polyester dress were hanging there, and there was an open, empty suitcase on the floor. I checked the shelf, but there wasn't anything there other than a pair of cheap faux-leather pumps. Frank was going through the chest of drawers, but there was nothing in it other than some socks, underwear, and T-shirts.

After the bedroom, we walked back into the kitchen and back into the heat. There wasn't a window unit in the kitchen—which didn't make much sense to me; why wouldn't you have an air conditioner in the room where you cooked? There was a pot on the stove with congealed spaghetti noodles floating in starchy water, and an opened jar of hardened spaghetti sauce on the counter. There was also some packaged hamburger in the sink, which had turned brown and smelled pretty bad.

Hamburger?

What kind of animal rights activist eats *hamburger?*

"Frank—" I started to say, but cut myself off when I heard the sound of another car pulling up the driveway. Frank and I exchanged glances—we had technically disturbed a crime scene—and I hurried back through the kitchen and peered through the blinds on one of the living room windows. The car was a small, dark blue Nissan, and it stopped right next to the rusted old car. I gasped when the car door opened and a young woman got out.

Hope Porterie.

I'd never seen her outside of on television, and I was surprised at how small she seemed in person. She had white-blond hair that hung to her shoulders, her forehead covered with bangs. She was wearing a purple LSU T-shirt and a pair of white denim shorts. Her skin was tanned a golden brown and she couldn't have been more than five feet tall. She was wearing Nikes, and a white canvas purse hung from her shoulder at her side.

"What is she doing here?" Frank muttered. "Returning to the scene of the crime?"

I didn't bother to remind him that she was being hijacked by AFAR around the time her mother was being murdered. But it was weird. *Fuck it*, I decided, and walked out the front door.

Startled, Hope reached for her purse when I opened the screen door. "Hi." I smiled ingratiatingly at her. "We've never met, but you know my mother, Cecile Bradley? My brother Storm?"

She relaxed a little bit, but I also noticed she didn't let go of her purse—which was more than a little odd. "Hi," she said hesitantly, forcing a smile.

I walked down the steps, holding my hands up so she could see I wasn't a threat. Mom had always taught me to do that in situations where I was somewhere alone with a woman who didn't know me—to let her know I wouldn't hurt her. I didn't hear Frank behind me. "So, what are you doing here, Hope?"

She licked her lower lip. "I—I, um…" She paused again, apparently not sure how to continue. Her eyebrows came together. "What are *you* doing here?"

I've always found honesty to be the best policy, primarily because I'm a lousy liar when put on the spot. I sat down on the steps. "My father was kidnapped, Hope, on the same day your mother was murdered." I spread my hands. "The only thing the kidnappers want is Huey Long's deduct box." *In for a penny, in for a pound.* "Now, I've come across your great-grandfather's diary—which is supposedly the key to where he hid the box for Huey. Did you know your mother sold the diary to a Houston millionaire over twenty years ago?" I reached into my shorts pocket and held up the little book. "He gave it to me a little while ago so I could try to find the box myself. But lo and behold, the page where Eugene Porterie tells where he hid the box is missing." *No need*, I figured, *to tell her I was able to read what was written on that page anyway.*

She bit her lower lip and shifted her weight from one foot to the other. "Yeah. I know. My mom told me all about it when she called me last week." She took a deep breath. "She told me the deduct box was her insurance policy, but I really didn't know what she meant." A tear slid out of her right eye. "Does that make any sense to you?"

I shook my head. "No, it really doesn't." I heard Frank's phone's ringtone—"Knowing Me Knowing You" by ABBA—going off behind me.

"So, why did you get in touch with your mother after all those years?" I asked, moving forward until I was standing very close to her. "I can't imagine your grandmother was too pleased about it."

"I was curious, was all," Hope said with a slight shrug. "Wouldn't you be?" She barked out a little laugh. "Your mom is great, you know. I always wondered what the deal with mine was... so I found out everything I could about her. My grandmother told me my mother never wanted to have anything to do with me, that she willingly gave up custody and never tried to see me." She shook her head. "*None* of that was true, I found out by looking up the court records. It made me wonder what else wasn't true. So I sent my mother an e-mail through the AFAR website. And she called me within two hours." Her jaw set. "So my grandmother can go to hell. At least I got to meet her before—you know." She choked up and wiped at her eyes with the heels of her hands.

"When was the last time you saw her?"

"Last weekend." She sniffed. "I mean, I'd seen her a few times over the years—she always wanted me to go live with her, go to work with her and all, but AFAR—AFAR wasn't for me. It was *her* cause, not mine, you know? I love animals—that's why

I majored in veterinary science, but I want to work for a zoo. I don't see zoos as prisons. But she was always cool about it, which kind of surprised me. She called me this past weekend, wanted me to come out here and meet her. She always stayed here when she was in Louisiana." Hope bit her lower lip. "My grandfather left this place to her—it's hers. She really liked it here, said she felt closer to nature here than she did in a city."

"You didn't know about her plans regarding Mike?"

"Of course not!" She shook her head so hard I thought it might jar loose from her neck. "I still can't believe she did that. She had to know the cops would figure out I was her daughter, and it wouldn't look good for me."

I didn't feel like pointing out to her that her mother might not have cared about that. I know I wouldn't have wanted to hear it if it were my mother.

"Anyway, so I came out here today because—" She paused and reached into her shorts pocket. "Mom gave me this when I came out here Sunday." She held up a folded piece of yellowed paper with writing on it.

The missing diary page.

"May I see that?" I asked, my voice shaking a little bit. She nodded and handed it to me. I unfolded it, and sure enough, on the front side of the page was the writing I'd unencrypted in the diary itself.

But there was writing on the other side.

I cursed myself for being so stupid. It had never even crossed my mind there might also be writing on the other side of the page.

Huey will know where I put the box because it is buried only ten paces toward the lake from where we always went to shoot ducks. We always went by ourselves, so no one else will know.

Well, *that* wasn't much help.

I said so, out loud.

"But I know where that is," Hope replied.

I stared at her as Frank came up beside me. "That was Taylor on the phone—Dad's come home, some of Rev Harper's men dropped him off at the Devil's Weed. He's talking to the police now—he was taken by state troopers, he thought he was under arrest."

Troy Dufresne.

"Where is the place they shot ducks, Hope?" I tried to keep my voice calm and cool. Frank gave me a look, but I shook my head slightly to let him know not to say anything further.

"I can show you," Hope said, starting to walk off to the left of the cabin. "They never built a duck blind. My grandfather used to bring me out here when I was a little girl, when he went duck hunting." She smiled, a little wistfully. "He told me it was the best place in all southwest Louisiana to shoot ducks and that his father used to bring him there when he was a little boy." She shrugged. "I figured that was the same place his father would have brought Huey Long to hunt."

It made sense, and I started walking after her, with Frank at my side. We'd reached the side of the cabin when we heard a car coming up the drive. "Were you expecting someone else?" I asked, and Hope shook her head. "Let's get out of sight."

"Inside the cabin," Hope said, and we ran up the front steps and closed the front door behind us once we were inside. I peeked through the blinds in the now-dark living room and saw the battered old red Cavalier pull up and park right behind Hope's car. Barney Fleming got out and leaned against the car, looked at his watch, and then started examining Hope's car.

"Is there anything in there that would identify you?" I whispered, glad we'd decided to park the Jag behind the house. Not, of course, that it wouldn't be found by anyone walking around the cabin, but at least it was out of sight for anyone driving up.

"My registration and insurance card are in the glove box," Hope whispered back.

Fortunately, though, she'd apparently locked the doors, because Fleming tried opening them to no avail.

I could hear Frank mumbling into the phone and hoped that he was calling the cops—but not the Tangipahoa sheriff, that's for sure.

And I heard the sound of another car coming up the driveway. Moments later, a Tangipahoa sheriff's car pulled up, parking next to Fleming's battered Cavalier. Donnie Ray himself got out, and he and Fleming started talking. They were too far away for me to hear what they were saying, but the argument was getting heated.

Until Donnie Ray pulled out his gun and shot Fleming twice in the chest.

I slammed my hand over Hope's mouth as she started to scream, and when Fleming looked over at the house, I worried for a moment that he'd heard her. But then he grabbed Fleming by the hands and dragged him to the edge of the swamp water. He shoved the body in, giving it a strong kick to push it away from the shoreline, and the body drifted out a little way before it tangled in some reeds. He stood there for a moment, his hands on his hips, and then the water started thrashing around as an alligator materialized and wrestled Fleming's body through the reeds into deeper water.

Had to give Donnie Ray some credit—that was one body that would probably be never found.

"I called Venus and told her what was going on," Frank whispered, turning his phone to vibrate and slipping it into his pocket. "I don't know what she's going to do, though—don't the state police fall under Dufresne's jurisdiction, too?"

I shook my head. I honestly didn't know—but even were it the case, I didn't think every state cop was corrupt or willing to do something illegal.

Of course, we'd just witnessed Donnie Ray murdering Barney Fleming.

And that meant if he found out we were there, he'd have to kill us, too.

We needed to get the hell out of there.

"Ms. Porterie!" he suddenly yelled, walking toward the cabin. "You want to come out of there? I promise you, nothing's going to happen to you! You know that Fleming killed your mama, right?"

I felt Hope stiffen beside me, and she started to walk toward the door. I grabbed her, whispering furiously, "What do you think you're doing?"

"He doesn't know you two are here," she hissed back at me. "If I go out there, I can maybe distract him. Your car's in back, right? Well, I'll distract him and you two go get in your car and go for help."

"I've already called for help," Frank replied.

She shook off my hand and went out the front door.

"Hello," she called. "What are you doing on my property?"

I gave Frank a little push. "You go for help, Frank. I'll stay here and make sure he doesn't hurt her."

Frank didn't say a word, just handed me his gun. "Shoot the bastard if it comes to that." And he was gone, not making a sound as he slipped through the rest of the house.

I took the gun and made sure it was loaded, then eased the safety off. Hope still stood in the doorway right above the steps to the yard. Donnie Ray was walking slowly toward her.

"You say that man killed my mother?" Hope asked, defiance in her tone. "How do I know that for sure?"

"I was here," Donnie Ray replied casually. "She had something we wanted, and when she wouldn't give it to us, he shot her." He sounded convincing, almost reasonable—if it weren't for the fact I'd seen him shoot Barney in cold blood just minutes before and then feed his corpse to an alligator. "Turned out she didn't have what we were looking for after all. I'm real sorry about your mama."

"You mean the diary page?" she said, and I realized she'd taken it back from me after I'd read it.

He was practically salivating. "Do you have it?"

She held it out in front of her, beckoning him to come forward as the sound of another car coming up the driveway made them both turn to look. It was a black Lincoln town car, and it stopped without coming into the front yard of the cabin. The windows were tinted so I couldn't see inside.

The driver's door opened.

Troy Dufresne himself.

He wasn't wearing a suit, the way I was used to always seeing him on television, but had on an LSU T-shirt and a pair of jeans. His hair was slicked back, and I had to give the man credit—he was good-looking, if completely untrustworthy. I also realized the way he'd parked the town car was blocking the driveway; there was no way Frank could get the Jag past it. I swore under my breath.

I didn't have a clear shot at either Donnie Ray or Dufresne.

That's when I heard it—the sound of an engine from behind the cabin. But it wasn't the Jag—the engine was too loud and uneven to be the Jag. The Jag's engine ran so quietly it barely purred. No, it sounded like a boat of some sort, coming up the bayou to the back of the cabin. *Who the fuck could that be?* I wondered, but Dufresne's reaction was not what I expected. He ran back to the town car, jumped back in, and started backing down the driveway at a really high speed, which probably wasn't very smart. Donnie Ray had a very sour look on his face—looked to me like maybe Dufresne was leaving him holding the bag.

Whatever was going on behind the house, Donnie Ray clearly wasn't taking any chances. In one fluid motion he grabbed Hope, put his arm around her neck, and put his gun up to her forehead. All the color drained out of her face.

"Put down the gun and put your hands in the air!" a voice boomed through a bullhorn.

"Do I look stupid to you?" Donnie Ray shouted back. He was sweating now, big round circles of sweat under his arms.

There was a gunshot, and dust flew up right at Donnie Ray's feet. Hope screamed, and Donnie Ray quickly tossed his gun to the ground, let go of her, and put his hands up. Several men in SWAT outfits came running around the building, and one of them retrieved Donnie Ray's gun while another handcuffed him. I stepped out through the front door, after putting Frank's gun down, and held my own hands up in the air.

My knees felt a little bit weak. It was all over—Dad was home, and if Donnie Ray was telling the truth, Veronica's murderer was not only exposed, but Louisiana taxpayers would be saved the expense of his trial. We wouldn't be so lucky with Donnie Ray, of course.

And I could hear him singing like a bird to the SWAT team man who'd handcuffed him—and every other word out of his mouth was "Dufresne."

Frank came around the side of the house, a big grin on his face. "You can always count on the FBI," he said to me with a wink. "Now let's wrap this whole mess up and see if we can find the deduct box."

I sighed in relief and leaned back against him. "Praise the Goddess," I replied. "May they catch Dufresne real soon, too. I wonder if he's going to try to make a break for it?"

"He's a politician," Frank replied grimly. "More like he'll deny it all and hire a good lawyer. And you know how Louisiana voters love a good scoundrel."

"Yeah," I replied as one of the SWAT team guys came walking up to us. "We might always vote for 'em, but a jury always convicts them. That's something to be proud of, don't you think?"

"Scotty Bradley? Frank Sobieski?" the SWAT agent asked, taking off his helmet and smiling at us. He was a nice-looking man, maybe in his late forties. "I got some questions for you."

"Ask away," I replied. "Ask away."

AFTERWARD

We never found the deduct box.
Either it was moved again at some point or Eugene Porterie took Huey Long duck hunting in a different place than he did his son, but we dug everywhere around the spot where Hope's grandfather claimed was the right one to no avail. Hope has given permission to a team of archaeologists and historians to dig on the property, but so far no one has turned up the deduct box.

Troy Dufresne never admitted to wanting the deduct box. The legislature did demand his resignation, and the governor appointed someone to his office until there could be a special election. A lot of people want Storm to run for attorney general, and he is considering it. It amuses me no end to think that my brother could be a very powerful man in this state. As I told him, "No matter who you end up being, Storm, you'll always be my asshole older brother."

Saying this to him, of course, resulted in my getting head noogies. I don't think he'll ever completely grow up.

Dad didn't seem any the worse for wear. Apparently Dufresne's men fed him well and took really good care of him.

Taylor is still with us and has fallen in love with New Orleans. Like so many others before him, he never wants to leave. We've gotten him registered and enrolled at Tulane, and he's still living in the upstairs apartment. We have moved all of Colin's spy toys down to our floor, and I always knock before I enter his place—lesson learned.

He's a great kid, really, and every day I grow more and more fond of him. My worries about being a bad role model for him were unfounded. He really can make me laugh, and he's also teaching me all the things my computer and my smartphone can do.

They really are *smart* phones.

The Feds came down on AFAR like a ton of bricks. Diana Killeen and her cohorts are in jail, and I'm hoping they never get out.

And Mike of course is back in his habitat. The athletic department at LSU was so grateful to me and Taylor for getting him back for them—even though we really didn't do anything—that they gave both of us a pair of football season tickets for life.

I'm looking forward to football season this year.

GEAUX TIGERS!

About the Author

Greg Herren is a New Orleans–based author and editor. He is a co-founder of the Saints and Sinners Literary Festival, which takes place in New Orleans every May. He is the author of over twenty novels, including the Lambda Literary Award–winning *Murder in the Rue Chartres*, called by the *New Orleans Times-Picayune* "the most honest depiction of life in post-Katrina New Orleans published thus far." He co-edited *Love, Bourbon Street: Reflections on New Orleans*, which also won the Lambda Literary Award. His young adult novel *Sleeping Angel* won the Moonbeam Gold Medal for Excellence in Young Adult Mystery/Horror. He has published over fifty short stories in markets as varied as *Ellery Queen's Mystery Magazine* to the critically acclaimed anthology *New Orleans Noir* to various websites, literary magazines, and anthologies. His erotica anthology *FRATSEX* is the all-time best-selling title for Insightoutbooks. He has worked as an editor for Bella Books, Harrington Park Press, and now Bold Strokes Books.

A longtime resident of New Orleans, Greg was a fitness columnist and book reviewer for Window Media for over four years, publishing in the LGBT newspapers *IMPACT News*, *Southern Voice*, and *Houston Voice*. He served a term on the Board of Directors for the National Stonewall Democrats and served on the founding committee of the Louisiana Stonewall Democrats. He is currently employed as a public health researcher for the NO/AIDS Task Force and is serving a term on the board of the Mystery Writers of America.

Books Available From Bold Strokes Books

Light by 'Nathan Burgoine. Openly gay (and secretly psychokinetic) Kieran Quinn is forced into action when self-styled prophet Wyatt Jackson arrives during Pride Week and things take a violent turn. (978-1-60282-953-4)

Baton Rouge Bingo by Greg Herren. The murder of an animal rights activist involves Scotty and the boys in a decades-old mystery revolving around Huey Long's murder and a missing fortune. (978-1-60282-954-1)

Anything for a Dollar, edited by Todd Gregory. Bodies for hire, bodies for sale—enter the steaming hot world of men who make a living from their bodies—whether they star in porn, model, strip, or hustle—or all of the above. (978-1-60282-955-8)

Mind Fields by Dylan Madrid. When college student Adam Parsh accepts a tutoring position, he finds himself the object of the dangerous desires of one of the most powerful men in the world— his married employer. (978-1-60282-945-9)

Greg Honey by Russ Gregory. Detective Greg Honey is steering his way through new love, business failure, and bruises when all his cases indicate trouble brewing for his wealthy family. (978-1-60282-946-6)

Jacob's Diary by Sam Sommer. Nothing exciting ever happens to David Jacobs until the day he and his son are thrown into the most fascinating and disturbing adventure of a lifetime. (978-1-60282-947-3)

Lake Thirteen by Greg Herren. A visit to an old cemetery seems like fun to a group of five teenagers, who soon learn that sometimes it's best to leave old ghosts alone. (978-1-60282-894-0)

Deadly Cult by Joel Gomez-Dossi. One nation under MY God, or you die. (978-1-60282-895-7)

The Case of the Rising Star: A Derrick Steele Mystery by Zavo. Derrick Steele's next case involves blackmail, revenge, and a new romance as Derrick races to save a young movie star from a dangerous killer. Meanwhile, will a new threat from within destroy him, along with the entire Steele family? (978-1-60282-888-9)

Big Bad Wolf by Logan Zachary. After a wolf attack, Paavo Wolfe begins to suspect one of the victims is turning into a werewolf. Things become hairy as his ex-partner helps him find the killer. Can Paavo solve the mystery before he runs into the Big Bad Wolf? (978-1-60282-890-2)

The Plain of Bitter Honey by Alan Chin. Trapped within the bleak prospect of a society in chaos, twin brothers Aaron and Hayden Swann discover inner strength in the face of tragedy and search for atonement after betraying the one you most love. (978-1-60282-883-4)

In His Secret Life by Mel Bossa. The only man Allan wants is the one he can't have. (978-1-60282-875-9)

The Moon's Deep Circle by David Holly. Tip Trencher wants to find out what happened to his long-lost brothers, but what he finds is a sizzling circle of gay sex and pagan ritual. (978-1-60282-870-4)

Straight Boy Roommate by Kevin Troughton. Tom isn't expecting much from his first term at University, but a chance encounter with straight boy Dan catapults him into an extraordinary, wild weekend of sex and self-discovery, which turns his life upside down, and leads him into his first love affair. (978-1-60282-782-0)

Raising Hell: Demonic Gay Erotica, edited by Todd Gregory. Hot stories of gay erotica featuring demons. (978-1-60282-768-4)

Pursued by Joel Gomez-Dossi. Openly gay college student Jamie Bradford becomes romantically involved with two men at the same time, and his hell begins when one of his boyfriends becomes intent on killing him. (978-1-60282-769-1)

Timothy by Greg Herren. Timothy is a romantic suspense thriller from award-winning mystery writer Greg Herren set in the fabulous Hamptons. (978-1-60282-760-8)

In Stone by Jeremy Jordan King. A young New Yorker is rescued from a hate crime by a mysterious someone who turns out to be more of a something. (978-1-60282-761-5)

The Jesus Injection by Eric Andrews-Katz. Murderous statues, demented drag queens, political bombings, ex-gay ministries, espionage, and romance are all in a day's work for a top secret agent. But the gloves are off when Agent Buck 98 comes up against the Jesus Injection. (978-1-60282-762-2)

Combustion by Daniel W. Kelly. Bearish detective Deck Waxer comes to the city of Kremfort Cove to investigate why the hottest men in town are bursting into flames in broad daylight. (978-1-60282-763-9)

Night Shadows: Queer Horror edited by Greg Herren and J.M. Redmann. *Night Shadows* features delightfully wicked stories by some of the biggest names in queer publishing. (978-1-60282-751-6)

Wyatt: Doc Holliday's Account of an Intimate Friendship by Dale Chase. Erotica writer Dale Chase takes the remarkable friendship between Wyatt Earp, upright lawman, and Doc Holliday, Southern gentlemen turned gambler and killer, to an entirely new level: hot! (978-1-60282-755-4)

Secret Societies by William Holden. An outcast hustler, his unlikely "mother," his faithless lovers, and his religious persecutors—all in 1726. (978-1-60282-752-3)

The Jetsetters by David-Matthew Barnes. As rock band the Jetsetters skyrocket from obscurity to superstardom, Justin Holt, a lonely barista, and Diego Delgado, the band's guitarist, fight with everything they have to stay together, despite the chaos and fame. (978-1-60282-745-5)

Strange Bedfellows by Rob Byrnes. Partners in life and crime, Grant Lambert and Chase LaMarca are hired to make a politician's compromising photo disappear, but what should be an easy job quickly spins out of control. (978-1-60282-746-2)

Fontana by Joshua Martino. Fame, obsession, and vengeance collide in a novel that asks: What if America's greatest hero was gay? (978-1-60282-675-5)

The Dirty Diner: Gay Erotica on the Menu, edited by Jerry L. Wheeler. Gay erotica set in restaurants, featuring food, sex, and men—could you really ask for anything more? (978-1-60282-677-9)

Sweat: Gay Jock Erotica by Todd Gregory. Sizzling tales of smoking-hot sex with the athletic studs everyone fantasizes about. (978-1-60282-669-4)

The Marrying Kind by Ken O'Neill. Just when successful wedding planner Adam More decides to protest inequality by quitting the business and boycotting marriage entirely, his only sibling announces her engagement. (978-1-60282-670-0)